DAGGER

OF

EONS

This is a work of fiction.   All of the characters, organizations, and events portrayed in this novel are either products of the author's imagination or are used fictitiously.

DAGGER OF EONS

Published by Damn Fool Press
www.damnfoolpress.com

ISBN 978-0-9950434-8-0 epub
ISBN 978-0-9950434-9-7 mobi
ISBN 978-1-989360-00-2 trade paperback

First Edition : November 2018

This is for Lynn and the cats.

CHAPTER ONE

Escape From the Goddess

After four days of hard marching, Bob and Celcilia arrived at the portal grove. They'd not heard or seen any sign of Kydos, the self-styled Goddess who was out for bloody revenge. It was possible—although unlikely—that she had decided to abandon the chase. However, Bob had both rescued Celcilia from captivity and inflicted serious injuries on Kydos herself. Even in her youth Kydos had not been the forgiving sort.

"It's beautiful," Celcilia said in measured tones, constantly scanning the surroundings for danger.

Bob nodded. "That's the idea. Supposed to create a zone of serenity."

After a few more steps Celcilia slowed her pace, her face tilted to one side in obvious pain. She soon was forced to halt, grunting with the effort to continue. Bob grabbed her by an arm and escorted her back a dozen steps.

"Sorry," she muttered. "Like walking into a brick wall."

"My fault," he insisted. "That's the repelling field around the area. You got through it before, so I'd forgotten that it would affect you."

"So how'm I getting to the portal?"

"Leave that to me," said Bob in a confident tone. "I'll instantiate the portal and tell it to let you in. Sit here and rest."

Fifteen minutes later, Celcilia called out, "Still waiting."

The prompt reply came back, "Still working."

A few minutes later Bob came trotting back to where Celcilia waited. She looked up at him with a wry expression. "You're having problems." It wasn't a question.

Bob sighed. "Sorry, sorry. This is an older type of portal. Very adamant about not letting just anyone through."

"Would it let me through if I still had my jewel?"

"Not sure if even that would do it," Bob admitted. "It's a stubborn old thing. A nice piece of craftsmanship, though, considering its age."

"Lovely. So how does that get me in there?"

"Well ..." began Bob before he lapsed into silence.

Celcilia sighed. "Just tell me the bad news."

Bob grimaced. "The good news is that I can get you in. The bad news is the how of it."

"Meaning?" she said, drawing out the word in feigned patience.

"I apport you in"

"Excuse me?"

"Ah, think of it as, uhm, teleportation. Yeah, that's it." He paused for a moment before adding, "Not exactly, but close enough."

She considered that for a moment. "Why not just carry me in?"

He looked pained as he said, "You'd be dead before we reached the portal."

"Ah."

"Well, I did say that we installed these things after a time of war. Security was very, very tight. And for good reason, I might add."

Celcilia pursed her lips in thought. "And the portal won't mind if I just kinda show up next to it?"

"That's it, exactly. Not happy about you approaching it, but quite content if you just happen to show up beside it with me."

She looked at him through narrowed eyes. "There's a price to this, isn't there?"

He sighed. "Yeah. I can apport well enough. Couldn't do it at all as a child, but turns out I was just a late bloomer."

Celcilia nodded. "Kydos called you a cripple. Sorry, but she did. Wondered what she meant. You don't seem crippled to me."

Bob gave her a lop-sided smile. "Thanks, Celcilia. In some ways I am a cripple among my own kind. Can't levitate at all, and my apporting is limited. But I can do other things the other can't, so it all evens out."

"When you say limited, that means what?"

He gave a small sigh before answering. "I can apport myself and a small payload ... like the clothes I'm wearing and a bit more. One of the reasons I've learned to travel light."

"And I'm something more than 'a bit more', aren't I?"

"Yeah. What it means is that it'll take a lot out of me. In practical terms, I'll probably pass out for a few seconds and then be not much good for anything for up to a few minutes."

Celcilia snorted. "Typical man. Do a little work and then lay back and moan about the effort." Her smile took the sting out of her words, and they both laughed. Then she became serious. "So we leave and Kydos keeps on doing her thing? What does she do with all those people she had me indoctrinate?"

"Good question," said Bob, "and one that I've been giving considerable thought to. I've managed to convince both portals to lock down after we leave. In fact ..."

Their discussion was interrupted by the sound of something crashing through the forest coming towards them.

Bob turned to Celcilia and snapped, "Hold on to me tightly.

We've run out of time."

Celcilia ran forward and hugged her companion. There was a brief moment of intense cold and disorientation, then things were normal once more. The only difference was the structure standing in front of her. It had strange angles that hurt the eyes to look at, and a cold sheen of oily writhing wrongness coated it. She felt slide to her feet and looked down to discover Bob's prostrate body. She knelt to check on him and for the first time saw a shimmer of sweat coating his face. That, and his lack of consciousness, worried her, but not nearly as much as the rapidly-approaching shrieks from the forest. Within a few seconds the shrieks began to take the form of words. Or, rather, a single word screamed over and over again, "Bob."

The Goddess had arrived.

"Wake up. Wake up," she urged her companion, shaking his shoulder with increasing firmness. "Time to go." She was rewarded by a soft moan, but his eyes remained closed and his body limp.

A bush next to her exploded into flames as a heavy weight landed two body-lengths away from her. She looked up to see a vision out of the most horrific stories of her youth. The Goddess had been a being of transcendent beauty and full of life. The naked creature before her was little more than a ragged collection of poorly-assembled skin and bones. The skin was mottled, with some areas black with rot. The configuration of her skeleton no longer looked human. The rib cage had bulges and dents that no human could have survived, and the spine had a definite s-curve to it. The head wobbled on a neck that was both stretched and had odd angles to it. The face was broken and shattered into something not human, with a mouth twisted into a permanent scream. Sections of skull poked through the skin, and the head itself looked battered and dented.

But it was the arms that drew Celcilia's attention. On one

arm the hand was missing but the wrist bones thrust out like twin knife blades. The other hand was replaced by a hollow tube that began to point towards her.

Still squatting, Celcilia swung her staff and batted the tube-arm away. The knife-arm lashed out and hit the staff, almost knocking it out of Celcilia's grasp. Uttering a low growl, Celcilia sprang to her feet and lunged at the demon-figure before her, hitting at it with her staff. She managed to parry a blow from each of the hideous arms before a downward blow knocked the staff out of her hands, bouncing it across her shins and onto the ground away from her. The demon-figure grinned at her and hissed. Celcilia sneered and assumed a fighting stance. Time seemed to stand still as the two women glared at each other.

Then a blow from the staff slammed up against the chin of the creature. That was followed up by a flurry of blows against the head, arms, and body. Bob was awake and had entered the fray. He spared a quick glance at Celcilia and snapped, "Back up." She hurried to obey.

What followed transpired faster than her senses could follow. Bob and the demon—Celcilia could no longer think of it as the Goddess—traded blows at speeds that were faster than the merely human eye could sense as anything other than a blur. What she could hear, however, were a succession of what sounded like tree trunks snapping as the staff hit against the limbs of the demon. Finally she saw Bob flick the staff against the chin of the demon, throwing the creature into the air. Several seconds later it landed heavily at the edge of the grove.

Bob turned towards the portal, leaning heavily on the staff as he stood upright and closed his eyes. He was breathing heavily and was obviously attempting to concentrate. A sound, more felt than heard, coming from the portal caused her to look towards it. A blackness was forming to one side. A blackness that was deeper than anything she'd ever seen. It was folding in and around itself, attempting to wrap itself into her mind.

"Don't look at it," snapped Bob. "It's a transdimensional construct."

Celcilia shook herself and turned to look at Bob. "What? Oh, not for the sight of the merely human, is it?"

"Pfft. No-one can look at it for long without getting a headache," he panted. The blackness filled with symbols that pulsed and writhed as if alive before being absorbed by the darkness. "There, I've set the destination. Hold my hand and we'll walk through it."

A wordless shriek from behind them caused them to pause. They turned to face the snarling demon as it hobbled towards them. Its mouth clattered and frothed, but no words came out.

"You didn't take the time to heal properly, Katie. That'll take a very long time to heal, now," said Bob in a soft voice.

In response, the demon lifted its tube arm and a shimmering stream of bright objects raced towards them. Bob threw the staff at her, spun around, then placed himself between the stream of darts and Celcilia. He felt several impacts on his arm and torso. From the spreading numbness, he realized the darts contained a toxin of some sort. He picked up Celcilia and ran into the safety offered by the blackness.

CHAPTER TWO

Out of the frying pan

They arrived at their destination and Bob stumbled slightly as the effect of the dart toxin and the weight of Celcilia threw him slightly off balance. She mumbled an apology as she pushed away from him. This time he allowed it, and she stumbled several paces before bending over with her arms on her knees to brace herself.

"Where are we?" she mumbled, trying very hard not to vomit. Her left arm was beginning to throb. When she got no answer she levered herself upright and looked around. The sun was low in the sky, and the sky itself had a distinct nasty yellow tinge to it. Turning further she saw Bob plucking at an arm and wincing as he withdrew what looked like thick needles. He saw her watching, forced a slight smile, and said, "Poison darts. Her parting gift to us. Nasty things. Rather painful, in fact. Got them all before they hit you, though."

"No."

"Sorry, what did you say?"

She managed to whisper, "Ya missed one." Then she collapsed to the ground, moaning as she hit it. Her arm felt like it was freezing and boiling at the same time. She felt, rather than saw, Bob kneeling by her side.

"Left arm?"

She nodded.

"Hurt anywhere else?"

She shook her head. Then croaked out, "How bad?"

He was silent for a few seconds before he answered. "Bad enough. Hold on while I check to see if the portal has a medical kit of some sort."

She was lowered gently to the ground, and she heard the sounds of him trotting away. The pain was beginning to demand all her attention when he came back and settled down beside her. She opened her eyes and saw a grim expression on his face.

"No luck?"

"Not much. Just some water, a couple blankets, some clothing we can use for bandages, and a couple of knives."

"Doncha have super dooper healing thingies inside ya? Gimme a few of those." Her speech was slightly slurred.

Bob shook his head. "They'd kill you faster and nastier than the toxin. We'll have to do this the hard way. Here, close your eyes."

She obeyed and asked, "Now what?"

"Think of England."

"Wha ..." was all she got out before the world went black.

When she awoke, her arm was swathed in blood-soaked bandages. It ached but not as badly as before. Her head felt thick and sore as if someone had hit her. She had experience with being knocked about.

"Good morning."

With some effort she turned her head towards the speaker. The sky was dimmer than before, but there was a fire bright enough to force her to squint. Off to one side sat Bob looking at the flames.

"Gah. Wha' scharggle ..." her mouth and tongue felt thick and tasted of last month's used laundry.

"Sip on this. Carefully now. Need some help?"

He held out a rough cup fashioned out of wood. It was filled with hot fluid of some sort and smelled rather like sewage. She gave a gasp of disgust and shook her head. Bob insisted, so she accepted it, took a sip, and decided that it tasted like last year's used laundry. But it was warm and took the edge off her pain. Smacking her lips and wriggling her mouth loosened things up enough that she tried speaking again.

"Where are we?"

That got a grim smile from Bob. "Good question." He looked around then back at her. "Probably a close approximation to your world's visions of Hell, I would imagine."

She nodded as she digested the information. "Why here?" she asked.

"Last place anyone would think to find me," came the soft-voiced answer.

Again she nodded. "Can't trace us?"

"Nope," he replied, sounding closer to his normal cheerfulness. "Put a lock on accessing the logs of the portal we just left. Won't stand up to anyone who knows how to run a diagnostic, of course. Also, this is a private portal than only a few people can access. By the time she finds someone like that we'll be long gone."

"Or dead," she said in grim tones.

"That's the spirit," Bob exclaimed with excessive cheer. "More tea while you're waiting for death?"

She looked into her cup, shuddered, then drained it. "Better not. Beginning to think death'd be better than this shite." She glanced at her bandaged arm. "Took the edge offa the pain, mind. What was it? And what'd you do to my arm?"

"Feels better?"

"Yah, some. Hurts like a bugger, but not throbby and feeling on fire any more. And don't dodge the question, you."

He didn't say anything and the serious look on his face began to frighten her. Her mouth tightened in anticipation of bad news. Then he sighed and shook his head.

"I did what I could. Which wasn't much."

Celcilia glared at him, clearly expecting a lot more information.

He sighed again. "I extracted the dart—there was only the one—but there was a lot of damage. The toxin is very nasty. Works by altering the structure of affected cells. Gets them to generate and secrete more toxin, passing it along to the next layer of cells, and so on. Producing the toxin kills the cell, and the target's body slowly necrotizes."

"Necrowhat?"

"Dies. One cell at a time."

"Ah. Sounds downright lethal. And you just happened to have the antidote handy?"

She realized what the answer was by the look of pain in his eyes. She turned to look at her arm, wrapped in the bloody bandages. "My arm ..."

Bob hurried to interject. "I saved the arm. It needs proper medical care at some point, but is fine for now."

"So what's wrong?"

He took a deep breath and exhaled it in a gust. "The arm is safe, like I said. But I had to excise some tissue."

"Cut away, you mean."

"Yeah."

"How much?"

He took and exhaled another deep breath. "Enough to save you and the arm. Worked around the blood vessels and nerves, but had to remove a good chunk."

"Meaning?" she said in tight tones, tired of the back and forth.

"About a third of the bicep."

"Oh, Goddess." Her eyes clenched shut. Despite her best efforts, several tears forced their way out and down her cheeks.

He face became stern. "You're alive and will stay that way. The damage can be minimized if we can get to a reasonably advanced planet in the not-too-distant future. Which we need to do anyway."

"But ..."

"You. Are. Alive."

The tone in his voice had echoes that made the words drill into her head, causing her to squeeze her eyes shut. She took and exhaled several deep breaths before trusting herself to speak again. Then she wiped her eyes on the sleeve of her uninjured arm.

"Alright. Fine. I'm alive. But how long can we expect to stay that way? The fact that we're still here means you couldn't just dial up a new destination, doesn't it?"

That got a broad grin out of him. "Yes and no."

"I am not in the mood for your crap, mister man. Neo-sort-of-god man. Speak plain or don't speak at all, you." She felt herself babbling but could only end the rambling with a giggle. The world began spinning, so she closed her eyes. That didn't seem to help too much until she felt a cold cloth pressed against her forehead. The light-headiness eventually passed. She opened her eyes again. "Sorry."

"Don't be. You're beginning to run a fever. Here, drink more tea."

Her sharp exhalation proclaimed her disgust as she turned her face away.

"Please, you've got to drink at least a bit more. It'll help with the fever."

Her face screwed up in disgust as she accepted the cup. After taking a small sip and gagging it down she looked at him and said, "I sip. You talk. Details."

That made him smile. "Fair enough. First, though ... you comfortable enough?"

She nodded. It wasn't much of a bed, but she'd had a lot worse. "What about the Goddess?"

He snorted a laugh. "Locked down both her portals for a month. Nothing in or out. She'll have to crawl back to her temple under her own power and heal along the way. And it'll take her a good long while to heal." He paused and looked thoughtful. "Judging by the way she looked at the end, though, I'm not sure she can heal without medical assistance. She wasn't fully adjusted to her new aspect and that adversely affected her healing factors. Very likely badly enough that she won't be able to control the alternate energies or access a portal. She's trapped there, I think."

Celcilia tried to laugh, but it turned into more of a cough. Bob leaned towards her to help but she waved him away. "Can we leave here?" she managed to say.

Bob nodded. "We can use the portal to leave but we have to wait for it to recharge. A couple of days, maybe three. It's an old one that my dad put here."

"Your da? That's good, right?"

"Not exactly. Things are going downhill a lot faster than I expected. My family's private portals are being hardened against me. Locking me out, in effect. Not just here, but everywhere."

She paused her sipping to ask, "And you know this how?"

"Dad left me a message."

The happy look on his face surprised her. "I thought you weren't on speaking terms?"

"We're not. We weren't. Uhm, but things seem to have changed. At least somewhat. Family politics spilling over into galactic politics, and vice versa."

"You're babbling worse'n me."

"Sorry." He took a deep breath and exhaled slowly. She had never seen him so rattled, and was curious as to what the news was.

"His message was brief but to the point. It appears that Mom, Set, and my elder sister have ganged up to force Dad to cooperate. He can handle any two of them, but not three. That would leave my youngest sister defenceless, and he would never do that. So he's playing for time, expecting me

12

to do something. According to him, even by just surviving I'm rattling cages and stirring things up. That's all well and good, but the others have decided to constrain me by locking me out of the exit function of our private portals. That is, I can use them to enter but not leave. Only he has the knowledge and experience to ensure that I can't bypass it, so they sent my elder sister along with him to ensure he does it right. Which he did, after a fashion. Turns out the sneaky old guy slipped in a loophole. I can use any of our portals to exit one time; then I am truly locked out."

"And the long recharge time?"

Bob waved an arm to encompass the area. "This is a testing planet. One entry portal, one exit portal. Each only works the one way. The slow recharge is a design feature to prevent someone from changing their mind."

"Except your da twiddled things."

"Yep. Told me he had full faith in my ability to turn that to a tactical advantage." Bob cleared his throat and turned away.

"Bob?"

He turned to look at her, his eyes unexpectedly bright. "Then he told me that he was proud of me." His voice cracked for a moment, but he was smiling. "That's the first time he's ever said that to me."

"And?"

"And he promised to defend my younger sister. Told me to focus my energies on everything else."

She just looked at him.

"Sorry, you don't understand. Whatever happens, he'll make sure she's safe. He knows that if I had any inkling whatsoever that she might be in trouble that I'd go to her, whatever the cost. Until now I assumed she'd be safe. Not too happy, perhaps, but safe. That situation has changed, but he'll take care of her."

"Uhm, and you're fine with that?"

"Oh, yes. Whatever else I may think about my dad, when he gives his word to do something, it is done. And he's probably one of the finest warriors in our long history. Which leave me free to do what needs to be done."

"Which is?"

"Stop Set from destroying my people. He's corrupted most of my family and many of the people I know—the Family at large. His new empire will destroy whole worlds of the younger races, and blacken the souls of my people. I won't let that happen."

"You. Alone."

"Yep," he replied. The edges of his mouth twitched as a smile threatened to break forth.

"Right. So all we have to do wait for two days or so until the portal recharges. On a planet you call Hell. Lovely."

His face became serious again. "I'll see that you get home, Celcilia. I promise."

She reached out her uninjured arm and patted his hand. "I know you'll do your damnedest, Bob. But ... you said this was Hell."

He looked around. "I survived here for several years."

Her eyes went wide.

He waved his hand. "This is the garden spot of the planet. All portals keep out the locals and ensure the integrity of the grove surrounding it."

She took a closer look around for the first time. The sun was above the horizon, but had a strange tinge to it. It felt warm, but not much more. There were wispy clouds, but their colour seemed off. The portal itself was gone and she could see that they were surrounded by rather scraggly-looking trees that were thick enough to form a rough barrier. The leaves varied from brown to green; some were broad and some were spiky. Overall, though, they blocked the view of what might lay beyond. Between the trees was scrubby grass, the tallest of which might reach her knees. The air was hazy but there were hints of hills in the distance. It all gave the impression of an ancient scarred world on the edge of death.

"This is the garden spot?"

He nodded. "It gets a lot worse beyond this."

"What about the people?"

His face became clouded. "It used to be a good planet, once upon a time. Quite lovely, in fact. Reasonably advanced—a little further along than yours in some respects, behind in others."

He paused long enough that she prompted, "And?"

Bob looked at her. "Disagreements. Civil unrest. Then, eventually, total war. Your own continent had something called the Hundred Years War, right?"

She nodded. "Uhm, ya. Centuries ago."

"Similar here. Except it never really ended. Year after year, decade after decade, century after century. Despite the wars, their industrial capability progressed and was enough to keep a good-sized population going. There were large socioeconomic entities that managed to keep people fed and reasonably content. Violence was mostly confined to the borders of the warring nations. "

"So why did you come here? The first time, I mean."

Bob uttered a sour laugh. "A final proving ground. To get tossed into that maelstrom of organized violence. Up to that point I'd gotten through every test, every scenario, without having to kill. Almost died a couple of times, but managed to out-think or gimmick or find a loophole in every single test. Looking back on it, it was Mom's way of trying to get me killed off. Oh, Set had gone through the exact same tests. But he'd always been older and better trained—and prepared to kill. I, on the other hand, was a pushy, mouthy kid who insisted on doing everything my big brother did and was determined to show him up. He knew it and took advantage of that more than once. You see, all my kind has to undergo a test of some sort to prove their suitability for adulthood. Create something or do something that is generally seen as a reasonable challenge. The applicant chooses the task, but it has to be approved."

He grew silent and she let the silence drag on for a couple of minutes before speaking again. In a quiet voice she asked, "Bob? What happened?"

"They sent me here as my final test. Dropped me in to do or die. This was the starting point, and was told the exit was somewhere on the other side of the planet. Tough but doable. After all, Set had done it."

"What happened?"

"What no-one expected—a sudden, total societal collapse within a few weeks after I arrived." He looked off into the distance. "Nations collapsed into city-states. Then those collapsed into tribes. Left-over caches of arms and equipment enabled warlords to run rampant over the tribes armed with lesser weapons. Imagine cavalry charges against tanks, or sometimes tanks against bows and arrows. Violence used to grab power for its own sake."

She shivered. "Sounds awful."

He turned to look at her. "It was worse than that, I assure you. Anyway, I got dumped here just before the collapse started. Took me several years to reach the coast. Another year to build a boat capable of crossing the ocean to the other major continent. A couple of years to reach the exit portal. Fighting all the way, nearly every day."

She looked at him with horror. "What? Non-stop fighting? Didn't anyone try to stop it, to make peace?"

"Of course," he answered, nodding for emphasis. "Many times. The warlords, and later the gangs, just kept attacking. The ones with the advanced tech tried to carve out empires, or even just a kingdom to rule over. Some were consumed by the hatred instilled by centuries of war. Some just liked the killing." He bowed his head and was silent for a time. "So much killing," he finally said in a whisper.

"Was everyone insane, then?"

He kept his head bowed as he answered, "No, not at all. Many good people lived here, once upon a time." After a moment he gave a soft sigh and raised his head to look at her. "One surviving group took me in. Cared for me. I'd been alone for a long time, you see, living off the land after the armies disbanded. Some of the soldiers went to the warlords, some to the gangs, and some ... some tried to make something better. I lucked into a band of those. They'd built up a nice little town, actually. A small mine, farms, light industry, that sort of thing. Fought off the marauders and gangs, and became pretty much left alone. Then it ended."

"How?"

"A high-tech mercenary corps came, demanding tribute. Got rebuffed, of course. What my friends didn't realize was how much heavy armour the mercenaries had, nor how many trained troops. Battle rifles are no match against a squad of heavy tanks. I was part of a scouting group on patrol when the attack came. Too far away to help. Oh, we tried, but the battle was over in less than an hour. The entire town was razed. No survivors. They ambushed my squad when we returned to the town and I was the only survivor."

"Then what?"

Bob looked away, took a deep breath, raised his head, and the expression on his face became fierce and predatory. "I wiped out the company of mercenaries. Every last one of them. Took me a few months to hunt down all of them, but I did it. The leaders, the tank crews, the armoured infantry, all of them."

He breathed deeply and a look of fierce satisfaction burned on his face. A look that frightened her to immobility. Then he released his breath in a rush and the savagery he had displayed vanished with it, to be replaced by a look of infinite sadness and regret.

"Then I began the long march home. And didn't let anything or anyone stand in my way."

The silence between them stretched out for a minute, interrupted only by Bob poking at the fire with a stick. Finally Celcilia asked, "What happened after you got home?"

Bob shrugged. "I'd passed the final test, so I was deemed an adult. Took on my final aspect ..." he gestured at his body, "... had my Naming Day, and left."

"Left?"

"Yeah. For us, a Naming Day is typically a big deal. New adult aspect, new adult name, everyone comes to formally recognize the new adult. A very big deal."

"And you did what?"

He smiled and uttered a short, sharp laugh. "Kept my childhood name. Made my aspect a duplicate of my childhood body. Declared my adulthood for the record with just my immediate family present. Didn't say much to anyone after I got back from here, and didn't say much to anyone when I left. What words I said were as angry and hurtful as I could make them."

"Where did you go?"

Bob shrugged again. "Did the usual Grand Tour of the friendly planets. Then branched out to the seedier ones. Lived for the moment."

"And did some of those moments include, ah, the company of young women?"

Bob gave a small, embarrassed smile. "You mean was I a brash, useless asshole who used women and then tossed them aside while sating myself with pleasures of the flesh? Yeah. For a time, that's exactly what I did. Who I was."

"What changed?"

"Got bored with it all. Bored with what I'd become. No, that's not accurate. *Ashamed* of what I'd allowed myself to become." He rubbed at his mouth for a time before continuing. Then he lowered his hand and looked at her.

18

"Also saw what was going on in the galaxy at large. Most of my kind stays at home or maybe does a short tour after their Naming Day to the friendly planets. Usually taking on a temporary human-form aspect to make things more fun. Nice and safe and sanitary. I saw the other places. Places where people—the younger races like yourself—were struggling. Most of them were decent folks, too. Working hard trying to get by, but all too often getting beaten down. Sometimes bad luck, sometimes natural disasters, but sometimes bad people came along and attacked them. Sometimes to conquer, and sometimes just for the fun of it. Just like here. Just like the townsfolk who had adopted me."

"So you fought them."

He shook his head. "Not right away. And not like I did here." He waved one hand to indicate the area around them. "Swore I'd never allow myself to lose control like that again. No, I kept bumming around from place to place but this time I kept my eyes wide open. Treated it like an intelligence operation, like I'd been taught."

"Just watched?" she asked in innocent tones, a smile playing on her lips.

Bob laughed. "Well, mostly. More or less. Quite a bit less as time went on, if truth be told. Did what I could to balance the scales. Wasn't much, most of the time, but made me begin to feel better about myself. I learnt to stop the really bad stuff by preventing it from happening in the first place. Learnt to trust the local sociopolitical structures to take care of things once I'd taken the edge off the worst of it. The Precepts of Survival teach us that 'perfection is the enemy of good enough'. That was a tough lesson for me to learn, but it eventually sank in."

She joined in with the laughter for a few seconds before sinking into an exhausted sleep.

* * *

19

The next several days passed well enough. Bob continued making potions with local herbs that kept the worst of the pain and fever at bay. Unfortunately, each day also brought less ability to move her fingers. She became somewhat obsessive about moving them until Bob bandaged her hand to prevent that, claiming it was to improve her healing.

He also managed to find enough for them to eat, so long as neither ate very much. Still, it was enough to keep them going. His time was spent foraging and looking after her. She spent much of the time dozing, but insisted on doing some of the lighter chores. That kept them busy during the daylight hours. Even so, Celcilia often caught him staring into the distance far more than was normal for him.

One day she found enough energy to take a short walk beyond the portal grove to stretch her legs. The barren landscape shocked her. The low mountains in the hazy distance would have reminded her of her native Wales except that here the vegetation was sparse and a grey-green. Between the grove and hills, the ground was a carpet of undulating mounds of various sizes. Here and there were tufts of something that resembled grass. There was a constant wind, but it smelled of desolation and death.

Celcilia shivered at the sight. "Feels haunted."

"Not far off," replied Bob. "Though to be honest, this always was a desolate place. The portal is the only source of water between here and the far side of those mountains. What little rain there is gets soaked up pretty fast."

"No wells?"

Bob shook his head. "Only in theory. This whole barren area forms a common border for several nations. Used to be a lot flatter, which made it a perfect shortcut for troops if water could be found. They all dug wells, but the other sides poisoned them as quickly as the wells got dug. Of course the poison leached into the water table, creating a toxic buffer zone around the mountains."

"Ick. So why is the portal here and not someplace closer to civilization?"

"Heh. That's part of the test. The closest cities are on the far side of the mountains. The haze prevents apporting to the mountains, and it's too far to levitate all the way."

"So you, what, walked? Without water?"

"Yes, indeed. Don't forget that I was trained for this sort of thing."

"Wouldn't those moguls or whatever they are make walking difficult?"

"It used to be quite flat, actually. When the collapse came, there were tremendous tank and artillery battles here. No point to it, but they'd been building up for battle here for so long that once started it just ... kept going." Bob shook his head at the memory of it.

"Didn't they have aircraft? Would have thought that'd do the trick better than tanks."

"Only to a limited extent. Their artillery and anti-aircraft weapons were so good that any sort of aerial vehicles never became more than a minor nuisance."

Celcilia shivered again. "Is the rest of the planet like this?"

"Not at all. Just very damaged. That's the result of a few atomic weapons being used further south. In addition to the immediate effects, they altered the major ocean currents. That, in turn, altered the prevailing wind patterns and climate. Farmlands became dust or mud, rivers became torrents or trickles, growing seasons altered ... nothing was the same. That reinforced the overall social collapse and it all descended into chaos."

Then he turned to her and said, "You should get back to camp and stay warm. Sleep if you can. I need to forage, and do that better on my own."

Celcilia glanced at Bob, and the look of pain on her friend's face tore at her soul. She nodded and returned to their meagre camp.

* * *

Although they managed to fill the daylight hours with chores, the nights dragged a bit. After her walkabout, though, Bob seemed once again willing to talk and Celcilia tried to find topics that would ease his pensive mood. At first she was hesitant to ask questions, but Bob was always forthright with his answers. Finally she asked, "Why are you telling me all this?"

He smiled at her. "Who'd you tell? Oh, don't look so sour ... I promised to take you home and I will."

"Yeah, but what if I told people about you? About what's happening out here?" she said waving her good arm at the sky.

That got a laugh out of him, the first outright burst of humour she'd heard from him since they'd arrived. "Tell anyone you like, anything you like. Truly. But who is going to believe you?" He waggled a finger at her. "Take care, or they'll lock you up as a raving lunatic."

She stuck her tongue out at him. "I'll write a book."

"Hmm. Well, I hope it earns you a lot of money. Still, no-one is going to believe it. And those that do aren't going to be anyone you'll want to associate with."

Celcilia sighed. "Yeah. The nutter brigades. Met enough of them when I was growing up. Our Order was fringe enough to attract a few of them no matter how secretive we were. If our parents kept us out of school to prevent us becoming 'polluted with foul ideas', as me mam liked to say, the local council would send around a social worker. Spend time in school, and the social workers'd get called if ya mentioned the Goddess. They weren't so bad, but Goddess help ya if the Wiccans got wind of it." She shook her head at the memory. Then she picked up a stick and flung it at Bob who was trying very hard not to laugh.

"Hey!" he said before collapsing in gales of laughter. She soon joined him, and the ruined world around them echoed to the sounds of two friends sharing some happiness. Eventually the giggles died down and they sat in comfortable silence for a time.

"So," she finally said. "What's this about 'aspects' that you keep going on about. You were going on about the Goddess—oh, stop glaring at me—having the aspect of a dragon. And you mentioned your aspect being a copy of your childhood body. What's that all about?"

Bob chuckled and she glared at him. He held up his hands as if to ward off a blow. "I keep forgetting that what I take for granted is totally alien to you." He thought for a moment before answering. "For us, a 'body' is what we are born with. And, yes, we are born in the usual way, just like you. As we get older and learn control, we get implants to do various things. Once we become an adult we get to choose a physical form ... our adult aspect. That clear?"

"As mud," she replied shaking her head. "You, what, transfer consciousness from your birth body into some artificial thing?

Bob gave her a horrified look. "What? No! That would be obscene."

She finally realized that he was seriously offended, and opened her mouth to apologize when he waved a hand to interrupt her.

"Sorry," he said. "I've explained it badly." He thought for a moment. "Alright, let's try this. We're born, just like you are, and trained as we mature. Implants are allowed to us as part of our training, to allow us to become familiar with the different powers available to us as adults. Upon reaching adulthood, we select a final form ... our aspect. It embodies all the power we have chosen to have access to. Each aspect has certain capabilities and limitations, with none inherently better than any other. One can't do, or be, everything. Not even us."

She considered that for a moment. "That is all well and good, but what is an aspect?"

"Ah. Yes, I think I understand your question. Okay, well, think of it of a chrysalis. You know what that is?"

"Like a butterfly?"

"Yes. You know how that works?"

"The caterpillar goes to sleep, then changes into a butterfly."

"Uhm, there's actually more to it than that. The caterpillar's body dissolves and is reformed into something else."

"Oh, Goddess. That's horrible!"

"Well, not for the butterfly. And for the caterpillar it is a perfectly natural thing to do."

"What? What's natural about dissolving?"

Bob sighed. "Look, work with me here. It is a perfectly natural thing for the caterpillar to do. Genetically programmed for it. In our case, we control the programming. Easy peasy."

Her eyebrows shot up. "Not natural for humans. Which you claim to be."

He chuckled. "It is how we do things. Natural for us."

She frowned as she considered that. "How does that follow?"

Bob's face grew serious. "It came out of the Great Wars. Our ancestors learnt how to modify their forms to suit specific battle requirements. Some for heavy gravity environments, some for zero gravity environments, whatever was required. Also to incorporate sensors and weaponry into the body."

She gave him a hard look. "You've mentioned, or implied, that. And talked about these Great Wars as if they were something holy. What happened at the end? You won, didn't you?"

"More or less."

"Meaning?"

"Yes, we won. But the human race was all but wiped out."

"Again, what are you talking about?"

Bob sighed. "Although each wave of Enemy was defeated, it came at a terrible cost every time. At the end of it all, only a few hundred humans were alive. On a handful of planets. Out of billions on hundreds of planets."

Her jaw dropped and she could only gape at him. Then she shut her mouth and said, "How did you survive? Breeding population too small to prevent serious genetic problems. Even I know that."

He grunted. "My ancestors had developed technology, including genetic technology, beyond anything you can conceive of. They took the genome of every surviving human and analyzed it. Then edited out every weakness, every bad recessive. Once that was done, they mixed every genome with every other genome to maximize the gene pool. Then they added every known positive survival factor to every genome."

"Excuse me. You're the result of a genetic experiment?"

"No. Not an experiment. A desperate attempt at racial survival. The ancestors had a small gene pool to work with, so they made sure that what remained was the best that it could be. Then they improved it. Carefully, with the full cooperation of each family."

"Everyone agreed to this?"

"Well, almost everyone. A few refused to take part in the blending of genomes, or the tinkering to remove the damaging recessive genes. These became known as the Refusal Faction, or simply Refusers. They eventually left to find their own way."

Celcilia shook her head at the inrush of information. "Okay, so they left to do their own thing. So then what happened, a civil war?"

Bob shook his head. "No. Neither side wanted anything to do with the other. We—my ancestors—saw them as betrayers of human survival. They saw us as abominations. Absolutely no common ground. Interactions became rare and unpleasant. Nowadays, no-one knows where they are or if they've even survived."

"Alright, so this blending business was to do what, exactly?"

"The culling made sure that everyone had the best starting point possible, taking care to emphasize variations as much as possible."

"So what about the aspects?"

"We have the technology to assume any form—any aspect—that we can imagine. But given our history, we're pretty much focused on forms useful for various battle functions."

"And yours is ..."

"Enhanced standard human configuration, with emphasis on general adaptability. Anything else is a specialist function."

"The Goddess ... you said she used to be a dragon?"

He nodded. "An interesting, if somewhat ornamental, aspect. There's a species that looks something like that ... the True Dragons we call them. A nasty, ill-tempered species for the most part. Don't much like humans. We never went to war with them, mind you, but there's no real love lost between us. Still, they are gorgeous and some people copied their form. And, no, that didn't help diplomatic relations in the slightest."

"So, choosing an aspect is a big thing. What about changing it?"

"Also a big thing. Impossible to do outside of a medical facility. Never something to undertake lightly. It takes time to learn to use one's physical form properly and take full advantage of its abilities."

"Is that why your aspect is the same as your original body?"

Bob nodded. "Exactly. I'd spent a long time acquiring a very fine level of control. Didn't want to throw that away."

"That, and it would confuse and piss people off."

That got a chuckle out of him. "Partly," he was forced to concede.

"And the Goddess—Kydos—used to be a dragon? Had the aspect of one, I mean."

Bob nodded.

"Was she a dragon when you dated?"

"Yep."

Celcilia gaped at him for a few seconds before she finally found her voice. "How ... how does that even work?"

He looked puzzled at the question, then smiled. "It all works out. Part of the fun of dating is figuring things out. Same thing with you folks, too, I gather."

"Yes, but ..." Celcilia started, but closed her mouth with an audible snap.

Bob's face took on a faraway look. "Now, meeting a girl's parents can get nasty. Especially if they've been around a while and have some of the more extreme combat aspects. In my experience, parents—of whatever culture and planet—can get awfully protective." He shuddered as memories resurfaced.

That earned him an askance look that turned into a glare. Then she grew thoughtful. "So how old are you?"

He was somewhat taken aback by the question. "Excuse me?"

She pressed on. "Seriously. How old are you? How long do your people live? Are you immortal?"

He considered the questions carefully before answering. "We aren't immortal. Long-lived, yes, but not immortal. We grow old and die. Then there are accidents and people who just stop wanting to live."

"And you are how old?"

"Age in your terms? I honestly don't know."

She glared at him.

"Seriously. As a child, time stretched on forever, like an eternal 'now'. I aged at what seemed to me to be a normal rate, but the years went by without counting. Truly. If you want to think of us in your terms ... well, our Naming Day is about equivalent to your eighteen years old. Like a high school graduation."

"So you came to this world when you were ...?

Bob considered the question before answering. "Just prior to becoming an adult. Call it sixteen or seventeen of your years. Physically I was much older, of course. But in societal terms, that would be about right."

"So physically you're older?"

He nodded as he pondered the question. "Yep. In your years, I'd estimate myself to be ... hmm ... several of your centuries old. Less than a thousand, though. Things often move at a slower pace when you've got lots of time available. I'm considered to be little more than a youth barely out of early adulthood."

"So your lifetimes are, what, many thousands of years?" Celcilia asked. Despite the fascination with all this new information, her eyelids were drooping.

"Uhm, yeah, in your measurements. On the order of ten thousand, on average, I'd guess. Some older, of course."

"Whoosh. So how long have your folks been doing this aspect stuff?"

Bob smiled. "A long, long time ... many generations. As I keep telling you, we've been around a long time."

She would have pursued the issue, but exhaustion claimed her and she drifted into sleep.

* * *

She awoke the next morning to find that Bob had acquired

and cooked a sketchy breakfast for her, complete with herb tea.

"Breakfast in bed. You're too kind."

Bob inclined his head. "We live to serve."

Celcilia would have offered a tart retort but her hunger kept her focused on the food before her. All too soon she was finished and became aware of a look of expectancy on Bob's face. "What?" she asked, wondering if she had a scrap of something on her face.

"It's time to go," he said.

She could only boggle at him. Then she gathered her wits and asked, "When?"

"Any time. No need to rush." He was smiling rather more than she had seen in a while.

"Where to?"

The smile vanished. "Been thinking about that. Need to go somewhere unexpected."

"Which means someplace that caused you pain, I gather?"

He winced. "Yeah. But that's my problem. The place I have in mind, though ... they might not like me very much."

She snorted. "That's supposed to surprise me?"

That got a grunted laugh out of him. "Fair point. Well, this place got hit by an attack from weapons left over from the Great Wars. I stopped it, but never did find out who was behind it. Anyway, it got very bad for a while until I fixed things. And, uhm, they know a little about my kind. Enough to not like us very much."

"And we are going there, why?"

"Know some people I can contact who should be able to help us. We need to get your arm looked at, you know, and they've got the tech for that. Or did. Probably still do. I hope."

"Stop babbling, Bob. How bad is it, do you think?"

"Well, we should probably be alright."

"Sounds grim. Better than the alternatives?"

Bob sighed. "Yeah. Wish I could offer something better, but this is the best bet."

"Then we do this." Her voice was firm, with no hint of hesitation or doubt.

He looked at her approvingly and nodded. "As you command."

After helping her to her feet, he instantiated the portal. After a brief frown of concentration, he defined the coordinates for their destination. Holding an arm around her waist to confirm to the portal security systems that she was a guest, they stepped into the black film.

CHAPTER THREE

Unwelcome Travelers

They arrived without stumbling, although the short walk had exhausted Celcilia. Bob helped her over to a nearby log and eased her down. She gave a grateful sigh as she sat, her eyes closed in an attempt to block her increasing discomfort. The brightness of the sun was irritating as well.

"Well?" she asked with her eyes still closed. "Things about what you expected?"

"Let you know in a minute after a look around. Wait here."

"Like I'm going anywhere," she muttered.

It took somewhat longer than a minute for him to return, and she was beginning to seriously consider whether to open her eyes. It was a new world, after all, and she felt that she should try to be just a bit curious about it. Suppressing the urge to sigh she opened her eyes and looked around, using her hand to block the glare of the sun. At first glance it all looked nice enough. The foliage looked green and healthy, and there was a soft rasping buzz of insects nearby. There was a soft breeze that bore the scents of healthy, growing things mixed with the slight tang of animal scents. The breeze rustled through the trees, and she noticed that there were several different varieties. Her headache began to recede a bit, or at least enough for her to feel a pang of homesickness.

She heard a rustle of brush off to one side and she turned around to see Bob moving towards her. "Was beginning to wonder where you were," she said. "Seems nice enough, though."

The tight look on Bob's face put a stop to her rambling. "I gather things aren't so nice, after all."

Bob shook his head. "No, they aren't. We're in no immediate danger, but probably shouldn't hang around any longer than we have to."

"What's wrong?"

"Remember I told you that the portals have a defensive system?"

She nodded.

"Well, someone has gone to a lot of trouble to probe the exact nature and extent of those defences."

"Meaning?"

Bob answered her by asking a question of his own. "Looks all nice and peaceful here, right?"

She nodded as she replied, "Peaceful enough, yes." Her eyes narrowed as she tried to guess what he was getting at.

"Well, someone has attacked right up to edge of the defences. Repeatedly and over what seems an extended period of time. Then built up a series of moats and fortifications around the circumference. Very much like the rings around a bullseye."

"With us as the target?"

"Yep. Well, the portal, actually."

"Why? What happened here?"

Bob sighed. "A while ago I was passing through here and helped with a problem." At the look on her face he hastened to add, "I didn't cause it. Honest. But someone from outside the planet did."

"What sort of problem are we talking about?"

"Uhm, a biological attack. The attacker seeded clouds with an agent that infected the rain. The agent was a

32

nanomachine of sorts that, in essence, weaponized rain drops."

"Excuse me?"

"Sounds bizarre, I know. As the rain fell, the drops coalesced into larger units that became more and more self-aware. The individual drops collected bits of whatever they landed on, delivered that material to the larger units, which then turned those materials into mobile weapons platforms."

Celcilia held up a hand. "Wait. Wait. So these nanowidgets infected the rain, the rain came down and tore strips off whatever they hit, then made weapons from whatever they collected?"

Bob nodded.

She shook her head, but kept a hand up to forestall any interruption from him. "Then they went on a rampage?"

"No," he said shaking his head. "It was a well-designed, military-style, area-denial operation on a planetary scale, not a randomized rampage."

"Who was behind it?"

"Never found out. With my help it got stopped, but not before a lot of people got hurt or killed. Tore up their infrastructure on a planetary scale, too."

"One of your people did this?"

"Don't know. Didn't think so at the time, as the portal hadn't been used in well over a local century. There were no manufacturing sites ever found, and we looked very hard to find them."

"How did you know what to look for?"

He looked uncomfortable. "It was something developed during the Great Wars."

"By your lot." It was not a question.

Bob sighed. "Well, yes. Keep in mind that my ancestors were engaged in a series of wars with aliens bent on exterminating them. Which they tended to be on the losing end of until they came up with something big enough to hit back with. Some of the weapons developed were for area denial, or to make life miserable enough to slow the Enemy down."

"This was one of those weapons?"

He nodded. "Yeah."

"So how do you know so much about it?"

"It's one of the classical lessons we're all taught as kids—how not to fight a war."

"What?"

"It's a pretty stupid weapon when you think about it. Kills indiscriminately, no control of it once deployed, and ruins the entire planet for decades if it recovers at all."

"So why'd they use it? Your ancestors, I mean."

"They panicked," he said in a soft, low voice. "That's the real lesson we were told to learn. Panic tends to create stupid solutions that are often impossible to live with afterwards. My people aren't gods, Celcilia, and creating this weapon was one of our biggest blunders."

"So what happened here?"

He shrugged. "Not sure. Best answer I could come up with was that a leftover munition hit the planet."

"By accident or design?"

Again he shrugged. "If it was a targeted attack, the attackers never revealed themselves at all. Not before, during, or after. That doesn't make a lot of sense, so I concluded that it was a one-of accident."

"Why only the one time? How could you make sure of that?"

"I had the portal transmit identification demands on all the different war-time communications channels, as well as on the modern channels. There was no response up to a dozen light years out."

"Excuse me? How'd you do that?"

"You've heard me speak of the alternative energies?"

She nodded.

"Well, we can send messages faster than light ... it's one of our greatest discoveries. Series of discoveries, actually, since there are a number of ways to accomplish it. The easier ways are only slightly faster than light, but the truly complex ways are much faster."

"Fine. Whatever," she said, shrugging to show her indifference to the technical details. "How does that explain their interest in the portal?"

A rustling off to the side caused them both to look towards the source of the sound. Celcilia braced her good arm against the log, and prepared to jump. Bob moved quickly to one side and assumed a watchful stance.

An old man shuffled through the brush towards them. His movements were stiff, and he was leaning forward as if fighting against a strong wind. He spoke, and his voice was slow and thin but firm. "Hello, Bob. It's been a long time."

Bob stared into the old man's eyes. "General. Yes, it has been a long time. I'm pleased, if surprised, to see you still around."

The old man smiled. It was a professional smile—not hostile but not warm. "You've seen our defences, have you not?"

"Yes, sir. Very impressive. Although I'm not sure why you would create them."

The old man gave a slight shrug. "Well, it seemed like a good idea. Not many other options."

Bob sighed. "Perhaps. But it is all rather futile, you know." Then he frowned and added, "But how is it that you are here? You should have been running away in terror long before you got to this point."

The old man gave a genuine smile as he reached up and removed his hat. Celcilia, who had understood nothing of the exchange, gasped at the scars on the man's head. Bob's face fell as he realized what must have been done. The old man slowly replaced his hat then looked at Celcilia. "Who is your young friend, Bob? She looks injured."

"She is. Is there any chance of her getting medical attention?"

"No." The answer was swift and delivered in a flat tone.

"General, she's an innocent in all this. I'm trying to get her back to her home."

"No," the old man repeated. "Just leave us, Bob. Leave us and never come back."

"Bob, what's he saying? Is it time be scared, yet?"

Without looking at her, Bob answered in a low voice, "We're safe for the time being."

"Who is he?" she insisted.

"Someone I worked with when I was here last."

"Those terrible scars ... what happened to him?"

"They probably observed that the portal allowed animals to wander freely, and did surgery on him to approximate their mental state."

"He sounds like he's had a stroke."

Bob nodded. "Not far off. Now quiet, please."

"Your pardon, General, I was just explaining things to my friend. Her name is Celcilia by the way."

The General turned and made a small bow to Celcilia, who answered with a tentative smile.

"General, what happened here? Were there other attacks?"

The General shook his head. "No, but there had been so much destruction that people needed to fight back against something. Before vanishing, you admitted that you were from off-world. Grateful as we were for your assistance, we needed to ensure our safety. So we searched for anomalies and eventually found this place." He made a small wave with one hand to encompass the forest.

"But why the fortifications?"

The General shrugged. "At first it was only to monitor. Then we dug those series of moats to delay anything that came out. Then it was decided that more was required, then more, then more again. What began as a simple military reconnaissance turned into a major civil works project that took on a life of its own. An almost religious zeal, if you can imagine such a thing."

"And your surgery?"

The General raised a hand and gently touched one side of his head before lowering the hand to his side. "After I lost my family the army was all I had left. I was deemed to be the expert on off-worlders, so I was put in charge of the observation side of things here. Restorations efforts moved on apace and eventually we made back most of what we had lost. Even made some extra advances. When I got too old for active duty, I volunteered for this procedure to try penetrating the forest itself."

"But it wasn't successful, was it?"

"Not entirely, no. This is deepest I've ever been allowed to come into the forest. I suspect it is because you are here."

Bob nodded. "Sounds about right. But how did you get here so quickly?"

"I have a small shelter not far beyond the forest. Small but it suits me just fine, these days. But enough about that. You and your friend must leave immediately."

"But she needs medical attention," Bob insisted. "Could you spare some medicines, at least?"

"I'm sorry, but the attack will begin very soon."

"Attack? What? Why?"

Celcilia had watched the exchange with growing unease. Things did not seem to be going well. It didn't help that she felt another wave of nausea and dizziness coming on.

"You came through. The protocols are quite firm about the required response. I came merely to satisfy my own curiosity."

"It won't succeed, General. There is nothing on this planet that could penetrate these defences."

The General nodded. "I accept that, Bob. But the protocols are in place. They'll try every weapon. You've seen the scars on the landscape beyond, of course. But the difference this time is that they'll use fission and fusion weapons."

"That'll poison the surrounding area for decades, even centuries, and won't affect this spot."

"I do not doubt you. But the effort will be made nonetheless."

Bob shut his eyes and concentrated furiously. This madness had gone on long enough. Opening his eyes he looked at the General and said, "If I destroy the equipment within this forest, will you call off your attack?"

The General's face showed confusion. "Equipment? Destroy?" Then his expression became wary as he gave Bob a hard look. "Why would you do this?"

"Your planet has suffered enough, General. My companion and I will leave, and the equipment will self-destruct. Everything from here to the first moat outside the glade will be vapourized. Not a blast, as such, but a gradual dispersal of material. There will be some energy released. Anyone within the radius of the first moat will be in danger. Further away will be safer, of course, but that is the minimum safe distance."

Their discussion was interrupted by a soft thud, as Celcilia slumped unconscious to the ground. Bob rushed to her side and examined her.

"I'm sorry about your friend, Bob. Truly I am. But how quickly can you leave? The attack, you see. It will be launched very soon."

Bob's face had begun to twist into a snarl, but he forced it into a neutral mode. "She needs medical attention."

The old man shook his head, obviously saddened by her plight. "I'm sorry, but you must leave as quickly as possible. When can you go?"

Bob took a deep breath and let it out slowly. "Give me two

minutes."

"You can have five. That much I can do for you, and wish it could be more."

"You won't be able to get far in that time, General. Not far enough."

The General gave a wan smile. "I'm a soldier, Bob. This is the one last battle I always wanted."

"I was never your enemy, sir."

"I know; I was speaking metaphorically. Good luck to you both." With that the old man turned and hobbled away as quickly as he could. Bob watched until the forest swallowed the General before he squatted to examine Celcilia. Her breathing was somewhat laboured and her fever had gotten worse. As he wiped the sweat from her brow and positioned her to ease her breathing, he pondered his options. None of them were good, but some were definitely worse than others. Of course, this world had turned out to be one of the worst ones and now he had to leave quickly.

After a moment of indecision he instantiated the portal. Before setting the pattern for his destination, he accessed the diagnostics section. Dealing with the layers of security protocols took longer than he expected, eating well into the five minutes promised by the General. He was at the final security layer when the portal announced that missiles were inbound, arriving in less than three minutes. He snarled as he went through the final security layer and set up the portal's self-destruct sequence. He had a choice of settings, from world-wrecking to minimal damage. Choosing the latter, he set it initiate after he had reached his destination.

Bob picked up Celcilia and stood waiting as the gateway film formed. The portal tonelessly informed him that the missiles were less a minute away. Several seconds later, he stepped through and exited into another world. He hoped that the portal's destruction would take out the missiles before they exploded and inflicted irreparable damage on that recovering world. He'd done what he could and the rest was up to them. Right now, he had problems of his own to contend with.

CHAPTER FOUR
Strange Tidings

Bob arrived at the destination and moved carefully so as to not disturb Celcilia who was cradled in his arms. He saw what looked like a reasonably comfortable spot on the ground and knelt to lay her there. She moaned softly as her injured arm brushed against the ground, and without waking up she moved to guard it. Feeling quite helpless, Bob stood up and faced the portal.

Accessing the control system he acquired the latest information on the planet's maps, geopolitical situation, and local customs. Without bothering to scan the information, he ordered the portal to produce suitable clothing for both of them. To his surprise, it refused. He checked the supply closets but found no food, water, or medical supplies. That was very strange for a public portal, but a query of the system revealed that through-traffic had consumed everything and supplies had not yet been replenished.

Bob frowned. That amount of traffic through a portal was unheard of, not to mention the using up of supplies faster than they could be replenished. On the other hand, portals only stocked a limited amount of supplies so it was conceivable that a single recent group could have consumed it all. He checked the logs and was shocked at the number of times the portal had been used over the past local year, almost all of it inbound traffic.

That merited a deeper look at the log, but first things first. He ordered the portal to create basic medical kit. The portal pondered the request for a moment then complained that energy requirements would force it to be offline for an hour. That took him aback and he demanded further information.

It turned out that the energy reserves of the portal were very low, and even creating the small medical kit would be a strain. Bob's eyes widened in surprise. That was not just unheard of, it should have been almost impossible. After taking a quick look to see that Celcilia was still resting, he ordered the creation of a basic medical kit. Then he concentrated on finding out what the problem was, given that there was a good chance that he'd need to make a quick exit.

It took him some time to complete his examination but the results left him shaking his head with indecision. The soft sound of an alert interrupted his musings. He was pleased to see that the portal had completed the medical supplies as well as a quantity of water. He checked what had been made and was relieved to see a selection of dressings, a topical analgesic, and a general-purpose healing salve. It wasn't much but it would do for the moment. The portal suggested that it be allowed to return to subspace to save power, but Bob ordered it to stay instantiated and offline until he said otherwise. The portal acquiesced—rather sulkily, Bob thought.

Bob took the supplies and water over to where Celcilia was laying. Pausing for a moment to delay the ordeal, he woke her up and explained that he was going to change her dressings.

"Any painkillers in your kit, luv?" she murmured.

"Soon. Got a salve that should help with that, though. It'll be rough for a minute while I take the bandages off. Ready?"

She nodded and he got on with the necessary business.

"How's it lookin'?" she asked, her voice thickening with pain.

"Not so good. What I've got will help for the short-term, but we've got to get you some proper medical care soon."

"Anything like that around here?"

"Should be. It's a high-tech planet. Hub of a small interstellar republic. Or was. Lemme check that." His eyes took on a faraway look as he reviewed the information the portal had given him. After a few seconds he returned his focus to her, smiled, and said, "Yep. Except they call themselves the Five Stars Empire now."

"Ah, a regular battling starships sort of place. Only the five though?"

Bob nodded as he concentrated on being as gentle as possible while he changed the bandages. The damaged arm looked red and swollen, and Celcilia hissed with pain as he applied the healing salve into the wound. Then he applied the topical analgesic around it before wrapping it all with clean bandages.

"How's that feel?"

She grimaced as she carefully moved it. "Hurts, but not as bad. Don't feel quite so feverish."

"The fever will come and go until we get you properly treated. I'll have something better for the pain and fever shortly."

"Don't these thingies of yours have a proper first-aid kit on hand?"

"Normally, yes. But apparently there's been a lot of traffic coming through that's used it all up."

She looked at him with narrowed eyes. "That's not normal. No, don't shine me on, boy-o. There's somethin' goin' on here. Yer face gets a happy look when there's a mystery afoot."

He laughed. "Didn't think I was so transparent as that."

She grinned as she replied, "At least there's no-one

shooting at us. By the way, what happened after I passed out? Last thing I remember is you and that old man talking. Then I woke up here."

The sad look on Bob's face elicited a gasp. "That old man ... is he alright?"

Bob shook his head. "Don't know. Apparently it had been decided to launch an all-out attack, including nuclear weapons, if and when anyone used the portal."

She gaped at him. "That'd destroy everything!"

"Yes, it would, but only the surrounding area. The portal's defences would have left it and grove intact."

"You told him that?"

"Yeah. They were pretty sure it wouldn't do any good but had decided that doing something was better than doing nothing."

"Another panic response, just like your people."

Bob nodded. "Exactly. So I offered to leave and destroy the portal."

"And?"

"We left. He said he'd try to stop the attack, but I have no idea if he was successful. No way of finding out, now."

"So you really destroyed it? That portal-thingie, I mean?"

He nodded.

"Not exactly the thing to do, is it?"

"Not at all. It's ingrained into us and into our culture that the portals are, well, sacred in a sense. Inviolate."

"Why?"

"During the Great Wars they were all that stood between us and extermination, at the end."

"But all the Big Bads are gone, aren't they?"

"More or less. A few small pockets of the various sorts have popped up now and again, but they were taken care of. Then nothing for a very long time, until recently. It was, uhm, a few of your centuries ago. A large battle fleet attacked the home planet of some relatives of mine. In the end, the planet was exploded to destroy the fleet. Only two people survived—my Aunt Freida and my Uncle Sid."

"How awful. What happened to them?"

"Well, Aunt Freida ended up on a planet that my Dad was looking after. A plague had broken out, and Freida's a medical expert, so Dad asked her to look into it. She managed to stop the plague and decided to stay on, out of sight in the back country."

Something in the tone of his voice made Celcilia realize that there was more to the story than that but she decided not to pry.

"And your Uncle Sid?"

"How's the arm feeling?"

"Fine, fine. Oh, give us some of that water, would you? Now, about your uncle?"

He passed the container of water to her and waited for her to finish taking a drink. "No-one heard from him for centuries and figured he was dead. Turns out that your planet was one of the possible places he might have ended up, so after a visit with Aunt Freida I popped over and took a look."

"Just popped over, huh? And did you find him?"

"I did indeed. He'd been on Earth all that time, actually."

She waited for more details, and when none were forthcoming asked, "And?"

Bob sighed. "Well, he ended up in Central Europe and hung out there." At a glare from Celcilia he took a deep breath before continuing. "He got there just before the Black Death plague and worked on stopping it. When that was done, he decided to hang around."

"Uh huh. You're holding all the good parts back on me, aren't you? Goddess damn it, Bob, I'm in this up to my neck. I think I deserve a bit more consideration from you."

The effort of being angry made her tired and sweaty, and she lay back panting. Pausing to take a gulp of water, she wiped her brow with her good arm and settled back to glare at Bob. He sighed and said, "It's complicated."

"Involves the Goddess and your brother again?"

Bob shook his head. "No. It's bigger than that. No, hold on, and I'll try to explain." He paused for a moment to collect his thoughts before continuing. "Alright. There's a lot of bits and pieces, but not much in the way of connections. Just a whole lot of oddities. First the Great Wars. You remember those, right?" She nodded. "Well, after that we—my people—went back out among the stars and found your lot. The younger races, I mean. We'd lost so much that everyone assumed those were survivors from crashed ships or military bases or lost colonies. Except they weren't really like us. Oh, human enough, but ... basic. Oh, don't look at me like that. It's true. The genomes of the humans on all those worlds were what we'd been long before the Great Wars. So my people just shrugged and went about the business of rebuilding and keeping to themselves."

"Yah, you explained that once before. But I still don't understand. A huge mystery like that was ignored? Weren't your kind reduced to just a few folks? Why ignore that gene pool?"

Bob sighed and looked miserable. "You have to understand what the war did to my ancestors. A population of billions reduced to a few hundred over many centuries of nearly continuous warfare. They survived, though, and rebuilt a society from scratch. Then rebuilt themselves, from the genome up. A new stage of evolution, in a very real sense. We didn't have billions of people so it was decided we didn't need a large population. The extensive portal network had survived and gave each person access to worlds of their very own."

"Sounds ... lonely."

He nodded. "That excess of possibilities almost destroyed us. Somehow they came up with something that worked, though. Each family took responsibility for a home world and as many other worlds as they felt comfortable in handling. The various Precepts were established."

She broke in to ask, "Like that Precepts of Survival you keep quoting at me?"

"Exactly. That and others. Think of them as sets of guiding principles, differing in method but similar in goals."

"Those goals being?"

"Staying alive as a species, to be blunt. Don't attack each other without a very good reason. Keep yourself ready to deal with any problems that might arise."

"Sounds reasonable, actually."

Bob nodded. "Yep. But over time people acted as though it meant keep to oneself, don't rock the boat, don't mess with what works."

"And the younger races?"

"It was generally decided that they were of no importance. Not our kind, so not worth bothering with."

"Oh, ta."

He gave her an annoyed look. "It's not my fault, you know. I was just born into the way things are."

"And what have you done to change it?" Her hand flew to her mouth. "Oh, I'm sorry. You really are trying to help people and fix things. It's just that ... that ..."

"It's alright, Celcilia. I understand. I really do."

They were silent for a minute before Celcilia asked in a quiet voice, "What about those other oddities you mentioned?"

Bob cleared his throat before answering. "That plague that Aunt Freida fought? It was actually a series of plagues made to look like the result of an old biological weapon from the Great Wars."

"Like that weird rain shit?"

"Exactly. Except my aunt determined that the plague changed over the years, and in ways that she thought indicated tampering. In addition she found through genetic analysis that there'd been at least three distinct waves of colonization of the planet before she arrived. But none had arrived via the portal, and there were no signs of interstellar ships or space-travelling capability of any sort."

Celcilia's face screwed up for a moment. "And your uncle who was on Earth?"

"Got there just before the Black Death plagues. You remember those?"

Celcilia nodded.

"You'll recall that there were several waves of that, each somewhat different. Even today, your own scientists aren't really sure what those plagues were and where they came from."

"So your Uncle Sid was a medical expert like your aunt?"

To her surprise Bob laughed. "Not at all. Everyone in his family studied medicine except him. By his own account he studied kicking around just trying to have a good time. But after seeing his own world destroyed he decided to help. To his great surprise he'd picked up enough medical knowledge to be useful, and managed to stop the plague. Then when it started up again he would fight it again. Went so far as to trace its source and found out that someone was involved in seeing it distributed. Nasty business, but he put a stop to them."

"So who was behind it?"

"He never found out, but was content to see it stopped."

"And he never contacted anyone in all those years? All those centuries?"

"No. At first it was shock and paranoia. Then the series of plagues that were obviously an attack. He had no idea who to trust, and didn't know that his sister was still alive until I contacted him."

Celcilia sat digesting the information. After a couple of minutes she raised her head and said, "Fine, but what about this place?"

"Ah, that's where things get truly weird. You see, according to the portal logs someone has been sending large amounts of something to this planet. Something large enough, and often enough, to almost drain the power of the portal."

"And that takes a lot to do, I gather?"

"An awful lot."

"Needs looking into, I would think."

Bob nodded. "But not until we get you fixed up. That's got to be our number one priority."

"So why didn't you come here first?"

"It's a high-tech world, Celcilia. Lots of prying eyes, lots of security, lots of paperwork. Places like this always increase the risk of being discovered."

"Like that last world, with the old man."

"Yes."

"But someone has been doing it, and on an industrial scale. Like Kydos, but even more so."

"Yes."

"Can't you do a dump of the records on your magic gateway thing and find out who?"

"Yes, but if I do that the portal will automatically tell them that it was me who is checking up on them. Basic privacy safeguards that can't be overridden."

"Ah. So we do this the hard way, then. Well, pack up your glad rags, boy-o, and let's be on our way. Help me up." She held up her good arm, which Bob grasped and used it to haul her up, being as gentle as he could.

Seeing the pained look on her face Bob said, "Let me fetch the pain medications. Then I'll dismiss the portal and we'll be on our way."

She nodded. "And some more water, if you'd be so kind."

He bowed with a flourish and said, "We live to serve."

* * *

Celcilia felt better after taking the pain medications and insisted that they go explore the new world. When the portal disappeared back into subspace they could see a well-defined, if rough, roadway leading out. As they walked through the forest she marvelled at how nice things were.

"You insist that this is a high-tech world, and yet this is like the forest on Earth."

Bob nodded. "Yep. That's partly because of this planet's ecosystem and partly what the public portals are designed to create everywhere."

"Even on the Hell World?"

Bob's face went blank. "No. Private portals tend to be more basic. They preserve and protect, but not to the same extent or finesse as the public portals."

Celcilia was about to ask more questions but her words trailed off at the sight before her. They had emerged out of the forest into a world of wheeled and aerial transport, roadways, and the noise those things bring. In the distance they could see a city of tall towers that nearly spanned the horizon. She stood there gaping until becoming aware of Bob grinning at her.

"Oh, hush, you. I'm not used to this sort of thing." She gazed about in wonder. "Like London, only worse." After a short pause she added, "So where do we go from here? And how?"

"Well, we could try asking them." Bob pointed at the wheeled vehicle coming towards them along the rough roadway. Within a short time it had reached them and stopped. A driver leaned out and yelled, "Get in. Only the pair of you? Nothing was scheduled or I'd have parked closer." He looked like a middle-aged gnome, complete with wizened face and pot belly.

Bob and Celcilia glanced at each other, shrugged, and got into the vehicle. As soon as they had closed the door the driver began to turn around to go back the way he'd come.

The excellent suspension of the vehicle absorbed all the bumps, for which Celcilia was very thankful.

"Any particular destination?" the driver queried.

"No," said Bob. "We need a decent place to stay. Near a medical facility, if possible."

The driver shook his head. "Not much for you, I'm afraid. The build-up has made billets hard to find."

"What about the Skiv District?" asked Bob.

The driver swivelled his head to look at them for a moment before returning his gaze to the road. "You sure about that?"

"I've been there before," Bob assured him.

"Recently?"

"Well, no. But I'm sure it will be fine."

The driver shrugged as if to wash his hands of the stupidity of his passengers, but otherwise was silent for the rest of the trip. Within a minute he'd reached a main road, and after waiting for a break in the traffic he headed towards the nearby city. Bob and Celcilia sat back in their seats and enjoyed the scenery. The driver was watching them carefully in his rear-view mirror.

"First time here?"

"As I said, I've been here before some time ago. First time for my friend."

"Hmph. See much that's changed?"

Bob gave the man a thin smile. "It was earlier in the build-up."

"Yah. Ain't that sumpthin'? Not like when I was in the Forces."

"Which unit?" asked Bob. "Mech brigades?"

"Nah. Ground forces. Drove an armoured vehicle. Not so bad, though."

"Out long?"

"Few years. They needed drivers for this new push, so I put in for it and got the gig. A good posting, actually. Meet all sorts. Which unit you in?"

Bob waved a hand in a dismissive manner. "The Guards."

The driver snorted. "Yah, that's what they all say. Where you from?"

It was Bob's turn to snort. "The real Guards. The only ones that matter. My friend and I need a place while we wait for the paperwork to catch up with us."

The driver laughed. "Fair 'nuff, friend, fair 'nuff. Just, ya know, keep that attitude to yourself in the Skiv. Gets rough in there, if you know what I mean. Lots of bored troops and annoyed locals."

Bob gave a friendly smile and nodded. "I'll keep that in mind, thanks."

They had reached the edge of the city by this time. Celcilia, unable to follow the conversation, had concentrated on the scenery. The lights and architectural wonders were indeed a sight to behold, and she smiled like a happy tourist. Traffic was busy but moved in an orderly manner. Then the form of the city began to change. Gradually at first then more and more. The lights became garish, the streets narrower and dirtier. The architecture became less ornate, brutally functional, and interspersed with what were obviously leftover pieces from ages gone by. Traffic became denser and slower, with the variety of vehicles ranging from dingy to modern. The storefronts began looking more like open air markets. Their vehicle dodged a series of broken-down stalls that looked to have taken root in the street. After a meandering journey into an increasingly dilapidated area, the driver pulled into a parking slot.

"Skiv District, just like you asked," said the driver turning around.

"What do I owe you?" asked Bob.

The driver looked at them carefully for a moment before shaking his head. "I'm on retainer. When they ask, tell 'em Garsh picked up you and took you where you wanted to go."

"Thanks, Garsh," said Bob. "Where do you recommend

staying?"

Garsh pointed with his chin to a dingy-looking building on the other side of the street. "Faiz runs a decent place. Not fancy, but clean. Tell him you're here for the build-up and he'll not overcharge by more than the usual."

"Medical services close by?"

Garsh pointed down the street with his chin. "A block that way. They can handle anything short of major surgery. Tell 'em I sent ya."

Bob smiled as he said, "I'll be sure to do that. And to keep in mind who sent us there." His eyes bored into Garsh's.

Sweat broke out on the older man's forehead under the intensity of that gaze. "They're good. Really. I've used 'em before. Tell 'em you're a friend of mine. Yeah, tell them that."

"I will, Garsh. Count on it," said Bob in friendly tones, keeping the smile on his face.

"Well, uhm, I gotta get back on the circuit, ya know. Uhm, good luck. Welcome to town."

Bob and Celcilia got out of the vehicle and Garsh moved away as quickly as traffic allowed him.

"What was that all about?" she asked, brimming with curiosity despite the fever that was threatening to claim her again.

"He was expecting people to come out of the forest. Something about a build-up that's been going on for quite a while. Come on. Let's see about getting a room, then medical attention. That's a hotel across the road and the medical centre is on the next block."

Noticing the sheen of sweat on her forehead he supported her on her good arm as they crossed the street. They entered the hotel lobby and were greeted by a barrage of noise and scents of too many people in a small space. Bob manoeuvred them through the crowd to the front desk, where a bored-looking clerk greeted them.

"Non-comms or better. Troops down the road and two

blocks over. Single rooms are all we have left. How may I help you." His words, uttered in a monotone, slurred together as he studied them through half-closed eyelids.

"Single room is fine. Need it for the duration."

"Fine. Sign here with unit designation and name of company purser. Thumbprint here. No, just you, sir. Here's your room's security chit. Enjoy your stay. Next."

Bob pulled Celcilia away towards the stairs while studying the chit he had been given.

"Whazzat? Key?" she muttered, the fever beginning to hit her again.

"Something like that," said Bob looking for the transport tubes. Spotting them, he hustled them both into one and held up the chit to the panel that lit up as a voice greeted them. The panel changed colour, and the voice thanked them for their patience. There was a brief sensation of movement, followed by a soft but abrupt stop. The door opened and the voice urged them to exit quickly. Bob pulled Celcilia out just as the door closed.

"Ow," she complained.

"Sorry, but these things are on a timer and return to the main lobby if you don't get out quickly enough. Filters the experienced travellers from the newbies. You really don't want to get tagged as a newbie with this lot."

"Bloody lifts. Worse than bloody London," she complained.

Bob managed to find their room, and waved the chit at the door. The door dilated and allowed them to enter, urging them to do so quickly. The room they stepped into was, as promised, reasonably clean but nothing much.

Celcilia wrinkled her nose. "Crossed the bloody galaxy to stay in a bloody flophouse. Lovely." She staggered to the bed and collapsed upon it. Bob let her sleep while he examined the room in more detail. There wasn't much there but it did have a working public communications terminal and, more importantly, a private bathroom.

After making sure that Celcilia was sleeping, Bob took advantage of the opportunity to have a shower. It felt rather good to have a hot soak and rinse, but that joy was muted when he realized that his clothes were rather worse for wear and smelled like it. He put on his clothing while vowing that getting new outfits was going to be at the top of his list of priorities. Celcilia was still resting so he passed the time using the terminal to gather information.

A grunt followed by coughing and low moans drew his attention. Celcilia was sitting upright, but not looking terribly rested.

"Don't feel so good," she muttered.

"We'll get you looked at right away. I found the place that Garsh told us about. It appears to be a walk-in clinic. You alright to walk a block or so?"

She sighed and muttered, "Yah, if I gotta." Putting her weight on her good arm, she levered herself upright while stifling a groan. "Let's do this."

They left the room and made their way to the street. Their next problem was to wade through the sea of humanity with minimal damage to Celcilia's bad arm. Bob solved the problem by leading the way and plowing a path while she followed close by in his wake. That tactic got them some angry looks and words which Bob cheerfully ignored. If a hand or arm reached out it was quickly withdrawn with a curse after being slapped by Bob.

Celcilia's fever was making her woozy and she focused her attention on following behind Bob. She passed the trip in something of a blur, which was relieved only when they stepped into what was obviously a clinic of sorts. The sterile decor and tang of antiseptic made her nose wrinkle despite her wooziness.

Supporting her good arm, Bob moved her with care to a row of chairs and deposited her in one. She sighed with relief as she sat, and fought to keep her eyes open. Bob had a discussion with a receptionist of indeterminate sex who peered around him to look at her. The receptionist frowned for a moment then stood up and walked over carrying a book-sized device. After waving it around Celcilia's head and arm the frown became an accusing glare aimed at Bob. He smiled and said, "We just came through. Our driver, Garsh, said you were the best medical facility in the area."

"Garsh said that, did he?" said the receptionist in a warm contralto. "Well, she needs immediate care of the sort she should have gotten some time ago." Another glare was thrown at Bob who tried to look innocent. With a sniff of disapproval, the receptionist led them into a small treatment room and instructed them to wait.

"Wha' sup?" said Celcilia. "Health card no good?"

"Shh," answered Bob. "It's all good. Here, lay down in the chair." He helped her to sit in a large well-padded chair that began conforming itself to Cecilia's shape.

The door opened and a harried-looking middle-aged man walked in. "I'm Medico Haltoah. She the patient? Can we remove those bandages, please?"

Without waiting for an answer he approached Celcilia and examined the bloody wrappings. "No recent bleeding." He lowered his head to take a sniff. "Doesn't smell rotten, but infected for sure."

Ensuring that Celcilia was aware of him, he gently placed the back of his hand on forehead. "Fever." After smiling kindly at Celcilia, the man turned to Bob and said curtly, "What happened?"

"Single dart containing a necrotizing toxin to the left bicep. Lacking any other resources, I excised the contaminated tissue with my knife. Packed the wound and kept it as clean as possible. Several days later I obtained a basic healing salve and packed the wound with that. We got here as quickly as we could."

As Bob had been talking, the man had been preparing

several trays of supplies. He paused to ask, "This toxin, is there any remaining in her system?"

"No. She'd be dead by now if there were."

The man grunted and pressed some controls on the chair. It tilted back then modified its shape to present Celcilia's left arm to him on a ledge that held the arm level. Celcilia moaned softly once, then forced herself to be quiet. The medico took a cloth, wiped her sweaty brow, and gave her an encouraging smile. Turning to Bob he snapped out, "Known allergic reactions to the standard medications?"

Bob shook his head. "Not sure. This is the first time she's needed treatment."

The medico sighed. "Of course. Never mind, we'll do a quick test then proceed to unwrapping and treatment. I gather she doesn't speak the language?" When Bob shook his head the medico sighed again. "Fine, we'll do this the hard way. As usual. Tell her that we're going to sedate her and make her sleep before unwrapping the bandages. Not sure what form of treatment I'll be using until I see the damage, of course. From what you describe, the arm will never be back to normal but we can repair a lot of the damage."

He glanced at Celcilia then back at Bob. Taking a moment to lick his lips, he blurted out, "She's not military. Payment's not covered for her. Sorry."

Bob gave a friendly smile and answered, "I'll pay whatever it takes, never fear. Shall I arrange the details with your receptionist while you work?"

Relief was plain on the medico's face as he nodded. "That would be most helpful, sir, thank you. Now if you could please inform your friend of what is going to be done, I can get started. The scans show that the standard medications are safe to use on her, so we can get started right away." He stepped aside to allow Bob to approach the chair more easily.

"Hey, Celcilia. The doctor is going to fix you up while I wait outside. He's going to give you a sedative before removing the bandages and starting treatment. Won't take long."

She nodded without bothering to open her eyes.

Bob turned to the medico. "She's ready. How long will this take?"

The medico shrugged. "A reasonably standard type of injury from what you tell me. If there are no complications, should be done in an hour. Perhaps less. Now off with you ... my patient is waiting."

Bob left and went to the reception area. He checked with the portal and discovered that there were a large number of different accounts that could be accessed. Selecting one of several financial institutions based in the city, Bob arranged for funds to be held in escrow until the completion of the treatment. Once the medico confirmed treatment was completed, the funds would be transferred. That was standard business practise on this world, and Bob readily agreed to the terms. Then he sat in a chair to wait.

He passed the time by observing the steady flow of patients into and out of the clinic. It was busy enough but not to the point of crowding. All in all, though, it gave the appearance of a sustained larger-than-expected volume of patients.

The patients themselves were interesting. There were a few that appeared to be locals—mothers with children, for example. The bulk of the patients, however, were tough-looking but carried themselves with an air of discipline. The uniforms that some wore confirmed Bob's suspicions that the bulk of the clientele were soldiers. It was the variety of uniforms that surprised him, as most of them were from planets that should never have been seen here. Something strange was going on and he itched to find out what it was.

He had enough experience to know that information should form the basis of any action, so he was content to sit and observe. His presence did not go entirely unnoticed, though. A number of the soldiers, eyes automatically surveying the area as they pass through, saw him and identified him as a predator at rest. All of them, including Bob, were careful not to make eye contact without making it obvious that they were avoiding it. Predators acknowledging each other on neutral ground.

The receptionist waggled a hand to catch his attention and he went up to her desk. "The medico will see you now. If you would please sign here to acknowledge the transfer of funds? Thank you. That way, please."

Bob went down the corridor to the treatment room. The door was ajar and he pushed it open.

"Close the door if you would, sir," said Medico Haltoah. Bob complied and the two stood facing each other. Celcilia was laying in the chair, and appeared to be asleep.

"Your friend's treatment went well. There was some necrotic tissue but no signs of any toxin. You did a neat job on that field surgery, by the way." Bob acknowledged the compliment with a nod, and the medico continued. "You left the blood vessels and nerves intact, and that healing salve prevented further damage, so she should regain use of the arm and hand in short order. Perhaps as much as seventy or eighty percent. To achieve better would require a full arm transplant. If you decide to go that route, I can recommend several good medical facilities that specialize in those procedures. No? Well, in any case she needs to heal up before any further work can be done."

"What about her fever?"

"Oh, treating the arm put an end to the infection causing the fever. I've infused her with some medications that should deal with the current symptoms, eliminate any bacteriological or viral infestations, and provide ongoing protection against any standard disease. By morning all traces of fever should be gone. The wrappings are the usual sort. Leave them on until they change colour. Affix one of the green patches to the forearm of her damaged arm every morning, after removing the old one, for the next week to encourage healing. As for pain, that should be minimal. Affix one of the blue patches on her injured arm after you get her home, then another in the morning. After that, use only as required." The medico passed a wallet of medications to Bob. "These are standard patches that monitor and infuse at the correct dosage. If any of the patches begin flashing, get her medical attention as quickly as possible. I don't expect any complications, though. She handled the treatment very well. Oh, and no food tonight, but encourage her to drink lots of water. Tomorrow she can have whatever she wants. She'll want to sleep when she leaves, so that shouldn't be a problem."

"Any follow-up necessary, Medico?"

"Not unless there are complications. Now, if there are no further questions?"

Bob shook his head. The medico pressed a button on the side of the chair, and after a moment Celcilia opened her eyes. She blinked rapidly for a few seconds, saw Bob, and grinned. "Hey. You're still here. Arm doesn't hurt anymore." Turning her head slightly she noticed the medico, who was smiling at her. "Thank you, doctor. Can I go home?"

Bob chuckled. "He doesn't understand a word you were saying, but, yes, we can go now. In fact, they insist on it. Can you walk?"

Celcilia carefully slid off the chair and stood up. "Yah. Hey, I feel good. Better than good. The doc does good work." She held out her uninjured hand to the older man, who hesitated slightly then carefully shook it as he made a slight bow.

"See, Bob. He understands just fine." Flashing a final smile at the medico, she and Bob left the room and exited the medical centre. The crush of bodies came as a surprise to her.

"Was it like this when we came here?"

Bob laughed. "Yep. Stay behind me as I break through.

The hotel isn't too far."

The trip back to the hotel was an eye-opening experience for Celcilia. She was careful to stay close to Bob, but took full notice of the people and her surroundings. The buildings were tall and packed close together. The shops on the ground floor were small, brightly lit, and promised an enticing variety of wonders. The gaps between buildings were packed with vendors hawking wares in loud voices.

Then there were the people. A crushing hoard, packing the streets so tightly that it would have been impossible for a vehicle to pass. All of the activity produced a cacophony of noise that made talking impossible until they entered the entranceway of their hotel.

Inside the hotel the crush abated, but there were still many people bustling about in the brightly lit interior. Bob continued plowing a path through the crowd so she followed him to a wide opaque cylinder that reached up into the ceiling. He removed something from his jacket, waved it, and a door opened in the cylinder.

"Get in," he said, leading the way.

She got in with care. "Now what?"

His only reply was a grin. A few seconds later there was a slight bump and the doors opened again.

"Our room's this way," he said as he led the way along the hall.

A few seconds later they were inside the room. "Recognize anything?" he asked.

"Not really. Oh, the bed. That looks familiar."

He chuckled. "I'm not surprised. You headed straight for it when we first got here."

"I wasn't feeling well," she answered in a tone of mock hurt. Then she laughed. "Actually, it looks damned inviting. Would you mind if I ..."

"Go ahead. Best thing for you, right now. Oh, that's the bathroom over there. The usual facilities. Thirsty?" He opened up a panel in the wall and removed a container of cold water. She accepted it, took a small sip followed by several larger sips.

"Oh, that tastes grand. Thank you."

"You're welcome. Now sit yourself on the bed and rest. You've had a long day."

"That's no lie, boy-o. Oh, that feels nice." She took another sip of the water then placed the container on the shelf next to the bed. Lying back on the bed she let out a contented sigh. "I think I'll pass out for a while."

"Before you do, I have to slap a patch on you."

"Excuse me?"

"Your medications. They come as patches here. Hold on." He took the wallet from his jacket and applied a blue patch. "These are for pain. You'll get another in the morning, then as needed after that. The green ones are to help the healing process. You'll get one every morning for a week."

"Seems simple enough." Her voice was soft and her eyes were closed.

"Advanced medical tech. A good planet for that."

"So, what'll you be doing while I get my beauty sleep?"

"Could go out shopping. Our clothes are getting pretty sketchy."

Her eyes sprang open. "Uhm. Could you not be leavin' me just now, Bob? I trust you to come back, but ..."

"Not a problem," he said in a soft voice. "I'll stay right here and we'll go shopping tomorrow. You probably just don't trust me to get proper clothes, is all."

That got a smile out of her, and her eyes closed. "Damn right. Men have no fashion sense." Her voice faded as she fell asleep.

Bob smiled and went to the comm-link unit. There was research to be done. It would be interesting to see what the official channels said and compare it to his observations and what the portal had told him.

* * *

Morning came, but the light entering the window was little different from the previous night. In fact, the sky could not be seen unless one was on the street and looked straight up. Celcilia woke up, took a deep breath, smiled and stretched. She immediately let out a small gasp of pain as she flexed her injured arm.

"Don't stretch it just yet. It needs to heal more."

"Oh, thanks ever so for the bleedin' obvious," she snapped back. Then she carefully moved her injured limb and let out a satisfied grunt. "Feels better, though. A lot better. Not so puffed up."

"Any pain?"

"Some," she admitted.

"Let me put those patches on. That should do the trick." Bob took the wallet of patches, removed the previous evening's blue one, then applied both a blue and green one. He wrapped the used patch in a piece of tissue and put it into his jacket pocket.

"Any reason you're saving it?"

"Never leave your DNA around if you can help it. Especially on high-tech worlds." He turned to look at her and grinned. "Old habit, but a good one to follow. Hungry?"

She opened her mouth to make a point about paranoia, then shut it as she looked thoughtful. That was quickly replaced by a smile as she said, "Famished. First time in days I've been really hungry."

"How's the arm feel?"

She moved it with care at first, then with more confidence. "Feels better. Whatever's in those patches works a treat."

Bob nodded. "Any food allergies?"

"Nope. So long's it's cooked, I can eat it. Gimme a minute to wash up and then we can go."

They collected their meagre belongings, including the

63

wallet of patches, and headed out. As they were headed out of the hotel Bob asked her, "Ready to face the hordes?"

Celcilia nodded. "No worse than London during a footie match. I'd appreciate you running interference, though."

Bob led her along the street as far as the first alley. They entered it and were greeted by the raucous cries of vendors peddling food and various wares. Bob stopped at a stall selling meat on sticks. He sniffed the air, picked up one of the edibles, sniffed and sampled it. He grinned and flipped the man a large coin. He took another stick of meat and handed it to Celcilia saying, "Starters." The seller went to hand two more sticks to them but Bob waved them away. "I'll trade the change for information. Where's a good sit-down meal to be had? My friend here is feeling delicate." The seller gave a knowing grin and pointed further along the alley. "Pantoh's. End of the alley and across the street." Bob gave a sketchy salute to the seller, then jerked his head to indicate that Celcilia should follow him.

"How's your meat?" he asked.

"Mmph," she replied, her mouth still full. After a hurried gulp she added, "Hope that's just a starter."

"Yep. The seller recommended a place down the way. We'll have a proper sit-down then shop for clothes."

"You trust him?"

Bob shrugged. "Most people are helpful unless there's cause not to be. Especially in places like this where reputation is everything." He jerked his head to encompass the area they were walking through. "Life's tough enough that people need each other to survive. They'll shave the edges if they have to, but get a rep as unreliable and they'll get forced out to the really bad parts of town."

"Not so different from London or any other big city," remarked Celcilia.

"That's right."

They passed a barrel filled with something or other

burning, even though the temperature wasn't that cold. Bob tossed in the tissue-wrapped patch and their now-empty meat sticks without breaking step. No-one took any notice.

In short order they exited the alley, crossed the street, and entered Pantoh's Fine Restaurant. At least that was what the sign claimed, and Bob's nose detected no off odours. A busy-looking waitress greeted them. Bob asked for a private booth, but she shook her head. He showed a coin and she suddenly remembered that one was available and led them there. There was no menu, but the waitress was looking at them expectantly.

"A large-sized breakfast for myself, and a medium for my friend. Something with meat, fresh fruit, water, and tea."

The waitress nodded and left.

Celcilia had a sour look on her face. "Not speaking the language is a real pain."

Bob shook his head. "They're used to it around here. Watch how the staff deal with the ones who can't speak it. Point at pictures, smile, frown, whatever it takes. But speaking in their own language makes things easier for them and often gets better service."

Just then the waitress returned, bearing two plates. The larger plate was put in front of Bob, the smaller one in front of Celcilia. The contents, if not the volumes, were identical. Bob smiled at the waitress and held up another coin. She shook her head and held up two fingers. Bob gave her a friendly askance look but handed over two coins. The waitress gave him a big smile and walked away with a flounce.

"You paid her too much," growled Celcilia.

"Not by much," said Bob. "I checked out the local prices and it's about right if one includes a tip. See how busy they are? Now she won't be in a hurry to get us out."

Deciding not to press the point, Celcilia sniffed at the food. "Smells good."

"Should be fine, especially with the healing patch keeping the nasties out of your blood. Sip on the water, though, until I check out the tea." He took a sip and pronounced it safe for her.

They ate in silence and presented the waitress with clean plates and satisfied smiles when she came back. The waitress hovered for a moment, her eyes looking towards the crowds waiting to be served.

"We'll finish our tea, then leave. Oh, we're in dire need of clothing. Anyplace you'd recommend?" Bob asked her.

"My aunt Shia owns a good shop not far from here—turn left when you exit. Can't miss the sign. Tell her Bru sent you." Bob thanked her and she trotted off.

They sat for a couple more minutes then drained their cups and left. Once again Bob led the way, showing no hesitation as to their path.

"Where to now?" Celcilia said in a loud voice so as to be heard over the noise level of the street.

"Clothing. Not far. Our waitress recommended a place."

"Hmm," was her only comment.

A brisk ten minute walk brought them alongside a shop featuring a garish window sign. "This is the place," said Bob, pulling Celcilia inside and out of the crushing crowd.

They shut the door and the noise level dropped so suddenly that it was almost deafening.

"May I help you?" asked a middle-aged woman from behind a counter.

"I certainly hope so," said Bob with his most engaging smile. "A lovely young lady named Bru sent us here. We're looking for clothing. As you can see, ours is rather worn after our travels."

The woman had begun to wrinkle her nose, but then sniffed and politely pretended not to notice the smell. Celcilia, of course, guessed what was going on and gave an apologetic shrug and grimace.

"We'll set you up proper—you and your friend. Bru sent you to the right place, no doubt about that. Now, what sort of clothing will you be wanting?"

"Something suitable for everyday wear, but suitable for travelling when the time comes."

The older woman put her hands on her hips and examined the two of them carefully for a moment. After a brief nod, she turned and began pulling pants and shirts from her stock and showed them to Celcilia. Bob was astounded at how quickly style and colour were selected without only looks and nods passed between the two women. As they went about their work, Bob wandered about and found clothing for himself. He turned in time to see Shia point Celcilia to a room to try things on.

"And for you, my lad? How are you getting on?"

"I'll take these, thanks. The legs on the pants are a bit long."

"I can do those in a flash, no problem." She examined him with pursed lips, nodded, then took the pants over to a large machine tucked in the corner. As she arranged the pants in the machine she asked, "Anything else?"

"Uhm, yes. Another pair of similar pants in the same colour. These shirts are fine as they are. A warm sweater for myself, and one for my friend. She'll need a coat of some sort, too. Something with a large hood, I think."

They were interrupted as Celcilia fairly bounded out of the changing room. She stopped in front of Bob and twirled, her face a study in joy.

"They fit beautifully. And they're clean." That last word was draw-out and practically purred.

Bob had to chuckle at her happiness. "Take those and get another set."

She rewarded him with a big grin before turning to select a second set with care. The older woman examined her carefully before selecting and handing over two sets of undergarments. The two exchanged knowing glances and rolled their eyes at the general cluelessness of males.

Bob, to his credit, took it all with good grace. He added a jacket of his own to their pile of purchases, adding a pair of sturdy shoulder bags to carry everything.

"Will you be needing footwear, sir?"

Bob nodded, and the two women were off happily looking at foot gear. "Sturdy boots would be good," he yelled over at them. They ignored him, so he went off to select a pair of boots for himself, with socks to complete the ensemble. Finally, everything was assembled and paid for.

Shia looked at Celcilia for a moment, ducked under the counter, and came up holding a knife by the blade. It wasn't large--just the length of her hand--but the blade looked sharp. "Every young woman needs a boot knife in this town." She handed it to Celcilia who made a happy sound and slipped it into her boot without another word. She spun around to admire its placement and ensure that it was sitting snugly. A fold of her pant leg hid it nicely.

Shia then turned her attention to Bob, giving him an evaluating look before asking, "What do you want done with you old clothing, sir?"

"Do you have an incinerator on premises?"

"I do, indeed, sir. And may I say, thank you." She wrapped the old clothes in some tissue to avoid touching them, opened up a slot in the wall and dumped the refuse in. When she turned to face them once more, her smile was friendly not just professional. "A pleasure doing business with you both." She gave a short bow first to Celcilia, then Bob. Celcilia gave her a smile and a brief curtsy, which pleased the older woman. She escorted them out and wished them well.

"Where to now?" asked Celcilia still glowing from the feel of clean clothes.

"There's a public square not too far from here. Let's sit for a while and watch the crowds."

"I like watching crowds," she said. Then added brightly, "So long as they're not chasing me."

Bob laughed and led the way to their new destination.

* * *

As before, they walked in single file with Bob leading the way. After a half-hour of walking they emerged into what passed for an open area in this overbuilt part of the city. There was a large open space, surrounded by planters of sad-looking flowers of various colours. There were a few ornamental fountains scattered at random throughout the space, dribbling and spitting unenthusiastic streams of water. There were a dozen or so food vendors on the periphery, carefully spaced out. Bob led them on a casual circuit of the food offerings then asked Celcilia if anything struck her fancy.

"Those taco-looking things looked nice."

"Want one or two?"

She considered for a moment. "Two. They're small."

Bob chuckled and led the way to the appropriate vendor and bought four of the wrapped edibles plus several bottles of water. There were numerous small benches scattered around and they found an empty one without having to wait. They ate in silence, watching the crowds pass by. Bob handed her a container of water which she took with a nod of thanks.

When their meal was finished Bob turned to her and asked, "Notice anything?"

She laughed and leaned closer. "We're being watched." Then she leaned back and continued to look at him, smiling broadly.

He returned the grin and nodded. "Well caught. But they don't seem to be focused on us. Seems meant to ensure that the riff-raff don't move beyond here into the good parts of town. And to keep an eye on things generally."

Celcilia's mouth creased into a slight frown. "Lot of uniforms around. They walk like soldiers, too. That normal for this place?"

"Yes and no." Bob's face had settled into a thoughtful look. "This is a minor interstellar empire based on military might to keep things humming. Not as bad as it might sound, actually, so long as one obeys the rules. The rules, by the way, are much what you'd see in a good military outfit, but looser for the general population."

"Not just a military junta, then?"

"Not at all. It's a military-based social system. Along the lines of, say, your continent's Norman Empire."

"So what's with all the different uniforms? They got that many different service branches?"

He shook his head. "No, most of them are from off-planet. And by that I mean outside their empire, and brought in via the portal."

"Why do you assume that? Couldn't they have come in a spaceship or something? It is an interstellar culture, after all. FTL ships will be common enough."

He looked at her with surprise. "Look at you, tossing around big words."

She sniffed and lifted her nose in the air. "Comes from hanging around over-educated riff-raff. So answer the question."

Bob chuckled. "Fair enough. Their FTL ships aren't that good, really. Maybe ten times the speed of light, tops. That puts a limit on the size of their empire, as well as how far they can explore."

"Excuse me?"

"Think about it, Celcilia. On Earth, the closest star is something like four light years away."

She nodded.

"Alright, that means a ship travelling at the speed of light would take four years to get there and four years to get back.

That's a long, long time to be cooped up inside a ship. So, if their ships go ten times faster they can reach ten light years per year of travel. Assume that's the radius of the hypothetical empire. Now, if you want to set up a political system that encompasses that radius of action, that means there is a two-year delay in the social control system. A lot can happen in two years, especially on a high-tech world. Or even a frontier world, for that matter. So, they've settled for something smaller and more manageable. Besides, the systems they control are the only inhabitable ones for some distance. So, no, I don't think these new troops came here by ship."

"Faster ships?"

Bob shook his head. "Nope. Oh, maybe by a bit, but not enough to make any difference."

"What about your people? Didn't you say they've got faster ships?"

"We've been around for a very long time, Celcilia. We started out with sub-light ships, but by end of the Great Wars we had ships that could reach nearly two thousand times the speed of light. With communication systems that could operate much faster than that. In addition to that we had the portal network."

She gave an appreciative grunt and nodded her head. "Sounds impressive."

"It was. But the Great Wars all but wiped us out, and now everyone just uses portals. Which brings us back to this interesting mystery."

"So, who did it? And why couldn't they be using those super-ships of yours?"

"To answer the second question first, there aren't all that many of those ships left. Certainly nothing the size of a troop carrier. Or at least none that I've heard of, even in rumours. As for the first question, don't know, yet. The portal was nearly drained of power when we arrived. That is unheard of, so I checked the summary logs--that won't set off any privacy alerts--and found that it had been used many times to bring in large masses of something. That 'something' would be these troops and their equipment, I'm guessing."

"That means your people, Bob. Like the Goddess and her lot."

"Exactly. That's why we need to be careful to blend in."

"Okay. So why not just check those logs to see who of your kind have come here?"

"Because the system would automatically alert them to the fact that I checked up on them. I'd rather not do that, not until I've got more information to go on."

"Why all the troops?"

"That's the mystery. There's no place to go from here, other than the other planets of the Empire. Nothing there worth fighting over, so far as I can find out. The public communications channels seem to be full of recruitment pitches for mercenary groups, plus some of the empire's own forces. Something is going on. I get the feeling that this is just a staging area for something bigger. There's enough troops and equipment here for a couple of good-sized planetary invasion forces. And that's assuming the target is another high-tech planet. Low-tech planets would be easier targets, of course."

"What about Earth?"

"Sorry, but it's perhaps at the top end of the low-tech scale. Besides, it's too far away to be of much use. Anyway, we've sat here long enough. Time to move on." He got to his feet, and Celcilia followed suit. Bob flicked his head from side to side to confirm his bearings, gave a slight nod, then walked off at a modest pace without checking to see if Celcilia was following.

She trotted up alongside him, slinging the strap of her bag around her neck while trying not to bang her injured arm. "What's this about?" she growled in a low voice.

Without moving his lips he answered in a low voice, "Keeping in character. Keep acting annoyed until we reach the edge of the square ..."

"Who's acting?" she muttered.

Bob continued as if she'd not interrupted. "... then put your arm in mine and smile." He took her grunt as an acknowledgement. They got to edge of the square, where Bob stopped, turned, and smiled at Celcilia. She put her arm in his and looked up at him, smiling broadly.

"Is my widdle oogums all happy now?" she cooed.

"Oh, yes," he cooed back. "Our new hotel is just a block away. Somewhat nicer, if the advertisements can be trusted. Be nice to put our feet up."

She nodded, a trace of weariness showing on her face for a fleeting instant. Bob noticed and made sure to angle his arm to allow her to lean on it if she needed to. Past the square, the cityscape became almost identical to what they'd left behind them. It was less crowded enough that Celcilia could manage to walk alongside Bob. The biggest difference, though, was that more people in this part of town wore uniforms, and the uniforms themselves were somewhat nicer.

The walk wasn't far, but Celcilia was feeling the stirrings of real fatigue when Bob guided her into a doorway. It looked very much like their previous hotel, but everything was just a little bit brighter and cleaner.

Bob walked up to the check-in desk and slapped the top for service. A harried-looking middle-aged man greeted them. When Bob mentioned that he'd made a reservation the man typed at a keyboard and shook his head. Bob slipped him some coins. The clerk typed some more, smiled, and handed Bob a pair of chits. Celcilia didn't need to understand the language to recognize what was going on.

Bob finished with the clerk, then motioned for Celcilia to follow him. Without a word, he led the way to a transport tube. They entered and she opened her mouth to speak, but

Bob gave a slight shake of his head so she stayed silent. The doors opened and they exited. Their room was a short walk along the carpeted hall. Bob pointed at the symbols on their door to make sure Celcilia recognized them before he opened it. After entering, he handed her an identification chit and said, "Here's a spare key. Just in case." She nodded her thanks as she put it into a pocket of her pants as she looked around.

The room was, as Bob had promised, the same size but overall nicer than their last one. She unslung her pouch and dropped onto the bed with a happy sigh. Bob took a brief tour of the room, and examined everything carefully. Celcilia watched through half-closed eyes, and wondered why he was moving his upraised hand over the various surfaces. She chalked it up to super-science god stuff and drifted off to sleep.

Bob heard the change in the rhythm of her breathing and smiled. She'd had a hard time of it and was bearing up very well. He continued his examination of the room and completed it a few minutes later. There was the usual assortment of listening devices, so he went from one to the next neutralizing them. He suspected they were placed there by the hotel as a way to make some extra money. He wasn't concerned about what they might find out, of course. What worried him were the ones who would be tapping into the hotel's systems. Celcilia's use of English couldn't be helped, but might be used to flag them for extra attention because it was an unknown language. That was the type of attention he was hoping to avoid.

While Celcilia slept Bob amused himself by using the communications terminal. He found it interesting that the sorts of advertisements shown to him were for higher-end mercenary units than at the other hotel. To help keep up appearances, he checked the listings for restaurants and found several close by that might be worth a look. He made note of those then went back to examining the advertisements.

She inhaled sharply as she came awake. Overtones of a rapidly-fading bad dream blurred her sense of place. She forced herself to focus and put aside the fear and ignore the dull ache of her injured arm. The mental rituals of her upbringing were always of use for these sorts of situations. The fact that the Goddess, and the faith itself, had been revealed to be fraudulent didn't negate the usefulness of the rituals as a way to achieve calmness.

Bob waited until her breathing was even before speaking. "Have a good nap? Feeling better?"

"Pretty good. How long was I out? Arm's a little achy."

"A few hours. You're due for another pain patch. Hold on, let me get the kit."

Celcilia insisted on doing the job herself. "Might as well learn to do it," she muttered.

Bob approved of that attitude and walked through the necessary steps before allowing her to do it herself.

After a couple of minutes she gave a contented sigh. "Stuff acts fast. Feels good, now." She flexed the arm slightly.

"Don't overdo it," warned Bob.

"I'll be careful, mother."

That got them both chuckling. Then she asked him how he'd been spending the time.

"Research. This is a better class of hotel, so the adverts are for a higher class of mercenary. If the ads and background info can be believed, this whole thing is larger than I expected."

"How so?"

"It's definitely not aimed at anything in the Empire, that's for certain. This is the home world but now it's become nothing more than a supply depot. It's making them very wealthy, and offers them a shot at influencing the movers and shakers."

"And what's the end game?"

"Invasions. Multiple ones, to different classes of planets from primitive to high-tech. Remember how I told you that my brother's goal was to set up a new empire with himself at the head? Well, this is the big play, I think. He's got basic supplies and an endless source of fanatical troops from his low-tech kingdoms. Now it seems that he's bought off a few high-tech planets, rather than conquering them, to get the volume of heavy weapons and trained mercenary troops he needs. Smart move, but I'd have thought it out of his league." Bob paused, lost in thought.

"And? What's the payoff?"

"What? Oh, sorry. Yeah, well, a bigger empire for one. For another, a more balanced power base. If he pulls this off, it'll create a good-sized self-sustaining interstellar kingdom. Not just a pocket empire, but a real expansionist political and economic force with the military to back it up."

"You said he wanted to re-create the old pre-war setup your lot had." She paused for a moment then added, "But what's in it for him?"

"That's what has me puzzled. At the beginning he set up temples on the low-tech worlds to worship him and his followers, and seemed content with that. I ended that racket here and there, but not enough to stop him. I always thought that the re-creation of the old pre-war setup was just talk." He leaned back in the chair, with steepled fingers tapping at his lips.

"You underestimated him."

"Yes, I did...and badly. But I can't help but think there's something else going on. Someone pushing, or at least influencing, him. Kydos hinted as much, when she mentioned new alliances. I've no idea who she was referring to, though."

Celcilia shrugged. "Others of your kind? Your brother isn't acting alone."

Bob nodded. "Good point. But, no. People like Kydos got into this to be worshipped and fawned over. That's their weakness, and how Set got them into his scheme. No, these are someone new."

"From the look on your face there's more to this puzzle."

He met her grin with one of his own. "Oh, yes. A lovely collection of mysteries. Set's organization is more extensive than I realized, and now includes those mysterious new allies. Then there's the whole setup that Kydos built up to condition increasing numbers of people. She spent a long time breeding people like yourself to be part of the processing tech, as well as fine-tuning the conditioning process itself. That drug she's using concerns me, too. Aside from the logistics of moving all those people through, where are they coming from and where are they going to? That's a lot of infrastructure and people spread out over a lot of planets, building up towards some grand scheme, and I've completely missed it until recently. Still, it's a big galaxy, I suppose."

"Hmm. It's a puzzler that's for sure. Well, is this something we need to worry about right away, or can it wait for later?"

Bob gave her a puzzled look.

"I'm hungry. Starved, in fact. And would kill for a beer. Anything like that here?"

Bob laughed. "Beer is the universal constant among humans, I can assure you. There appears to be a few choices. There's ..."

"A pub. I want a proper pub. With beer and pub grub." She gave him a stern look.

Bob made a formal bow and said in an overly cultured manner, "As m'lady commands. In fact, I'll just take the med-wallet and we'll leave the rest here. Live dangerously. Take your cloak, though ... we're going outside and you'll want to keep your arm warm."

* * *

They reached the promised establishment within a few minutes and went inside. Celcilia looked quite pleased as she surveyed the clamour and packed tables. She took a deep breath and exhaled a satisfied sigh.

"This," she said with a nod. "This is how civilized people get together."

Bob laughed and led them to a table in a far corner where he had a view of anyone entering or leaving. They sat and waved at the bartender. The latter held up a small tablet, waggled it, and pointed at the wall behind them. Celcilia turned and picked up a similar device off a rack, then turned back to the bartender and gave a short wave of thanks.

"It's a tablet with an ordering app," she said while examining the selections offered. "All the posh places have 'em."

"So how is it that you know about it?" teased Bob.

"Hush, you," Celcilia retorted, pointing a finger but not raising her eyes. "You're here to pay the tab, not make rude comments. My turn to select the grub." She poked at several selections then leaned back. "Done."

Bob pointed her attention to the bartender who was trying to catch their attention. He held up a pitcher of beer and gave it a waggle. Celcilia held up two fingers, then waggled a finger at herself and Bob. The bartender nodded and bent to his task.

She rubbed her hands together briskly. "Lookin' forward to this, me."

Bob grinned. "Feeling better, I gather?"

She grinned back. "Feels almost normal, so long's I don't exert the arm. What'd the doc say about long-term healin'? You've been canny about mentioning that."

He leaned forward and she did the same. "It'll be healed enough to be fully functional, but you'll never have the strength you used to have. Sorry."

"Not to worry, Bob. I've gone from bein' in a secret cult to the property of an alien witch to chasin' through the galaxy. It's been a grand adventure." Her face became serious. "Once I learned the truth about the Goddess and her temple, I figured to be on borrowed time. And that damn short. You saved me, and I'm more grateful for that than you can know." She reached over with her good arm and patted his hand. Then she leaned back, the very picture of contentment. "And here's our grub and beer. Just in time—I'm perishin'."

Bob laughed and helped their server place the plates, pitchers of beer, and glasses on the table. "Sure you ordered enough?"

Celcilia shrugged and replied, "If not, there's always more." She bent forward to focus her attention on the meal before her. Still grinning, Bob dove into the food with gusto. While he could eat and digest anything organic, well-prepared food and drink was always enjoyable.

After a time they both sat back with satisfied sighs and pushed the now-empty plates away. Bob topped up their glasses and they sat there soaking up the ambiance. He leaned forward to say something to her when five large, well-muscled men walked by. They stopped and surveyed the crowded pub with frowns. The eldest of them looked at Bob. With a tilt of his head and motion of his hand he asked if it was alright to sit at the table. Bob nodded, and the newcomers gathered chairs and dropped heavily into them. The eldest had turned to signal at the bartender when Celcilia held out the tablet. The man nodded his thanks as he accepted it.

Bob glanced at Celcilia, but she appeared to be comfortable with the situation. She had pushed her seat closer to the wall, where she leaned against it radiating disinterest and calm. She took occasional sips from her glass, but Bob noted that the level within didn't drop at all. As for himself, he drained his glass and refilled it. Then he tweaked his metabolism to neutralize the alcohol.

A server arrived carrying a pitcher of beer and glasses for the newcomers, then left. The elder of the group apportioned out the beer, leaving the smallest measure for himself as he emptied the pitcher. They sat back in their chairs with less-than-happy expressions and sipped on their beers. While Bob and Celcilia remained silent, their tablemates exchanged the odd comment and barked laughter. That led to some roughhousing, which ended up with Celcilia's pitcher of beer being spilled. She favoured them with a string of curses. The men might not have understood the language, but they understood the tone and the look on her face well enough. One of them took offence at her words and got up to lean towards her, snarling in a language she didn't understand.

No-one saw him move, but Bob was on his feet knocking aside a hand that was reaching towards Celcilia. It was retracted with a howl of pain, born of shock more than injury, and all his companions sprang to their feet. Bob held them with a calm steely-eyed glare until one of them spat out a curse and threw a punch that was easily blocked. That brought howls from the pack, and knives came out. They each had a predatory smile and adjusted their positions relative to each other. It was obvious that these were soldiers used to fighting as a unit.

In response, Bob snorted a laugh. The pack moved forward only to be stopped before the attack had properly begun. They were sitting back in their chairs rubbing bruised arms and hands, as their knives rattled to a rest on the table top. Bob had a slight scratch on his right hand which he wiped with a napkin, afterwards placing the napkin into a pocket. The wound itself was completely healed.

The eldest of them stepped back and assumed a position of parade attention. "Sir! Forgive us, we didn't know ..."

Bob took a quick glance around before hissing a command, "Sit down. We're attracting unwanted attention."

The man nodded as he dropped into the chair, sitting at

attention. He turned to utter a command to his fellows, but stopped with his mouth open. Bob realized he'd forgotten about Celcilia. He turned in time to see her calmly wiping her boot knife on a napkin while looking as calm as a cat licking its paws. She finished wiping her knife, then tossed the napkin at a man holding his bleeding hand. While everyone was looking at him, she slipped the knife into her boot and covered it using a fold of her pants.

Celcilia saw Bob and the older man gaping at her. "What? You think this is my first football match crowd? Please." She picked up her glass and took a dainty sip before putting it back onto the table. "I won't put up with anyone spilling my beer." Then she leaned back and regarded the others through half-closed eyes. Her expression fairly radiated her disdain.

The elder man's eyes narrowed a fraction until he saw that his comrade's injuries were more cosmetic than serious. That worthy had wrapped the napkin about his hand and was gazing at Celcilia with respect. He had also squared his shoulders and was sitting upright in his chair, the very image of a perfect gentleman.

Bob grunted as he signalled the barman that a cleanup was required along with several pitchers of beer. After the cleanup was done and glasses filled, Bob turned to the elder man and snapped, "Identity." His tone was sharp, rich, and filled with subsonics for emphasis.

The man looked straight ahead and rattled off a unit identifier. Then he added, "Tanzan. Battle-Sergeant. First Class."

Bob nodded. In a soft voice he asked, "Battle-Sergeant Tanzan. If you would be so kind, explain your actions."

Tanzan gulped. He recognized an officer when he heard one. "Sir. We have no-where else to go. It's warm here."

"When did you last eat?"

"Yesterday. Sir. The Brigade is low on funds, and we're all scattered about, and ... well, you know how it is. Sir."

Bob found a tablet and ordered a supply of food. In arrived in short order and the men dove in. For her part, Celcilia took a bite of food from each man's plate, washing it down with a sip of her beer. She gave a small shrug when she noticed Bob smiling.

As was the nature of soldiers, the meal was finished in short order. The men nodded their thanks to both Bob and Celcilia. One started singing what sounded like a shanty, and the others joined in. To their great delight Celcilia joined in with tonal harmony, her rich voice melding well with theirs. Battle-Sergeant Tanzan motioned Bob to lean closer and they talked while the others sang.

"Thank you for feeding the men, sir. I was at my wit's end."

"I thought all these places charged everything to your unit?"

Tanzan gave a sour grunt. "They're supposed to, that's for sure. But some units get treated better than others. We're still looking for a room."

"How long have you been here, Battle-Sergeant?"

"Nearly a week."

"Staying where?"

Tanzan jerked his chin. "Places like this, sir. They're warm. Served us food until a couple of days ago. I scraped together some coins, but ran out yesterday."

Bob considered that for a moment. "It is crowded, what with all the mustering of troops."

"Mustering," Tanzan spat out. "Sorry, sir. I suppose I've seen worse mustering but I can't recall just when."

Bob raised an eyebrow.

"You said you're part of a brigade?"

Tanzan said with pride, "Yes, sir. A good one, too. Heavy and medium armour." Then his face fell. "Was a good one until our last battle."

"What happened?"

Tanzan drained his glass, which Bob quickly refilled. "Was supposed to be a quick in and out against light opposition. It turned sour and we retreated as best we could. Saved just over half the brigade. Then heard about this contract, and here we are." He looked around, an unhappy look on his face. "The Battle-Colonel did the best he could, I know. But this ... this is feels like being inside a stockade for all the ways they treat us."

"So, who do you think I am, Battle-Sergeant? Speak freely, please."

The older man gave Bob a wry look. "I know an officer when I see one, sir. And those moves of yours plus the accelerated healing. I was present at a demonstration when the Brigade got recruited. You're one of the God's Own Elite."

Bob smiled. "It could be a trick." He raised and flexed the formerly-injured hand.

That got an amused grunt out of Tanzan. "I saw your wound when I cut you. Yes, it was me. Now there's not even a scratch. I've seen some amazing hand combat skills in my time and yours is at least the equal of the best of them. I've been shown what the Elites can do, and was told to obey any orders they might give."

"What about your men?" Bob nodded at the other men, still happily singing with Celcilia.

"They're my crew, sir. I command a Class-Three heavy tank. A fine crew, sir. I stand with them." The man radiated a fierce pride.

They paused to listen to the singing for a time. Then Tanzan leaned in. "Strange thing is, sir, we aren't the only damaged brigade."

"How so?"

"Been talking to others. Lots of brigades recruited, and a lot of them suffered recent losses. And now we're all packed in here waiting for some promised big action."

"With no place to billet?"

"No, sir."

Bob considered that. "Ready to call it a night, Battle-Sergeant Tanzan? I might be able to find something for you. Probably cramped, though."

Tanzan grinned. "I'm a tank man, sir."

Bob grinned back. He'd spent some time in tanks and understood the sentiment. He stood up and motioned Celcilia to do the same. Tanzan's men, initially annoyed, snapped to alert with large grins as Tanzan explained. Leading the way, Bob took them out of the pub and back to the hotel. He marched up to the registration desk and got the clerk's attention.

"I need another room for my associates."

"No room." The man didn't even bother making a show of typing at his keyboard.

"Oh. That's too bad. They were so looking forward to getting a room. They get very anxious when they have no-where to sleep."

Tanzan began a detailed examination of the decor. His men began doing the same.

"No rooms. Sorry. Next?"

Bob persisted. "Something next to mine would be best, but I'll take anything on the same floor."

"I'm sorry ... you there! Stop assaulting that plant!"

One of Tanzan's men had been sniffing at a large potted plant. At the shrill command of the desk clerk, the soldier began snapping leaves off and dropping them to the floor.

"I'm willing to pay a premium," Bob said in a calm reasonable-sounding voice.

Celcilia began pushing items off the desk onto the floor behind the counter. Push, pause, push, pause. She looked at the clerk. He shook his head. She shrugged and continued flicking items off the counter. Tanzan began examining one of the chairs in the lobby with the aid of a large knife.

"My friends are very tired," Bob explained in a sad voice. "They get cranky when they're tired."

"Fine, fine. A room. Next to yours. Small room. Triple price. One night only."

"We'll take it, thank you. And they'll stay for as long as we do. Now give me the security chit."

Bob led his new-found associates up to their room. He handed Tanzan the security chit. "Take five minutes to get settled, then come see me." The Battle-Sergeant grinned, nodded, and escorted his crew into their new quarters. Bob led Celcilia to their own room.

"They seem like a decent lot," she said. "What's their story?"

"Mercenaries. Recruited for some big operation."

"You think there's more to it?"

"Oh, yes. But first things first. The leader of the group is Battle-Sergeant Tanzan. Uhm, equivalent to a Master Sergeant on your world."

"Earned his rank, then. Oh don't look so surprised. I've met some military types in my day."

"You never fail to surprise me, Celcilia. Anyway, he commands a tank and the others are his crew. He's part of an armoured brigade that suffered heavy losses just before being recruited. According to him a lot of other mercenary brigades suffered heavy losses before being recruited."

Celcilia's head jerked up. "That's quite the coincidence, isn't it?"

Bob nodded. "There's an awful lot of those piling up. I need to do some serious investigating."

"When do we leave?"

"Not 'we', just me. No, don't argue. I can move faster on my own. And I'll be meeting with too many dangerous characters in situations where I can't protect you."

"You mean your people."

Bob nodded. "Not just them, though. Tanzan thinks I'm

part of an elite group serving the gods."

She covered her mouth with a hand and her eyes went wide. "Oh, shit."

"That about covers it, I'm afraid. I have to get more information about what's going on."

A knock came at the door. Bob turned to Celcilia and spoke quickly. "Your name is 'Dyta' ... it sounds local enough to pass. My name is 'Zahnruf', but you'll always refer to me as 'Zahn'. Got that?"

"Yep. So they think you and I are ..."

"Combat companions. Nothing more. I'll make sure they understand that." With that he turned to check the door. It was Tanzan, and Bob let him in.

"Battle-Sergeant, are you and your men up for a minor contract?"

Tanzan looked at him carefully. "I cannot break the oath given for the current contract."

Bob smiled. "Provide protection for my battle companion, Dyta. She is recovering from injuries and I must attend to urgent matters."

"Leaving, sir?"

"I need to talk to this Battle-Colonel of yours. Something strange is going on and I need to find out what. How can I get in touch with him? Wait ... do you accept the contract to provide protection?"

Tanzan smiled. "Sir, it would be an honour. I'll station two men here at all times, on two-hour shifts. Will that be sufficient?"

Bob nodded. "Perfect. Now, about contacting your Battle-Colonel?"

Tanzan gave him the contact information. Bob turned to Celcilia. "I'm off. The Battle-Sergeant and his men will be providing you protection. No, don't argue. He'll station two men here at all times. Now, here's the wallet with your drugs. You've got a security chit to access the room. Oh, here's some money." He handed her a pouch with coins. "You shouldn't need it, but just in case. I'll try to be back by morning. Evening by the latest. Any questions?"

She glanced at Tanzan, who gave her a curt nod. She returned her gaze to Bob and said, "Just make sure you come back."

He gave her a quick grin as he left the room. It was time to get to work.

CHAPTER FIVE
Tipping Point

The first thing Bob needed to do was to gather more local intelligence. The portal's resources had been a good start, but he'd seen recent instances where it was woefully out of date. The local equivalent of a public library was not far away and was his destination. The problem, however, was that the library lay just inside the better part of town from where the riff-raff (such as himself) were excluded. He used the time spent on the walk in communication with the portal, arranging for a more solid identity and the local economic credentials to back it up.

His encounter at the security perimeter indicated to him that the latter was much more important than the former. That was an interesting datum that wasn't in the portal's data. It also suggested several new lines of enquiry to follow up on. Entry to the library required passing through yet another security check, but it seemed to be more for the sake of form than real security.

Once inside, he enquired about a private office and arranged to rent a small room. A nondescript librarian of indeterminate sex escorted Bob to the office. It was located in an area set aside for such offices, and the bland decor wouldn't have been out of place in any number of worlds. The room had a desk, communications and data-access equipment, and a wall-sized display that could be configured as required. There was also a small tri-D unit for visualizations. The librarian handed Bob an authorization chit, bowed, and left him to his own devices. It was clear that anyone requesting a private office was expected to be able to fend for themselves. Bob spent a few minutes learning the controls and configuring things to suit himself, then began working.

After an hour of furious activity Bob leaned back and examined the various charts his research had generated. He minimized those, then arranged for a series of maps to be displayed. The maps included an overview of the city, the local spaceport, and the planet. He flicked through them, sometimes zooming in to view specific areas, sometimes zooming out to get an overview. After another hour of research he felt prepared enough to meet with the Battle-Colonel. It was also time to leave the library in case his various, and extensive, avenues of research had begun to catch someone's attention. He'd left the various monitoring systems—both listening devices and data taps—intact. For one thing, disabling them would have most likely raised an immediate alarm. For another, he wasn't familiar enough with this particular tech to ensure that he'd neutralized everything. Best to grab and go, which is what he did.

When checking out of the library, he discovered that the payment for the short time he'd been there was more than a week's lodging at the hotel. Time was getting short, so he had the guards at the facility's security call him a taxi. He directed the taxi to take him to the warehouse district. Bob was interested to note that the fare included hazard pay for requiring the driver to enter a less-desirable part of town. This all fit into the alarming pattern he'd discovered.

The Battle-Colonel was located in the warehouse district, along with his command staff and equipment. The leadership of many other brigades were also located in the same area.

Their troops, on the other hand, were scattered throughout this and other cities. Bob thought it was an interesting, and effective, way of keeping the brigades in check without being too offensive about it. The problem was that all the cities were beyond saturated with the mercenary troops, and he suspected that things were bound to be rather testy where he was going.

It turned out to take longer than expected to get to his destination. The taxi dropped him off some distance away, and would go no further whatever amount of money he offered. Bob asked about other taxis, and the driver just gave a harsh laugh and said that no-one had a death wish. Another datum on how bad things were getting here.

Bob sighed and began a brisk walk towards the warehouse that housed the Battle-Colonel. When the crowds thinned out he increased his speed to a jog, keeping it at a speed that a professional soldier could maintain. A half hour of running brought him to what was definitely a lower-quality part of town, so he began running in the middle of the road. The buildings were run-down and working lights were becoming increasingly sparse. The road itself had seen heavy use over a long period of time without being properly repaired. Some of the potholes looked to be the result of weapon fire.

He spotted an increasing number of watchers in the shadows as he ran. They all looked like soldiers, and an increasing number of them began looking like organized groups rather than random individuals. Within a few blocks any pretence of casual observation vanished with the appearance of formal security lines. Judging by the uniforms, there were several different groups. The soldiers looked disciplined and alert. Each line of security was well-lit and fenced with a simple gate providing the only obvious means of access.

Bob slowed his pace to a steady walk as he approached the nearest checkpoint. Upon reaching the guardhouse he stopped and said, "I'm here to see Battle-Colonel Frudyan."

The soldier examined him carefully, maintaining his rifle at the ready. When he spoke, it was a curt, "Next intersection in the direction you're walking, other side." Bob gave a formal nod, turned and walked at an easy pace to the indicated intersection. He could feel the hard stares of the various soldiers watching him. These were soldiers who took their security duties seriously, unlike the government forces he'd encountered earlier. Arriving at the designated checkpoint he once again said that he was here to see the Battle-Colonel.

The large soldier at the barrier sneered slightly as he looked Bob up and down. "Identification," he demanded.

Bob looked back at the soldier with an eagle-eyed glare ... this was no time for levity. "I believe that he's expecting me. Battle-Sergeant Tanzan will have contacted him. It might be a good idea to check with his staff."

The soldier made no attempt to hide a sneer as he opened up a link to his superior to relay the situation. That done, he stood awaiting orders. The longer the wait stretched out, the larger the sneer grew. After a minute the soldier began fingering his rifle and his comrades began to fidget slightly. Bob stood there assuming a neutral expression, radiating calm assurance, with his hands folded in front of him.

A slight sound coming from the soldier's helmet broke the tension. Within seconds the soldier's sneer was gone to be replaced by a look of shock. A few seconds later he slammed to attention and saluted Bob. "Sir," he snapped out, the very model of a soldier about to undergo inspection by a high-ranking officer. "I'm to escort you to the Battle-Colonel. Sir." Bob acknowledged the salute with a formal nod. The soldier relaxed from the salute and gave a nod to his comrades, who opened the gate.

"Let's be off," said Bob as he strode in through the gate, without looking at the soldiers. The first soldier spun on his heels and hurried to keep up. "This way, sir. If you please, sir," the soldier gulped out, pointing towards a low building not far away. Bob didn't speak or acknowledge the soldier in any way, but changed his direction slightly to angle towards the indicated structure. Just before they got there, the soldier hurried forward to open the door and saluted as Bob entered.

The building itself looked like a standard industrial warehouse, with nothing on the inside to contradict that appearance. The lights inside were adequate, but not excessive, as he walked into what looked like a small reception area. There were three doors, each guarded by a pair of armed soldiers. The pair on the right hand side came to attention and saluted. Bob acknowledged them with a nod, and one of them opened the door while the other continued to salute. Still unsure if he was heading into a trap or a meeting Bob steeled himself for any eventuality. The door opened into the end of a large room, with Bob facing the far wall.

"Good evening," a strong resonant voice said, coming from his right.

Bob turned to face the speaker. There were a number of uniformed men sitting behind a long table. Soldiers with battle-rifles at the ready, but not aimed, were placed at regular intervals on either side of the table. There was a walkway halfway up the wall behind the table, lined with soldiers carrying heavy assault rifles. As with the others, the rifles were held at the ready but not aimed.

"Where did you wish me to stand, Battle-Colonel?" asked Bob, being very careful not to make any other movement.

"Approach the table until you are halfway here. Slowly, if you please." The words were delivered in the precise manner of a professional soldier, but otherwise betrayed nothing.

Bob approached the designated position with care. He considered the situation and decided to allow the others to set the agenda...for now. Just to be on the safe side, he did a quick simularity scan of the ends of the walkway, a position behind the table, and the doorway where he had entered. As he walked, the armed soldiers tensed slightly. At first Bob worried about an ambush, but the overall feeling he got was of fear.

"That's far enough," came the order. "I don't know who you are, but you have made a grave mistake in coming here while impersonating one of the Gods' Own Elite. There is no record of you."

There was the sound of weapons being brought to bear. Bob took a deep breath and apported to the far right side of the walkway. He spun and backhanded the rifle out of the soldier's grasp. Without making a sound the soldier's right hand flicked and a knife appeared in it. He stabbed at Bob, who stood there and met the point of the knife with the palm of his left hand. The knife sunk in to the hilt, but despite the strength and momentum of the soldier Bob's pose never wavered. Then Bob's right hand flicked upward and knocked the soldier's arm out of the way, while leaving the knife embedded in his hand.

Bob took another deep breath and apported to a position behind, and close to, the seated officers. Bob said in a calm voice, "You wanted proof of my identity? Fair enough. I'm not here to fight you unless I have to. Now tell your troops to lower weapons ... they'll just hit you and the others if they fire. I'll be fine, but you'll be dead."

An older man in the centre of those seated turned away from Bob and nodded at the troops. "Stand down, but be ready." Then he turned to Bob and said, "Good enough?"

"That will be fine, sir. Now, if you would be so kind, please watch." Bob grasped the knife and pulled it out of his hand. He held up the left hand, palm out, to show that there was neither wound nor trace of blood. Then he altered his grip on the knife in his right hand so that his thumb pressed the handle while the blade rested against his palm. A quick press of his thumb caused the knife to snap in half. As he opened his hand the pieces fell to the floor with a metallic clatter, and he displayed the hand to show that there was no injury. The knife, or rather the pieces thereof, had no trace of blood. He rotated both hands to allow the older gentleman to verify the lack of damage.

"Satisfied?" asked Bob, a slight smile on his face.

The older man slumped back into his chair. "Stand down, all of you." Then he got to his feet, came to attention, and saluted. "The responsibility for this is mine and mine alone. My troops were just following my orders, sir. I accept my punishment, but please spare those under my command." All of the others present, officers and troops, stood at attention.

"Battle-Colonel Frudyan, I presume?" asked Bob.

"At your service, sir. I stand ready to accept my punishment."

"Ah, yes. About that. Why, exactly, should I be punishing you? For confirming my identity?"

The officer gave a curt nod.

Bob considered that for a moment. "You were doing your duty, sir. These are strange days and precautions must be taken."

The eyes of the Battle-Colonel widened. "You take no offence?"

"Not at all. I just came here to talk with you and exchange information. Nothing more. Would you like to do it here or someplace else? Feel free to include as many others as you might want, of course."

Frudyan continued to stare for a moment before giving his head a small shake. "Here is as good a place as any. Now, if I may rearrange things in a more suitable fashion?" Without waiting for an answer he turned and barked a series of terse orders. The table was broken up into smaller sections and re-arranged into a square, so that participants could all see each other. When this was done, the troops came to attention, saluted, and left in precision order.

Pulling a chair out, Frudyan asked, "Would you care to sit?"

Bob nodded and took the seat. In truth, the apporting had tired him more than he wanted to show. A group of soldiers came in bearing trays of refreshments which they passed out to all those present, then removed themselves from the room. Noticing that he was the only one seated, Bob urged everyone to sit. While waiting for the others to get settled, Bob helped himself to some tea and sandwiches without trying to look as famished as he felt. The alternate energies supplied the power for apporting, but it still took a toll on the body especially when performed in rapid succession.

Frudyan cleared his throat and Bob finished the last of the sandwich and swig of tea before turning toward him.

"Ah, what should I call you?" asked the Battle-Colonel. "I mean ... you're not one of the Elites. You're one of the gods, themselves."

Bob took another sip of his tea before answering. "Well, my name is Bob. Why don't you call me that?"

Frudyan looked startled and the others muttered among themselves. "Ah, I wouldn't want to seem overly familiar ... ah ... Bob," he said after a moment's consideration.

Bob's face became serious. "Battle-Colonel Frudyan, we have important matters to discuss. Matters which impact you and the other brigades. This is no time for trivialities or pretentiousness. We don't have much time." That got their attention and the room became quiet.

"First of all, let me tell you how I see the situation here," he began. "There are too many mercenary troops packed into the city. Into every city on the planet, in fact. They bought your contracts promising action, but there's been just one long buildup. Tensions are building and are approaching a critical point."

Everyone around the table nodded. One spoke out, "Then

there's the damned tribute. That wasn't in the contract."

Frudyan growled when he heard that, and clenched his fists. Bob indicated that he should continue. The Battle-Colonel took a deep breath before speaking. "It was supposed to be a voluntary thing ... and was, at first. Join up for a special corps, with promotion to the Elites for any that could prove themselves worthy. Then came the demonstrations by a small cadre of the Elites. Very impressive." There were nods from all around the table.

He turned to Bob and said, "The Battle-Sergeant took you for one, and from his description of your abilities so did we. Anyway, there were a few volunteers. Some from most of the brigades. Many, but not all, came back after a few months. About what you'd expect from advanced assault training. But they came back changed."

"Changed how, exactly?" asked Bob.

"Not one of us, anymore," said someone from around the table.

"Stuck to themselves," said another.

"Took up strange worship practises." That got a murmur of agreement from all.

"That went on for a time, but it wasn't too long before the volunteers dried up," continued Frudyan. "Not unexpected, of course. Most of the troops were happy with their regiments, and not everyone wants to get advanced training. So we were told to ensure a supply of recruits." He snorted at the memory. "All of the brigades just laughed at them. Then the troops quartered in the city began reporting about lack of food or shelter being provided. Some got so desperate that they volunteered."

"As tribute?" asked Bob.

"Yes. Brigades that didn't offer enough tribute had supplies cut. Oh, they dressed it up as mere glitches in the supply process, but we saw it for what it was. Dug in our heels ... us and a lot of other brigades. We're making do but the situation is getting grim. The only thing keeping the troops in check is the promise that action is coming soon, on multiple fronts."

Bob allowed his surprise to show. "Hadn't heard about that."

"Not been here long?"

"No. Just a couple of days. Been trying to get the lay of the land."

That earned Bob a quizzical look, but after a moment Frudyan continued. "All the brigade leaders were told about it a few weeks ago. Been tightening things up in preparation, but it hasn't been easy." Frudyan's mouth tightened. "Those supply issues are still in effect, it would seem. Doesn't help that we don't have any intel about the targets. Just know that some targets are low-tech planets and some high-tech. I don't like it but we signed the contract. Seemed like a blessing at the time and allowed us to save much of the brigade. Besides, there's no way home except what they allow through the portal."

The casual mention of using the portal surprised Bob, but he didn't let that show. "I don't know how much you know about the local situation ... the politics of the Empire, I mean."

"They don't encourage fraternization," growled one of the officers at the table, and there were murmurs of agreement. Frudyan nodded but said nothing.

"Not surprised," said Bob. "Here's the basics. It's called the Five Stars Empire, but there's more to it than that. This is the central planet, and it holds the best of everything. The other four amount to semi-autonomous states. Beyond that, it's expanded to include several other solar systems that amount to little more than vassal-colonies. Three of those have developed along enough to form the basis of a solid planetary economy, if given a boost and protection from retaliation. It's that threat of retaliation that's been keeping them in line ...

that and the blasted remains of a several colonial cities that tried to declare independence. Anyway, despite those threats there is a very strong desire to break away from the graft and corruption of an ossified Empire. They'd welcome an influx of trained, disciplined, well-equipped immigrants."

There was silence at the table for a minute. Then Frudyan said in a quiet voice, "But would they welcome mercenaries?"

Bob nodded. "I think so. A number of the settlers there are ex-military types, or their ancestors were. They're being treated shoddily right now but can't fight back. Their economy is stuck in low gear until they can bootstrap themselves in the face of opposition from the Empire. A well-equipped group of immigrants could allow them to leapfrog ahead on the economic front and give them a chance at the independence they crave. I won't say it would be easy, but it would give both groups a fighting chance."

"Why come to us with this offer? We're mercenaries."

Bob looked around the table, at each officer in turn. "I've studied your record. It's a good one. You fight hard, yes, but you behave honourably towards defeated opponents and the civilian populations. In occupation scenarios you've always tried to use tact and diplomacy, with force as a last resort. If anyone deserves a chance, it's someone like yourselves. Assuming that's the sort of thing you want to do."

All eyes turned towards the Battle-Colonel. Everyone was holding their breath. Finally he chuckled. "Imagine it ... us as the incumbent troops. Planetary protection of our own home world." His eyes looked far away for a few seconds. Then he sat upright and looked around the table. "We've talked long and hard about what it means to be mercenaries, especially since coming to this forsaken world. A chance to make a home for ourselves sounds awfully good right now. Probably still enough fighting for those of us that want it, too."

That unleashed a barrage of discussions around the table. Some of it heated, but most of it merely intense. Bob and

Frudyan sat back in their chairs and listened to the mood of the room. Finally Frudyan leaned towards Bob and said in a quiet voice, "It won't be easy, you know. We still need to get off this world. And it's a bigger job than a single brigade can handle."

Bob nodded. "Agreed. That's why I said that this discussion affects all the brigades. Not all of them are worthy of a chance like this, but enough to give those three planets a good chance. Besides, the Empire is about ready to fall apart all on its own. They were on the hairy edge when someone approached them to act as a staging area."

Frudyan's eyes went wide at that. "I thought we were working for the Empire. You mean they're nothing but contractors to someone else? Who?" Then he paused, and his eyes narrowed as his face hardened. "Someone has been recruiting down-on-their-luck units for a while. There are an awful lot of mercenary brigades here, and a lot of them are top-line groups. I now wonder if that was all bad luck or manufactured circumstances. Again, who is behind this?" His voice had become flat, but his eyes burned.

"Not sure. I do know who's in the next layer up, though." Bob sighed heavily and shook his head. "Some of my own people, I'm afraid, caught up in dreams of glory. I know who those leaders are, and would have thought this level of planning to be beyond them. And beneath that of others."

"So they're being used, just like the Empire?"

Bob shook his head once more. "Not as such, I don't think. More like an unseen power behind the throne, content to wield the real power while others bask in the glory. Haven't found them, yet, but working on it."

Both men fell silent at that, a silence soon broken by Bob's throaty laughter. The sound startled everyone enough that they fell silent to look at him. He looked around the table still grinning. "There'll be time enough to ponder the deep mysteries later. Right now, though, we have a rescue mission to plan."

The others looked at him blankly, but Frudyan's face betrayed the beginnings of a smile. "I think I understand. The Empire is doomed no matter what. We've got a chance to save those outland worlds from the coming collapse."

"And to make a home for yourselves," said Bob in a quiet voice that was heard by all. "It's not just them that you'll be saving."

The room erupted into cheers, which the Battle-Colonel allowed to last a few seconds before rapping loudly on the table with his knuckles. Everyone quieted down but their grins spoke volumes.

"This all sounds wonderful, but there's a war's worth of details to work out," began Frudyan. "We're ready to move out with little notice, of course. But this is too big a task for just us ... we need to bring in some of the other brigades. All of us are going to need to be resupplied before leaving, too. Then there's the small matter of transport. How were you going to arrange for the ships?" He looked at Bob.

"Bring in the leaders of the other brigades as quickly as you can. While that's being done I'll set up the financial side. You'll have all the funds you need." Bob spoke with a quiet assurance that calmed their questions, at least for the time being.

* * *

Within an hour Bob was facing the leaders of eight brigades. Frudyan swore that these represented the best of them and Bob's own research agreed with that assessment, more or less. These were mercenaries, after all, not humanitarians. Not a perfect solution, but workable and useful enough. It just remained to convince the others. It turned out that working out an agreement proved to be both easier and more difficult than Bob had imagined. The leaders were able to work together with surprisingly little friction.

The problems lay with his proposed solution.

"I don't see why we can't just go back home," hollered one brigade commander who was getting louder and louder with his demands.

"It took years to get you all here," explained Bob, and not for the first time. "Even sending just these eight brigades home would take months, perhaps as much as a year. The portal needs to recharge after a significant transfer of mass. Besides, not all of you come from planets with portals which means delays while arranging for transport. The Empire will collapse within months, possibly weeks. Even before that, societal conditions will be degenerating to the point where you'll be fighting regular battles for survival."

"He's right," spoke up one man who looked more like an academic than a soldier. "We're an intelligence brigade, and have been seeing the signs for nearly as long as we've been here. Just kept hoping for a way out to come along. This is going to be our only chance, I think."

"But what about ships? Supplies?"

Bob spoke up, his voice cutting through the chatter of multiple conversations. "I've given control of the finances to Battle-Colonel Frudyan. Ordering of supplies can start immediately. As for ships, there are some commercial ships available. Not enough to transport everyone, but a good start. I'd hoped that some military vessels would be available for a price. They'd know, better than anyone, how close the Empire is to collapse. Perhaps the offer of a new home and a fresh start could tempt some of them. Anyone have contacts with them?"

"Aye," said the loud commander who had wanted to go home. "Some of my junior officers have made contacts, even friends, among the local navy. The ground forces are blindly loyal to the Empire, but the Navy tends to see further. Not all of 'em, mind ... not even most. But quite a few, especially among the younger ones. Don't think you can buy 'em, but you might be able to sell them on building a new future."

"What about the Empire's ground forces already on those colonies?" asked a young officer. "They might not want to be part of a new, free world."

"In that case," said Frudyan, "they'll find out what it means to face the best damned brigades in the Galaxy."

This was greeted with enthusiastic cheers by all present, except Bob. He'd seen war and had hoped never to see it again, much less be the cause of it. Still, he was well aware that this was the only chance to preserve and protect those worlds from the societal disintegration that was coming very soon. So he smiled and nodded and helped the leaders of the mercenary brigades to plan.

It was approaching the evening of the next day by the time the informal committee was ready to recess. Agreements between brigades had been made, alliances formed, and a command structure set up. It was time for the general staffs of the brigades to get together to hammer out the details and begin ordering supplies. The leaders of the other brigades had returned to their encampments, leaving Bob and Frudyan alone.

"Battle-Colonel, now that we've got a bit of privacy I've got a few questions if you don't mind."

That earned him a small smile, "Only a few?"

Bob gave a small, tight grin before answering. "You know I'm not part of the organization that created this, correct?" He waited until Frudyan nodded before continuing. "What can you tell me about the Elites? I've not heard anything of them until I got to this planet."

Frudyan studied him for a moment before replying. "Can't tell you very much, actually. They're a relatively small group, so far as we can tell. Drawn from a pool of special forces that take part in the tribute. They get the best armour and weapons, some of it new to us. There's some bio-modifications involved, but we don't know much about that. Their reflexes, strength, and healing are better than normal but not to your level."

Bob nodded. "How are they deployed?"

"Typically in squads of three to eight, although I've seen reports of a few on their own commanding groups of regular soldiers. A lot of their time here seems to be doing publicity, as living examples of what a soldier can aspire to be if they volunteer as tribute."

"I've not seen any around. Are they not stationed here?"

Frudyan shook his head. "Enquiries about their activities are actively discouraged. By them. Still, we—the brigades we've gathered here—keep tabs on them as best we can. They normally come and go on a regular basis, but right now we think all are off-planet. There are a couple of small squads operating within the Empire to discourage rebellions and encourage reticent governors to stay loyal. The rest seem to be preparing the way for the big operations that have been promised us."

Bob considered that for a moment. Then he asked, "What about your interactions with my kind? You call us 'gods', but you know we aren't. At least I hope you do."

That earned him a small, but real, smile and a shrug. "That's what they tell us to call them. After the first couple of demonstrations no-one argues the point. I've only interacted with the one who recruited us. Seen a few more from a distance, though. Not all of them were human or even humanoid."

It was Bob's turn to shrug. "We come in all shapes. It's complicated. Any names for them?"

"Our recruiter called himself Glaaki. The only other recruiters I've heard about from the other battalions are Hastur and Zhar. I'm sure I've not got the pronunciations quite right, but that's as close as I can make it. They each claimed to serve a great cause and invited us into their service. Do you know them?"

"Not sure," said Bob with a small shake of his head. "I'd have to meet them to find out for sure, and that'd be a very bad idea. Any on the planet right now?"

"Unlikely. They rarely visit here anymore. We keep a pretty close watch on the portal and monitor them and the Elites."

"You missed me."

Frudyan frowned. "Yes, we did. But you don't act like them. They—the Elites and the gods—strut around in their finery demanding obedience if not worship. You treat us as equals."

"You are," said Bob in soft, even tones. "My kind has been around longer and has learned a few more tricks. Nothing more. Make sure that everyone understands that." He paused for a moment then added, "On a more tactical level, the Elite still within the Empire will pose a danger to you. Can you handle them?"

Frudyan gave a predator's smile. "Oh, yes. They may be exceptionally tough, but they are quite mortal. We can handle them." Then he frowned as he added, "Not sure about your kind, though."

Bob shrugged. "We're mortal, but have made sure that we're very hard to kill. Your best bet is to keep away. Evacuate off any planet they are on and leave no ship behind. I'm quite serious."

Frudyan looked startled, then nodded as his expression became thoughtful. They stood in companionable silence for the space of a few heartbeats. Then Frudyan said, "There's something I've been wanting to ask you, Bob. If you don't mind."

"Go ahead."

Frudyan turned so that he was looking straight at Bob. "Why are you doing this?"

Bob struggled to keep a neutral expression on his face, but Frudyan noted the flashes of sadness. "I've seen civil wars, Battle-Colonel. On a local and planetary scale. Anything I can do to stop or alleviate that type of horror, I will do."

"Are your people in a civil war?"

"Not yet," said Bob. "But there are forces that seem to be trying to arrange just that." He puffed out his cheeks and shook his head. "Or perhaps it is just a bunch of foolish people who need to be stopped before they do any more damage." He smiled a crooked grin. "In any event, the troops here won't be invading other worlds. That'll upset an awful lot of plans. It's a good start."

"But the portal will still be here, won't it?"

Bob grimaced. "Maybe. Maybe not."

That earned him a hard look. "You can destroy it?"

"Yeah. If I have to," Bob said, his voice miserable. "It's not supposed be that way, though. Not supposed to hurt anyone."

"Lad, it already has. Here for sure, and elsewhere from the sounds of it. If you leave it intact, someone'll start using it again."

Bob looked into the distance, his face neutral. "You're right," he said in a soft voice. "I can't have that hanging over your heads. It'll be bad enough here without it." His looked directly at Frudyan. "Things are going to get very ugly here. The main planets are going to get hit hard when it all starts to fall apart. If you've got any spare money, maybe try to transport some of the other brigades outplanet. Might act as a stabilizing influence to prevent the worst of it. Not all, of course, but might preserve something."

Frudyan nodded. "I'll do what I can. You're not sticking around?"

Bob shook his head. "I need to deal with the portal. And with the ones who set this horror up. Good luck, Battle-Colonel. I doubt we'll meet again."

"Good luck to all of us, Bob. Good hunting. I'll have someone drive you back inside the city. We're recalling the troops, so it'll be on the way." They shook hands and went their separate ways.

Bob arrived outside his hotel, and told the driver to wait. "There's some of your men in here. I'll send them out."

"Thank you, sir," the driver said, grinning broadly. "It'll be good to be all together again." Bob answered the grin with one of his own and went inside. Arriving at his room, he hesitated a moment, knocked, and waited. The door opened almost immediately, and he saw that Tanzan and his crew were crowded inside. Celcilia was holding a guitar-like instrument and it appeared that they'd been passing the time in the time-honoured fashion of soldiers and travellers.

Tanzan leaped to his feet and braced to attention, followed a fraction of a second later by his crew. Bob acknowledged them by inclining his head and nodding.

"Orders sir?" Tanzan said in a happy tone, noticing the smile on Bob's face.

"There's a driver downstairs collecting lost lambs. Time to rally with the rest of your brigade, Battle-Sergeant. You'll receive detailed orders there. Collect your gear and double-time it."

"Yes, sir," was the enthusiastic response from Tanzan. At a gesture from him the other soldiers cleared the room, leaving only him and Celcilia.

"You took your own sweet time getting back. The battle-sergeant and his lot were doing their damnedest to keep me cheered up, which was beginning to worry me. It went well?" Her eyes were bright, but her face was smiling.

Bob nodded. "Yes. And we're leaving, too. I'll explain later when we've got more privacy."

He was interrupted by the arrival of the soldiers, who stood milling in the hallway. They were eager to get on their way, but insisted on saying proper goodbyes. Celcilia gave each of them a hug, which they accepted as one soldier to another. Then she dashed inside, returning with the musical instrument she'd been playing. She handed to Tanzan, saying,

"You take this. Remember us when you play it." She looked over at Bob, who translated. Tanzan came to attention and saluted her, then Bob. The others followed suit before trotting off.

The two re-entered the room and shut the door. "That was very thoughtful of you, Celcilia. Thank you for that."

"T'were your money," she said, blushing. "We went for a walk to stretch our legs earlier, and the lads stopped to gape at it in a window. I gathered it was something they knew well, so I bought it for them. Grabbed some takeout grub, then came back here to wait. They seemed nervous and waiting on something, which I figured had to do with you. So I had them teach me some of their songs and I taught them some of mine. They're good people, Bob. I can't speak but a few words of their language, but that much I can tell."

"They are that, Celcilia. Now, gather your kit. Events are in motion and we don't want to get caught up in them."

Celcilia gave him a questioning look, but began gathering her meagre belongings. "Got some grub left. Take it?"

"Yes," Bob replied. "That'll be useful. Put anything heavy into my bag ... don't worry about balancing the loads."

She nodded and distributed the gear as he had requested. He was pleased to see that she had already packed his belongings and had only to pack the food. She filled several empty bottles with water and packed those as well. "Not going to run short of water again, if I can help it," she said, flashing a grin.

"You're learning," Bob laughed. "Ready?"

In reply she tossed his bag at him as she shouldered her own. "Let's boogie."

Bob didn't understand the colloquialism, but the meaning was plain. They left the hotel without bothering to check out, acting as if they were just going for a stroll. They got outside where they were greeted by another military driver. The man saluted and said, "Battle-Colonel Frudyan's compliments, sir.

He told me that I was to place myself at your disposal."

Returning the salute, Bob said, "That's very kind of him. Well, we won't take up much of your time. Drive us to the portal, please. Then you carry on with the recall."

He and Celcilia got into the vehicle and off they drove. If the city was busy in a normal way when they had arrived, it was fully abuzz now.

"Any problems finding everyone?" Bob asked the driver.

"No, sir. Slow at the start but the word spread quick. Bit of trouble from soldiers whose brigades aren't in the mustering, but nothing we can't handle." The driver grinned at that.

"Any pushback from the regular troops?"

The driver lost his grin as he answered. "Here and there, sir. Nothing more than posturing, though."

Bob nodded. "It'll get rougher— and faster than you might expect. Might be an idea to travel with backup. Not a good time for a soldier to be caught alone."

"Yes, sir. Thank you. I'll pass the word."

They travelled in silence until they reached the area not far from the portal grove. Bob and Celcilia got out of the car and dismissed the driver. They watched him drive away before going into the grove. Once again, they had to stop at the edge when Celcilia became affected by the warding field.

"Wait here," said Bob. Celcilia stepped back a couple of paces and nodded. He trotted off into the grove, returning a few minutes later.

"Try it now."

She took a few tentative steps forward, then smiled. "It's letting me in," she said in a pleased voice.

"Good, let's go," replied Bob as he led the way to the portal. "I figured this portal could be configured to allow people to pass after it let us walk out without any problems. Turns out it'll let any number of people leave, but takes a bit of twiddling to let it pass people in. Not much of a twiddle, seeing as they've been bringing in a lot of people through both ways."

"I take it you've found out some useful information as well as putting the cats among the pigeons."

"Such an interesting turn of phrase, Celcilia, but yes. Some of the soldiers were taken off-world for training and indoctrination. Came back not the same and with strange new worship practises. Sound familiar?"

That piece of news caused Celcilia to stumble, and would have fallen if Bob hadn't caught her.

"Careful. We're almost there. Just around that bend."

In a few moments they stood before the portal. Bob had left it instantiated, and Celcilia stared at the hypnotic interplay of patterns on it. After a few seconds she shook her head as she looked away and blinked several times. Turning to Bob she said, "It looks different than the other ones."

Bob nodded. "Manufactured in a different era. This is one of the newer kinds. Couple of interesting points. Its energy reserves were nearly depleted not too long ago."

"Didn't you say it was powered by tapping into that weird magic stuff?"

"The alternative energies, yes. Think of the portal like the battery in your car. Needs to be charged up before it can deliver the sudden burst of energy needed to start the car. Anyway, it gets depleted a little bit after transporting a single person. To deplete the energy reserves, though, takes a lot of people over a short period of time. People or equipment, that is. Then it needs to recharge before it can do it again. This particular portal has been doing a lot of those high mass transfers for years."

"All these soldiers, you mean?"

"Exactly. And their equipment. All brought here in preparation for a large number of attacks on various planets."

"Wait a sec. Wouldn't it take as long to send them out as bring them in?"

"Not exactly. The troops and equipment were trickled in as they became available. In a push, the portal could get most of them out in under a year."

Celcilia thought about that for a moment. "Why not just plop them into a big spaceship and fly that into the portal? Or just keep the portal open and march 'em all in at once, instead of piecemeal in a series of transits."

"Good questions," Bob replied, nodding. "The problem is that the energy requirements go up exponentially with mass and size. Sending a few medium-sized battle tanks, or a single continental siege unit, is about the limit for a single transit before the portal has to cycle again. The recharge time between transits would start to increase as well."

"So any invasion would take time, right?" she asked.

Bob shook his head. "Keep in mind even that a limited number of troops and equipment could be successful against a low-tech world. Which in turn could be used as self-supporting staging areas. The Empire, here, has been accumulating mercenary troops for a long time. With that quantity of reserves, and a few low-tech worlds for supply, they can go after the high-tech worlds. With a few of those in hand, that'll form the nucleus of a major interstellar power. It was set to begin in a couple of weeks."

"So, the Five Stars Empire is behind this?"

"No. They're just being used as a glorified holding pen for the mercenaries. Many of whom signed on in desperation after an unsettling run of bad luck. The Empire itself was on the rocky road to ruin when this opportunity fell into their lap."

"Set." Celcilia's voice was flat. "Him and the Goddess."

Bob nodded. "And some others of my kind. The brigade leaders know about us, and call us 'gods'. Not out of worship, though, just as an acknowledgement of our powers." His voice had become bitter.

"So how do we stop all this?" she challenged. "Figure

you've got a plan."

"Oh, yes," Bob said, a tight smile on his lips. Then he fell silent long enough for Celcilia to prompt him to continue.

"And?"

"And I've arranged with the brigades for them to relocate on other worlds within the Empire. Worlds that are chaffing under the yoke and could use some good people to help them out."

"The Empire is going to allow that?"

"The Empire is dying, Celcilia. Even as we stand here it is beginning to fall apart. Has been for a while. I'm hoping the brigades will be enough to stabilize parts of what remains and build something better."

Celcilia looked at him, aghast. "You're talking civil war. Just like that other place. Goddess, Bob. That's ... I can't think of words to describe how horrible."

"It'll be worse than you can imagine. Total civil collapse at best. Planetary suicide at worst."

They were silent for a minute before Celcilia spoke in a small voice. "Bob? This scheme of yours to have the brigades go to other worlds within the Empire. Is that speeding up the breakdown?"

After a moment Bob looked away and nodded. Then he turned to look at her. "Yes, Celcilia, it is. The breakdown was bound to happen. Beginning to happen, actually, but slowly over a period of a few years. The arrival of the mercenaries sped that up somewhat, but my plan will bring it all to a head in a matter of weeks. But without this plan the breakdown would have been sudden and catastrophic, destroying everything. This way some planets here get preserved, no interstellar power base gets created, some very powerful mercenary groups get taken off the market, and Set is reduced to temples on a handful of low-tech planets. He'll never be able to re-create this level of troop deployment again."

"But the Empire? What about all the people here?"

Bob shook his head. "I've done all I can for them, except for one last thing." He turned to look at the portal, shimmering in the dappled light of the grove, his face a study in sadness and loss.

"You destroyed the other one," she reminded him.

"Yes. Yes, I did. That will earn me the condemnation of my people. Destroying this second one, though, will be almost unforgivable." He turned to face Celcilia. "Yes, it has to be done. Yes, I will do it. But I don't have to like it. They're a direct link to our ancestors, in a very real way. One of their gifts to us, their descendants. A gift of hope to a future they wouldn't see." He shook his head and sighed. Then he cleared his throat and forced out a laugh. "But time's a-wasting and there's work to be done."

"Do you know where we're going?"

"I'm taking you home. Making one stop along the way to muddy the trail, then on to Earth. Just a couple little chores first."

"Which are?"

"Download a detailed history. That'll alert everyone who's been here that I've been checking up on them."

"And the other?"

"Send a message to them. Let them know that I'm coming to make them pay for this and everything else. It ends."

It took almost a half an hour of effort to make the preparations. Grinning at Celcilia, he set up a destination and the two of them stepped through to another world. Shortly after they left, the portal collapsed upon itself with a flash of light that signalled the start of a revolution.

CHAPTER SIX
Training Ground

They emerged out from the portal transport field, stumbling as they came out.

"That was a bit rough," grumbled Celcilia. Then she giggled. "Heh. Moving between stars in the blink of an eye and I'm complaining about a stumble." Then she made a mock-accusatory face at Bob and said, "Still."

Bob grimaced. "Supposed to be smoother than that, to be honest. Matching the intrinsic velocities is a big part of what the portals do. It eats up almost as much energy as the transfer itself."

"Problem with the low energy reserves of the Empire portal?" suggested Celcilia.

Bob shook his head. "Shouldn't have allowed the transfer unless it could match velocities. Let me check with the unit here." He turned to face the portal mechanism and got a faraway look.

Celcilia took the opportunity to examine the portal. She was beginning to fancy herself something of a connoisseur of them. This one was rather plain and stark. The whorls of patterns glowing from within were less complex and not as rich in texture as the others. Still, there was something familiar about it. She decided to get more information before making any comments about its plainness. By this time Bob was blinking and looking perplexed. She took the opportunity to ask, "Are we where you planned to take us?"

"What? Oh. Oh, yes. That's not the problem." Then he fell silent.

"So where are we, then?"

To her surprise, Bob smiled and made a small wave that encompassed the area. "One of my Dad's planets. Spent a lot of my childhood here. Lots of good memories."

"Oh, like a resort?"

Bob snorted a laugh. "Hardly that. It's a dedicated training facility."

Celcilia blanched. "Not like ..."

"Oh, no," Bob hurried to interject. "That was a final test after training. No, this is an uninhabited planet where most of that training took place." Then he grinned and said, "Came here just for fun, too. Just have to take care where you go." He became serious as he added, "So don't wander off for anything. There are safe paths, but going off them can be dangerous or even fatal."

"Ah. Point taken. So what was with the puzzled looks earlier? Something wrong with the portal? Thought your da fixed them so we could pop out."

"Yes, he did. But not on this one. He left me a note, you see, apologizing. Seems that both Set and my elder sister were watching him tweak this one. But not to worry—there are several more scattered about and we can leave by one of those."

"And? That's not the only thing ... that much I can tell."

"Heh. You know me too well. Two things, actually. The first is that the logs show that no-one has been around since my family came here to twiddle the portals. So we're the only ones here—and that makes things a lot easier. The other thing is that this portal sent a message out to all the other portals on the planet, but not to any of the off-planet ones. Just a simple, non-specific alert. Don't know what that's about."

"Not something standard, I gather."

"Not at all. Might be something Dad added for a training exercise after I left home. He offered training courses to the other families from time to time, even when I was a child. I'm sure he'd have kept that up." Then he took a deep breath and let it out in a whoosh. "Never mind that. The closest portal is that way, on the other side of those hills. Locally it's mid-afternoon. There's a good place to camp that we can reach before sunset if we march at our regular rhythm. Unless, of course, all that big city living has made you soft."

That earned him a snort as well as a backhanded blow that he avoided with ease. They set off at a jog, with Bob leading the way. They travelled in companionable silence. Celcilia found the rustic surroundings rather restful after the clamour of the Empire's cities. She could understand how Bob might enjoy being here. After the running interval, they reduced the pace to a brisk walk. Once she had evened out her breathing Celcilia asked, "That portal we came through. Its design seemed familiar, somehow. But not like any of the others."

Bob kept a neutral expression on his face as he paused for a moment before answering. "You've seen a similar one before. On the Hell planet. You weren't in very good shape, though. Surprised you remember any details."

Celcilia nodded. "Remember some parts of the trip. Saw the portal before the infection had fully taken hold. Just remember thinking it was different from the one I took from Earth. Seeing this one brought that back." She shook her head. "Hard to believe that this place prepared you for a hell-hole like that. It's beautiful here."

"Yes it is. But never, never forget that this is a training environment designed to teach many different lessons. Some are military, some are bush craft, and some are philosophical. Usually a combination of them. Oh, be sure to watch the skies as well as everything else."

"Excuse me?"

"There's a species of bird-like creature here that hunts in packs, called blood-kites. Think of them as small wolves with wings. Rather lovely things, though. My dad's favourite kind of bird, too. Was very serious about never harming them, no matter what the provocation. Tanned my hide when he caught me throwing rocks at them. I only did that the once."

"What? Get caught, you mean?"

"Oh, Celcilia. You wound me." Bob placed a hand over his heart. Then he laughed and added, "Nah. Learned to appreciate them for what they were and how they fit into the ecosystem."

"They dangerous to us?"

"Not usually. Just keep an eye out for them and watch how they're reacting to us. They'll only come after something our size if they're upset about something."

"So, like most things ... leave them alone and they'll leave you alone."

"Very good. I see that your time with me has increased your wisdom significantly. But not your speed ... time to run."

They made good time despite the hilly country. The terrain was rocky, but Bob led them along a sketchy trail. A couple of run-walk cycles later they came to a wide chasm. It was several body-lengths deep, and held a jumble of sharp-looking rocks and gravel on the bottom. They stood at the edge while Celcilia caught her breath. Bob stood off to one side, smiling, clearly expecting Celcilia to say something. She examined the surrounding area with care before again looking into the chasm.

"Well?" asked Bob. Celcilia thought his smile to be quite irritating, given the situation.

"Nasty place to tumble into," she said, indicating the chasm with a jerk of her chin. "There's a couple of easy-looking paths off to the sides ... there and there." She pointed at one, then the other.

"And?"

Celcilia sighed. He really was becoming irritating. She peered at the chasm again then grunted before answering. "Those large boulders ... there, there, and so forth. They form a rough path across the chasm, if you want to risk jumping from one to the other."

Bob just stood there in silence, still waiting.

"Ah, c'mon, Bob," she said in irritation. "I'm not here to do these silly tests of yours."

"You're taking this the wrong way, Celcilia," said Bob, shaking his head. "Seriously. Life is a series of challenges and opportunities to learn. Now, which is the correct path?"

"Seriously? Fine. That one over there," she said pointing to one of the easy-looking paths.

He shook his head. "In the interests of saving time, I'll tell you that it leads to a dead end. Lovely flowers along the way, though. Nice view, too."

Celcilia rolled her eyes. "Fine. What about the other path?"

"Another dead end, I'm afraid. Very pretty rock formations, though."

"Gah," she exhaled with some force. "You're joking, right? We have to jump from boulder to boulder to reach the other side? Wait ... those sharp stones on the bottom are fake, right? Some sort of illusion?"

Bob shook his head. "Not at all. Failure leads to injury—that's one lesson to take away from this. Those easy-looking paths? The lesson there is that the easy routes might be scenic, but are all too often a dead end. Sometimes one has to screw up one's courage and make the first leap, then one after that, then another after that until the goal is achieved."

"Uh huh. And those lovely flowers are poison, I suppose."

"Yes, actually. Well, more akin to your poison ivy or poison oak, but you get the idea. Those pretty rock formations hold sharp crystals almost as hard as diamond. They'll rip clothes and flesh in an instant. Beautiful things can be deadly. Dad liked to pack a lot of lessons into every test."

"Yeesh. How much training did you have before he let you loose on this one?"

"This was my first test. Was told to go from the gate we just left to the spot where we'll stop for the night."

"How old were you?" she asked with some horror.

"In your terms, about six. Perhaps a bit younger."

Celcilia's eyes went wide. Her mouth worked for a moment as she swallowed hard. "Lovely man, your da."

Bob chuckled. "He was an old-school adherent of the Precepts of Survival."

"The gap between boulders look easy enough for an adult, I suppose. But for a child? How'd you manage?"

Bob's face took on a faraway look. "Took me a few tries, but eventually I made it."

Celcilia's gasp of horror brought him back to the here-and-now. "He let you fall into that?" she said, pointing at the jagged rocks below.

Bob shrugged. "Part of learning to control my healing factors. But you've caught your breath. Time to go." Then in a gentler voice he added, "Think of it as walking on stones across a stream. I've seen you do that many times. This is the same thing. Easier, since they aren't wet. Take a deep breath and focus. Head out when you're ready."

Celcilia gulped a couple of times, closed her eyes, and stilled her mind. She took a couple of calming breaths then walked briskly forward to the edge and hopped to the first boulder. She wavered slightly but recovered by using her arms for balance. Taking another deep breath, she hopped to the next. After a brief pause she hopped to the next. Each time her pauses became shorter and her need to catch her balance all but disappeared. When she reached the other side she stood bolt upright and still for a moment. Then she made a small jump up and did a double fist pump, uttering a quiet but heart-felt, "Yes." When she turned around, Bob was standing next to her.

"That was well done, Celcilia. Congratulations." There was no trace of mockery or condescension in his voice, only the quiet pride at a friend's accomplishment.

She cleared her throat and looked embarrassed but proud. "Not so bad after the first few hops, is it?" Then chuckled as she added, "But that's another lesson, right?"

Bob grinned and nodded. "Ready to go? It'll be sunset in just over an hour, and it'll come sudden in these hills."

Celcilia nodded, and off they trotted. "No more traps or tests?" she asked.

"Not after that first test. Just in case, though, I've been scanning. You should keep an eye out, too—I might miss something."

She snorted. "As if."

"I'm quite serious. I'm overly familiar with this place and it's been a long time since I was here. A second set of eyes is always a good idea."

The sun wasn't too far away from setting when they came to the place that Bob declared to be their destination. It was a small glen, a horseshoe-shaped grassy area surrounded by woods and the rock of the hills.

"Why here?" asked Celcilia. "We've passed a few places that look as nice or better."

"This is the only one with water, shelter, food, and safety. Speaking of the latter, hold up while I scan the area for potential surprises."

Bob gave a shrug of his shoulders to loosen up as he partially extended his sensorium. There were no surprises on the passive sensors, so he made several cautious probes with his active sensors on their lowest power. Detecting nothing untoward he retracted everything. He turned to give Celcilia the all-clear, only to find her shuddering and trying not to gag.

"What's wrong?" he asked in a puzzled tone.

"I'll never get used to those tendril thingies sticking out of you." She shuddered once more before getting control of herself. "Sorry, but it just looks like something out of a horror movie. Yes, yes, it's normal for you. Yes, yes, I'm just a silly merely human person. So, what'd you find out?" Her tone was brisk and no-nonsense.

Controlling both laughter and the urge to crack a joke, Bob explained that he was just checking for surprises. "Dad always kept this area clean, but I've been away a long time. Always pays to check."

He directed her attention to an area on the side of the hill. "There's a small cubbyhole over there under the ledge. Easy enough to make a snug lodging for the night. Want to help?"

She nodded.

"Gather bedding like we did in that other forest," he continued. "There's some trees equivalent to evergreens just over there, so hack off however much you think we need. Then gather up firewood. I'll get something for the poles and the sides. Then you're in for a treat." He refused to say anything more, claiming it was a surprise. In a short time they had a rough, but serviceable, shelter complete with a large fire.

Celcilia made a contented sound as she warmed her hands. "Fire feels nice. Starting to get chilly. Say, you mentioned something about a treat? Hope it's food."

Bob grinned at her. "Give me about five minutes." Then he vanished into the gloom.

Celcilia shook her head and amused herself by keeping the fire going and listening to the sounds of the local wildlife. Then she looked up at the sky where the stars were just beginning to show up and gasped. "Goddess, that's a lot of stars," she muttered. She'd seen stars at night in the countryside before, on Earth and the planet of the Goddess, but this put them to shame.

"Beautiful isn't it?" came Bob's voice from beside her.

"Gah," she said jerking around to glare at him. "Damn, but you move silent as a ghost. Give a girl some warnin', will ya?" Then she noticed that he'd coming bearing gifts. "Ooh. Whatcha bring us?"

"Berries. The red ones are the ripest, so just eat those. The green ones won't hurt you, but taste awful." He handed her a couple of heavily-laden branches, saving a couple for himself. "While you work on those, I'll go get us some fish."

"What is it with you and fish?" she muttered. "Every damn planet we're on you just eat fish. Besides, I've still got that snack food. Or were you wanting to save it?"

"Eat some if you like, but save some for just in case. As for fish, they're usually easy to catch. And you know very well that we've had other things when we've stumbled on them. Besides, these fish are something special and go very well with some of the local herbs. You'll see." He vanished into the gloom once more, leaving her to munch in peace.

As promised, the berries were tasty and took the edge off both hunger and thirst. She'd finished her own lot of berries and was eyeing Bob's when there was a slight rustling of branches preceding his appearance. "That better?" he asked. Then he held up his catch of fish and a medium-sized animal of some sort.

"Ah. Very nice, Bob. What's the lumpy thing? I'm guessing not a fish."

He held it up for her to see, obviously rather pleased with himself. "This will add a taste to the fish that will amaze you." He handed her the fish. "Gut and spit these while I prepare this fine fellow." He handed her the fish which Celcilia took while suppressing a sigh. In her experience Bob's idea of culinary delights were less than appealing. Still, she did her share and soon had the fish ready to go.

"All done," she said, and held out the spitted fish.

"Great," he enthused. "Now we wrap them with these herbs." He wrapped long grassy-looking bits around them. "Then we wrap the fat from the snuffler—that's what I always called it and Dad never corrected me—around the fish. Then some more herbs." His actions matched his description, and in a few minutes all the fish were wrapped up. "Now we cook them. It'll take a half hour or so." Then he glanced at her. "Maybe closer to an hour to cook all the way through."

Celcilia rolled her eyes. "I'll be wanting a properly cooked meal. Not one of your raw or half-cooked efforts. We're not being chased by nightmare creatures, so let's do it right just this once."

That got a chuckle out of Bob. "Fair enough. I guess I owe you that. This really is good, though. I think you'll enjoy it."

They lapsed into silence, each lost in their own thoughts. The only sound was the crackling of the fire and the hissing of the meat as it cooked. Every so often Bob would turn the skewers so as to evenly cook the meat.

Seeing the look on Celcilia's face Bob said in a soft voice, "You have questions. Ask anything."

To his surprise, Celcilia blushed ever so slightly. "It's a bit personal."

"Ask anything. Truly."

"That test of your da's that we went through. That's a horrific thing to put a child through. No, don't make excuses. He were awful rough with you."

Bob nodded. "Off and on. It wasn't all military and survival training, though. He put equal weight, if perhaps a touch more, on scholarship. Made sure I knew my history and science and engineering and such. Insisted that I learn the reasons behind why things were the way they were. And, believe or not, he enjoyed games and even cracking the occasional joke."

"And your mam?

Bob paused for a moment before answering. "We had a more complex relationship, my mother and I. You have to understand ... we were not the usual sort of family, even among our kind." He paused for a moment to collect his thoughts. "I've told you that we live a long time. That makes people put off having children, or even having children at all. Most couples have no children, or perhaps one or two. My parents had four."

"Wait," Celcilia interrupted. "That's not replacement level, is it?"

Bob shook his head. "Not really, but for a society with very long lifetimes it isn't that simple. We don't have a central census as such, but my impression is that we're very slowly dying off faster than we can replace ourselves. But my parents were part of a movement that wanted to bring back the old days ... not like Set, but more along the lines of the pre-war egalitarian system. There was a very brief surge in the birthrate before people lost interest. My parents were at the forefront of it, and had a record-setting four children. I was the third."

"You say that like it means something special, Bob. I get that having a large family, or any family at all, was a big thing. But what did it mean to you?"

Bob chuckled. "It's complicated. Mom loved the thought of being the centre of a revival and all the attention it brought. Dad was ... what he was, I guess. Traditionally, the eldest gets the most attention, as they are typically the only child. The second is expected to be, not subservient, but certainly the second among equals. Not much tradition to go around a third."

"So you played fast and loose with tradition then did what you bloody well wanted, I expect."

"More or less. Didn't have much to do with my elder sister, who stayed very much in Mom's keeping. Elder brother, Set,

123

and I were at odds almost from the start. I've never been one to bow to authority."

"I never would have guessed," muttered Celcilia.

"Harrumph. Anyway, I figured anything my elder brother could do, I could do better. Mom encouraged that attitude and encouraged Dad to go along with that. That meant that I went through the same training that Set did, but at an earlier age."

"Wait. She arranged for you to undergo training that was beyond you? That's not just horrid, that's plain evil."

Bob shrugged. "Won't argue with you. When things got too tense, Dad would send me away to stay with relatives until Mom cooled off. I didn't really mind and learned a lot from them. Sometimes I'd go with Dad on his jaunts to check on the private portals he'd made."

"But what happened when you returned home and resumed your training?"

"Got quite good at thinking my way out of the traps and tests. Set just bulled his way through them using his superior physical abilities. Being younger and weaker, I came up with novel solutions. Set called it 'cheating', but Dad just sighed and told me that I'd missed the point."

"And yer mam?"

"Urged Dad to come up with harder tests."

Celcilia shuddered. "And I thought me own Order were tough."

"Everyone has to bear the burden of the ancestors they're born into. Anyway, the food looks done. Let's eat."

To her surprise the fish tasted wonderful. They washed it down with some of the water of the Empire. There was enough for tomorrow's breakfast, which they carefully put aside out of reach of the local wildlife. They stayed up for a time and Bob pointed out some of the wonders to be seen in the night sky. Eventually, though, Celcilia declared that it had been a long day and she needed her beauty sleep. Bob stayed awake for a few minutes longer then dropped off into a light sleep. It had been a busy and eventful few days.

* * *

They started out the next day at the crack of dawn. That is to say, they had a light sit-down breakfast before heading out. Sometime during the night Bob had gone out and collected some herbs that made a passable tea, which pleased Celcilia immensely.

Bob set the pace at a brisk walk. There was a chill in the air and a light dew on the countryside. Celcilia missed the warmth of the fire but the exercise soon warmed her up. He pointed out various scenic highlights as they travelled, but otherwise the trip passed in silence.

The path was reasonably smooth and wide enough for them to run abreast. They were on an uphill portion and the path was a series of switchbacks that eased the effort. They emerged from the current switchback onto a fairly straight section. Celcilia came to halt with a suddenness that caused her to skid. She put out an arm to block Bob and said, "Wait." She began looking around with great care, puffing as she caught her breath.

"What is it?" Bob asked, standing erect. He, of course, wasn't winded in the slightest.

"Not sure, exactly. It's different, though."

"How, exactly?"

She shot a look at him. His face betrayed no emotion but his tone had taken on the cadence of a teacher quizzing a pupil. She pursed her lips and looked back at the trail. To their left was a steep drop. To their right was the hill's gentle slope; grassy next to the road, changing into trees and bushes further up. She peered at the area where the trees began.

"There," she said. "There's something in the trees that I can't quite make out. And there, on the trail just ahead." She pointed at a section ahead of them. "The surface changes colour a little bit. But just that two metres or so stretch." She examined the area again for a moment before continuing. "And, look. That part of the trail is directly down-slope of that strangeness in the trees. If I were a paranoid woman—which I am—I'd say there's something not right here."

Bob nodded. "Very good. How do you suggest we proceed?"

Celcilia heaved a large sigh. "Really? We're doing this?"

In answer, Bob just stood there unmoving.

"Fine," she said, squatting to get a better angle on the trap. Then she stood up and repeated the examination from either side of the trail. Finally she stood up and said, "There's a narrow strip of normally-coloured trail to either side of the discoloured portion. Not very wide—maybe twice the width of my foot." Then, despite herself, she smiled. "How'd I do?"

Bob returned her smile. "I'm impressed that you caught that, Celcilia. And pleased. Yes, that's a trip-point for a cache of logs up the hill. Hit it and the logs come tumbling down." He chuckled. "I caught Set with that, once, when I got him to chase me. Good times."

"Brat. Then and now," Celcilia said shaking her head. "So, are those the safe zones?"

"Yes. The narrowness was to get me used to walking a narrow path. Subsequent tests had increasingly narrower paths, which also became higher off the ground and over longer distances. Eventually just a finger-width wide, over a deep valley, taking several hours to traverse." At the look on Celcilia's face he laughed. "No, we won't encounter anything like that. That's second-level stuff."

After they'd successfully gotten past the trap, Celcilia asked, "Second-level? How many levels were there?"

"Four," Bob answered. "Then came the advanced levels. Those were a lot tougher."

Celcilia's eyes went wide. "Do all of your kind get this sort of training?"

"No," Bob said, shaking his head. "The Precepts of Survival are considered rather old fashioned these days. Oh, most people pay lip service to them, but Dad's one of the few who truly lives them."

"So only your family trains like this?"

"Oh, no. Dad offers training to a lot of other families—Mom sees to that—but most only do the first level. A very few do the second level, and rarely the third. As far as I know, only Set and I did the whole course."

"So, each level gets harder and harder tests like the ones we saw?"

"Only the first two are like this. The third emphasizes hand-to-hand combat, and the fourth emphasizes weapons. The advanced levels bring it all together for tactics and strategy training. Of course, in between all this were the academic lessons. And regular home life."

"Of course. Oh, my. Well, any more surprises up ahead? I'm not sure I'm up for these sorts of tests."

Bob laughed. "You're doing fine. If we push it, we can get to a nice picnic spot for lunch. There's nothing that I know of between here and there, but there's a couple of tricky tests after that. Best to be properly rested for those, I think."

"Oh, ta," she said with only the faintest hint of sarcasm. "Well, if I'm to risk life and limb, I expect a proper lunch."

"I can promise you that. Now pick up the pace, trainee."

* * *

As promised, lunch was plentiful and tasty. Bob insisted that they sit to let the food digest before moving on.

"Those tests are that bad, are they?" asked Celcilia, suppressing the urge to sigh. "How much longer to the portal?"

"There's three more tests before we reach a place to camp

for the night. Then one before the portal ... it's there as a lesson not to drop one's guard when the end is in sight."

"Not going to say anything more, are you?"

"What, and ruin the fun?"

"Fine," she said. "Let's be on with it then." She got to her feet. "But we're starting off at a walk so I can get the lay of the land."

"Wisdom is best when it comes slowly," Bob intoned, dodging the clod of dirt thrown at him.

They reached the next test shortly thereafter. It was similar to the first one, except it used a series of narrow bridges instead of stepping stones. Celcilia, well aware of the dangers of overconfidence, took her time and crossed with ease. Upon reaching the other side she heard Bob clapping. Without turning around she flipped him the finger and continued walking. He caught up within seconds.

"Eyes open and scanning," was all he said.

The trail led them into a forested area, and the dappled light was a quite a change from the open trail. Bob let Celcilia set the pace. She moved at a steady, but not fast, pace. Her head moved back and forth in a controlled way as she scanned for potential problems or traps. A couple of times Bob stopped her to point out problematic plants or insects.

"Thanks for those. But why the help?" asked Celcilia as she paused after the second caution from Bob.

"You don't know the local ecosystem. I was always given that information ... at least for the first level and much of the second."

"And after that?"

Bob shrugged. "It was expected that I had learned enough to be careful. Training for landing on other planets."

"Don't the portals give you that information when you arrive?"

"Yes, they do. But Dad wanted me to be able to survive if I

found myself without that information. Now, eyes sharp."

"Yes, sir, harsh taskmaster, sir."

The trail narrowed slightly after this point and Celcilia took the lead. The brush was rather thick and the effect was to force them to walk single file. There was a sharp right turn up ahead which Celcilia suspected might be the danger point. She moved forward with great care as she peered around the curve.

"Uhm, Bob. I see the trap ... but something's in it."

"No, the trap is a bit further on."

"No, it's just ahead of us. Turn around and we'll walk back until we can switch positions."

They did as she suggested and soon Bob was peering around the corner.

"This is a new trap," he said after a few seconds of observation. "A simple snare. That animal, whatever it was, has been there a long time, too." He paused for a moment then added, "It isn't like Dad to leave an active trap lying around."

"You're saying he didn't set traps like this?"

"Oh, it's like something he'd set. But he'd only set them up just before one of us was to go through. And he'd always chase away any animals that might get caught in them. The only exceptions were the last of the advanced training levels. In any event, after each training session was over we'd go back and deactivate them."

"From what you tell me of your da, I'd of thought he'd consider the animals to be just collateral damage."

Bob whirled around to face her, his face showing the first real anger towards her that she'd seen. He opened his mouth then closed it with a snap. When he spoke, his voice and face were calm. "You have a good point. But you don't know him. Dad, whatever you may think of him, finds the idea of collateral damage abhorrent. Technically, it shows a lack of skill and precision. Morally, it shows lack of character, even cowardice. No, this isn't Dad's doing. Someone else did this, but not recently."

"Your brother?"

"Possibly. Or someone he was training."

"Why here?"

"That is a very good question. It's not something that should be in this section of the first level. We need to keep moving, but I'll take point. Stay sharp."

They moved out with care but didn't encounter any more traps. The path led them out of the woods and back into the open. Bob called a sudden halt as he pointed off to the side. "That's Dad's trap, there. Notice how much you're sweating? That's because of the high humidity level in these woods. There's a nice, cool stream there. Very inviting, but it's surrounded by a plant like poison ivy. Can't get to the water without walking through those plants."

Then he frowned. "Stay here," was all he said. He moved forward with care then peered into the brush on the other side of the creek. He stood motionless for a few seconds then came back to where Celcilia was waiting.

"There's another snare-trap a ways into the brush. Been tripped by an animal, but not recently. Let's follow the path. Stay behind me. The second test is about a half hour away."

They kept to a moderate walking pace until arriving at the test. It looked to be similar to the first one except it had been filled in. Bob's mouth was set into an angry frown as he took in the ruined test. "Wait here while I check the way across."

He approached it with care, scanning all around as well as the debris itself. Then he picked his way across, testing each spot where a foot or hand was to go before putting his weight upon it. A minute later he as on the other side where he repeated the careful scan before crossing again.

"It seems to be just debris meant to fill in the chasm. Not detecting anything untoward. Just be careful how you cross in case something shifts."

Celcilia nodded and watched as Bob repeated the crossing before attempting it herself. When she reached the other side she dusted her hands to clean them before brushing them along her pants to finish the job. "Well, that wasn't too bad. Almost like a simplified version of a real test."

Bob gave her a startled look. "I hadn't looked at it that way. All I saw was destruction. Hmm, you may be correct."

"Well, don't sound so surprised," she said, grinning and feeling rather pleased with herself. "Speaking of changes, how do we know this is the only one? Maybe it's time to go off the official trail?"

"Tough to do." He pointed uphill. "The forest gets very dense, very quickly ... almost impossible to get through with any speed." Pointing the other direction he added, "That leads to valleys that go nowhere near the portal. The trail was designed to offer the only real path."

"But I've seen the odd side trail. Oh, wait. Those are dead ends to teach you not to stray?"

Bob nodded. "Just so. However, I spent a lot of time exploring this area and found a few off-trail paths that we can use. And some places to camp out. There used to be a very good place just a couple hours ahead of us. I suggest we skip lunch and make an early camp, if you don't mind. The detour is about an hour ahead of us."

Celcilia shrugged. "You know the lay of the land."

They reached the detour sooner than estimated. Bob halted and pointed to the edge of the cliff. "We go over the edge."

Celcilia looked at him with narrowed eyes and pursed lips. She went to the edge and looked down. Then she frowned, shifted position, looked again, then chuckled. "Oh, that's cute. There's a ledge there that's almost invisible because it matches the texture so well. Just over an adult's height down, too. How'd you ever stumble on it?"

"Stumble would be the operative word, if I'm to be honest.

Was horsing around while following this path, as small children tend to do, and fell. Dislodged some stones that went over the edge and heard them hit something. Checked out the mystery and saw the ledge. Now, it is a bit narrow and you really don't want to fall off of it. You up for this?"

Celcilia examined it again. "It'll mean single-file walking, but, yeah I can do this. What's the footing like? Hard to tell from here."

"Easy walking, actually. Solid rock on the cliff face to act as handholds if you need them. I'll lower you so you won't have to drop onto the ledge."

A minute later they were both on the narrow ledge with Celcilia leading.

"If you get off balance, yell out and I'll catch you," he said.

"I know the lesson to this," Celcilia said in a confident tone. "Pride goeth before a fall. Heh."

She marched along, becoming more confident with each step. The sheer drop on her left-hand side was disconcerting but no longer bothered her after all the tests on the narrow trail they'd just left. "Which was probably another lesson," she thought to herself.

They walked in silence for some minutes. Bob called a halt to warn her of a winding stretch up ahead. "Just keep a hand on the rock face to steady your sense of balance. This section is designed as a test."

"Uh huh. So this isn't really just a secret little path then?"

"Very little in the test areas is secret. But this area is where Dad let his whimsy show. There are a lot of little nooks and crannies and wonders to amuse a young, active child. There's waterfalls and ponds that are perfect for swimming, wide open fields for running, and strange secret places. We're heading to one of those latter ones."

"Did we pass those waterworks and you didn't tell me?"

He laughed. "Oh, they're just past the portal we're heading to. The best play areas can only be gotten to after passing through the various series of tests. OK, time to focus."

Focus was essential for passing through this stretch of the narrow trail. Celcilia found the colours and striations of the rock and trail played strange tricks on her eyes. It was only by following Bob's suggestion of holding onto the rock face that she managed to make it through.

"Whew. That was truly strange," Celcilia said as she paused and blinked her eyes several times. "You come by your devious mind honestly, I must say." She gave her head a final shake and began walking. "Much further?"

"No. See that rock-slide up ahead? That's our destination. And thank you for the compliment. My Uncle Sid tells me that I take after both my grandfather and my father."

"Uh huh. Say, that brings up something that's been bothering me. It's your name ... all your names. They're so ... excuse me for saying this ... normal. Not alien, I mean."

Bob chuckled. "No offence taken, I assure you. Well, part of the reason is that you can't hear what our names really sound like. It's like bird-song. You hear their chirps and tweets, but there's a rich complexity of notes and phrasings that occur too rapidly for your ears to process. Our names have all that plus cover frequencies you can't hear."

"Fine, but even taking that into account your names sound like ours. Or something out of legend. Wait ... are you saying that those ancient gods were you lot?"

"Uhm, no. Well, on a few worlds, yes, but not on most. The best explanation we've come up with is this. In any population of humans there will always be those who are sensitive to some forms of the alternative energies, at least to a limited extent. Think of what's experienced as whispers that lurk just below conscious awareness. They come out, sometimes, in dreams. Those people try to explain to others what they've heard, often inventing whole mythologies. It's not an area that I've looked at much, though. That's the realm of the Precepts of Philosophy."

"Wait, so you're telling me that our nightmares and mythologies come from eavesdropping on your minds?"

"Well, no. Maybe. Look, I told you I don't understand much about this sort of thing. Some early philosophers thought that we were the source of all those things. But later philosophers dismissed that as too egocentric, and now believe that everyone taps into a shared stream of echoes of thought that bounce around all the human worlds. I prefer to stay away from such mental gymnastics ... too easy to fall into intellectual holes. Brr."

Celcilia laughed. "So maybe all of our fictions are based, however loosely, on something real that the writers tap into? Uh huh. Next you'll be telling me that Cthulhu is real."

"Who? Oh, Uncle Lou. Yeah, he's a strange one. Took on a large aquatic aspect and prefers to live in deep oceans. Spends a lot of his time in an induced dreaming state trying to tap into that shared stream of thoughts that I mentioned."

Celcilia stopped suddenly and held on to the rock face before turning her head around to look at him. "Are you serious?"

Bob nodded. "Honest. Only met him a couple of times when I was young. Very strange man, even by the standards of the Eldest Ones. Not unkind, just ... totally wrapped up in his philosophical ponderings."

She turned to face the path forward, gave a slight shudder, and continued walking. "So what do we do when we reach the rockslide? We're almost there."

"Stop and hang onto the rock face. You'll see."

She could get nothing more out of him and concentrated on walking. They soon reached the rock-slide and had to halt. "We're here. Now what?"

"Pick up a handful of pebbles," was all he said.

With a minimum of grumbling she did as he asked.

"Now toss them, one at a time, across the rock-slide."

Bob heard a soft but distinct, "Sod this", as she flung the

handful of pebbles in an arc. Then he had the satisfaction of hearing a sharp intake of breath followed by, "What in the name of the Goddess ...?"

She turned her head to look at him. "Only some of the pebbles bounced. How ...?"

"Camouflage field," he replied. "It's quite safe to walk into it. That's our destination."

Celcilia walked carefully to edge of the rock-slide, examining it with care. "Looks like rock." She carefully felt along the width of it starting with the outside edge. "Feels like rock, feels like rock, holy shite it ate my hand." She pulled her hand out from where it had disappeared and wiggled her fingers. Then she turned to him and grinned. "Cool. Very cool." With that she turned to face the rock and sidled forward with an arm outstretched.

Within seconds she found herself in a good-sized space inside the cliff. She moved forward and to the side so as to not block the entrance, then walked around tapping the walls. At the far end was what looked to be a small fire-pit, with the remains of a fire. She held her hand close to the remains, but they were as cold as the stones around it. Standing up, she brushed her hands together to get the ash off. A slight noise caused her to turn towards the entrance. Bob stood there grinning.

"I did almost the exact same thing when I first found this place," he said.

"Your da made this?"

"Grandfather, actually. Built it for my dad when he was young."

"Did he—your grandfather—build all the tests?"

Bob shook his head. "Only some of them. Dad expanded on it."

"How can that fire burn without filling this place with smoke?"

"There's a hidden ventilation system. Even disperses the

infrared signature so we can have a fire to keep us warm at night. A small one, mind you, but warm enough. There's some brush a bit further along the ledge. I'll leave you to explore while I go get some for fuel. Make yourself at home." He exited into what looked like solid rock.

Celcilia shook her head at the truly amazing otherworld technology. She looked around, this time more carefully. What she had taken for random bumps and boulders proved to be contoured chairs made out of stone. There were some bumps further up the wall that confused her until she realized they were places to put lamps or hang clothes. She hung up her pouch and jacket, and shrugged her shoulders to get the kinks out.

Just then Bob walked in carrying a large armful of branches which he placed next to the fire-pit. "This should be enough. It doesn't get that cold in here thanks to the moderating effects of the stone."

"This is really wonderful, Bob," enthused Celcilia. "I can see how anyone ... especially a child ... would love a place like this."

"Yes it is," Bob said, his face looking happier than she'd seen it in a long while. "But it seems smaller than I remember. To me, as a child, this was like a castle."

"Oh, it still is, I assure you. How is there so much light here?"

"Piped in from outside via light pipes. One-way, of course, so no light from here shows outside."

"And are there ... facilities?"

Bob laughed. "Oh, yes. Complete with running water. Go to that far corner there and feel around. The entrance is hidden by another camouflage field."

"This is amazing. Did the rest of your family ever come here?"

"Well, Set did, but he didn't like it much. Elder Sister got some first-level training, but I don't think she ever found this place. She has never been fond of the outdoors."

"And your younger sister?"

Bob grimaced. "My parents ... mainly my mother ... didn't want her 'contaminated' with such training."

"So you brought her here." It wasn't a question.

"Of course I did. Taught her the basics of all the different levels. Mom never found out about that. Suspected that Dad knew, but he turned a blind eye if he did." Bob cocked his head for a moment. "Storm's coming. Think I'll gather some more wood while it's still dry. Care to come along?"

Celcilia nodded and off they went. They returned a few minutes later carrying more wood, just ahead of the rain.

"That was sudden," she said.

"That's how it happens in these parts. Shouldn't last too long, I hope. Could make the path too slippery to be safe." Then he shrugged. "We'll find out soon enough."

Celcilia dug into her bag and pulled out a couple of pub sandwiches wrapped in plastic. "Better eat these before they go bad." She unwrapped hers, took a bite, and made a face. "Too late."

Bob sampled it and declared, "Not gone off, but a little stale. They'll do."

"Your idea of edible and mine are rather different," she grumbled. "But, yeah, I've eaten worse."

"I've told you about my life. Mind telling me about yours?" asked Bob.

She nibbled on her sandwich for a few seconds before answering. "Sure." Then she smiled. "As you say, ask anything. You've been upfront with me."

To her relief, his questions were forthright, honest, and came from a genuine desire to understand her life. They discussed the philosophy of her Order, which prompted her to ask how much of it came from Bob's people.

He pondered the question for a moment. "Some of it is pretty common stuff, you realize, even on your own planet.

The esoteric bits, though, are taken from some of our teachings. But the bits about obedience, well, those are all hers. Or rather, common among Set's idea of worship and adapted to her own brand of it."

That rather serious vein of talk weighed on them and they fell silent for a time after that. Sensing a need to lighten the mood, Celcilia asked, "You've mentioned that you used to tease Set and have him chase you through the traps. Didn't your da ever say anything about that?"

"Heh. Oh, yes. Told Set that it was a good lesson in situational awareness.

"What did he tell you?"

"Said to watch my back."

"Did you?"

Bob winced at the memory. "Not always well enough. Set got his revenge over the years. Once he made some new traps in the training areas. Advanced stuff that I'd never seen. Dad punished him very severely over that. Then he helped me recover from the wounds using his own healing factors. That's not really following the Precepts, but he did it anyway. Also hurt rather a lot. The healing factors are highly tuned to the individual and can't usually be transferred. From necessity I learned how to use mine to their best advantage, and then how to incorporate foreign ones into mine."

"Don't you have hospitals?"

"Something similar. But Dad never held with those mechanical methods. Insisted that we learn how to use our healing factors to their maximum. You already know that some of my other abilities are somewhat lesser than those of most of my people. Dad's training forced me to understand and use those that I had to a very fine degree of control. Turns out I can handle the alternative energies better than most. So it all worked out in the end."

"And your mam? What did she do in all this?"

Bob shrugged. "Made polite enquiries as to my health.

Then helped Set learn that a better way to play the game was to play on my ego. To taunt me into trying things beyond my abilities or stage of learning. Worked rather better than I care to admit. But Dad made sure that my mistakes weren't fatal. A near thing, a time or two."

Celcilia shuddered and muttered, "Families can be cruel." From the faraway look in her eyes it was evident that she wasn't referring only to Bob's family.

In a gentle voice Bob said, "And yet here we are, Celcilia. Alive and kicking. And most of all, enjoying life. That's the very best revenge."

She matched his grin with one of own. "Speaking of revenge, what's your end game? After you stop Set?"

Bob stared into the fire. "Don't know. Never really had a purpose in life until I decided to put an end to the horrors he was committing. Been working at that, and cleaning up other messes, for a long time. Always figured I'd make peace with my family and the whole Family at large. That's going to be a lot harder now that I've destroyed two portals. Maybe keep wandering around helping out where I can. Maybe just take a long vacation."

"Vacation? You?" Celcilia's voice mirrored her disbelief that such a thing was possible.

"Hey, I'll have you know that I used to be very good at just bumming around doing nothing. It's been a long time, but I'm sure I can dig deep and re-discover my inner wastrel."

They had a good laugh at that, then Celcilia began to yawn. By mutual agreement they decided that a good night's sleep was in order. There was a lot of ground to cover come morning.

* * *

The morning, as always, came early and quickly. They rose when the cave caught the light and had a light breakfast of the last of the pub snacks. After refilling their water bottles from the spring in the cave, they set out. Either the rain hadn't been too severe, or the natural drainage was very good, but the narrow path was fully dry. They made good time along the ledge then returned to the main trail.

"The portal's just over the top of the next ridge," said Bob as they stopped for their noon break. They had no food, but water and a chance to catch their breath was a welcome break nonetheless.

"Seems near enough."

Bob shook his head. "The test here is to teach patience. You can't see it from here, but there's a downhill section that leads to the base of the hill with the portal. The temptation is to hurry down the hill, but at the bottom and around the portal lies a field of broken ground. Very treacherous footing. You must go slow or else risk injury. There are also noise-traps to watch out for. Not dangerous as such, but once set off make quite a racket. Very unnerving and tends to interfere with concentration." He gave a wry grin. "I speak from experience." Then he grimaced. "At least we won't have to deal with an angry older brother levitating above us as he showers us with taunts and debris."

"Now, why ever would he have done that to such a sweet, innocent, little brother such as yourself?" cooed Celcilia.

Bob did his best to look innocent. It was actually so good that Celcilia laughed. "Yeah, yeah. Be careful, yada yada. I know the drill. Let's do this."

An hour later found them at the top of the hill. Bob held out an arm to stop Celcilia from proceeding. "Wait. Look at the ground. The rain's soaked in and slicked the stones underneath the dirt and dust. Believe me when I say this can be treacherous."

Celcilia, to her credit, managed to learn the lesson without falling although it was a near thing. She glared at Bob, daring him to say something. He held up his hands and said, "Not going to mock a mistake I've made myself."

They made it to the bottom of the incline then had to make a sharp turn around a rock face. The path ended and they faced an uphill climb over a daunting array of broken ground. There were stones and rocks of varying sizes and sharpness, the odd broken tree trunk, and to top it all off it was all still slick from the previous night's rain.

"You know this already, but I'll say it anyway. Be careful," warned Bob. "You lead and set the pace, I'll follow behind you. There's no best way here. Just avoid the noise-traps, if you can."

Celcilia gulped as she nodded. She walked to the edge of the broken stone field and carefully picked her way up the hill. They had made it nearly three-quarters of the way up when Celcilia lost her grip and stumbled. She was beginning to slide into a deep ravine so she reached up to grab a rocky protrusion. Unfortunately she used her damaged left arm, which proved not strong enough to hold her weight. The strain of the attempt caused her to gasp in pain and release her hold. She slid to the bottom and gasped with pain when she hit.

It took only a matter of moments for Bob to reach her. "Are you injured?"

"My right leg. I felt it get sliced by the rocks."

He examined the leg and saw that it was bleeding from several deep gashes. Taking the spare clothing out of his sack, he used it as both dressing and binding for the wound. Celcilia had a couple of other minor scrapes on her hands and arms, which he bound up despite her protests.

"Sorry, sorry, sorry," she kept repeating through clenched teeth.

"Shush," he said in a quiet tone. "This is what we're going to do. I'm going to slice up my bag and remaining clothes to make a harness. My coat will serve as the padding to hold you securely. No, don't argue."

In a few minutes he had created the simple harness and

arranged her in it. To her surprise it only took him a couple of leaps to reach the top of the rise. A few more long-range leaps took them to the top of the hill. Another surprise was to see him sweating with the effort.

"How'd you do that? That was ... not natural. What'd you do?"

"Levitate." He held up a hand. "Well, sort of. I can't fly, but I can reduce my weight and make it easier to climb or jump. Like apporting, it gets a lot harder the more mass I have to deal with."

"So what you're saying is, I'm fat." Then she began giggling. "Sorry, sorry. But the look on your face was worth it."

Bob looked at her with a sorrowful expression. "I blame myself. I've obviously been a bad influence on you." They both laughed for a moment until Celcilia winced.

"Got any of those Empire pain patches left?" asked Bob.

"Saved one."

"Now's the time to use it, I think," said Bob. "You're almost home and I'll get you to a hospital. But I don't want you going into shock before we get there."

She fumbled at her pack until Bob gently pushed her hand aside and retrieved the medication wallet. He put the pain patch on her bad arm. "You were right—that's the last of the patches, I'm afraid."

"S'okay. Deal with the portal. The patch is kicking in." She lay back on the ground and closed her eyes.

Bob concentrated but the portal only instantiated enough to form a hazy outline. He frowned and closed his eyes. The outline of the portal wavered but didn't become any more substantial.

"What's wrong?" asked Cecilia.

"It's locked. Won't fully instantiate without a key."

"Set's doing?"

Bob shook his head. "Not this time. It's my elder sister's

doing. Remember when we arrived I mentioned that mysterious message that was sent to all the local portals? It was a command to lock them down. My attempt to instantiate it caused it to relay a message to me. A very public message that will be displayed to anyone using a portal from now on."

"Well, what's it say?"

Bob sighed. "It's in our language, of course, and doesn't translate well. Basically it sneers at me for thinking that I'm so smart but she's smarter and that I'm a big poo-poo head for daring to go against her. Or words to that effect."

In spite of their circumstances Celcilia had to chuckle. "Ah. Sibling rivalry rears its head. So now what?"

Bob just smiled. "This is her idea of an impossible-to-break key. Give me a minute."

In half that time the portal instantiated and stood before them. Bob let out a contented sigh and said, "There we go. Easy peasey."

"You going to leave her a taunting message in return?"

Bob looked shocked. "I would never stoop to such a childish display. No, I merely added an addendum to her message pointing to the log entry that shows how long it took me to crack her unbreakable code."

"In big, glowing letters no doubt."

"Well," said Bob, "I wouldn't want her or anyone else to miss it. It's important information. A learning moment, if you will."

"So why the thoughtful look just now?"

"What? Oh, I was looking at how she implemented the lock and that messaging code I mentioned. Now if I ..." he stood still for nearly a minute before taking a deep breath and giving his head a small shake. "That will do it, I think."

"Do what, exactly? Stop looking so damned smug and explain yourself."

"Reset all the locks to a new code. A different code for

each portal on this planet. Even better, anyone looking at the status will see that the locks are active. What's more, her sorry attempts at being clever made a hash of Dad's lockout changes. That means I can use these portals as much as I want."

Celcilia laughed. "But only you know the magic words to make them work. Clever boy."

Their conversation was interrupted by the distant cawing of crows. Bob's head spun to the direction of the sound, and his face became tense.

"What?" asked Celcilia. "It's just crows. You said they were common to most human worlds."

"Not this one. They shouldn't be here at all." He paused for a moment as he interrogated the portal. "Someone arrived at our entry portal before we reached this one. Time to go."

Bob set an address and by the time the film of mind-wrenching blackness had formed he had scooped up Celcilia into his arms. Making sure she was secure, he walked into the film. After a series of indeterminate sensations they emerged into another grove. Here, the sun had long set and the grove was in darkness.

"Well," said Bob, "you're home. It's just after two in the morning."

"Oh. I suppose I was expecting something a little more, I don't know, exciting."

"Heh. I know what you mean, Celcilia. But there's rarely any fanfare upon arrival. If there is, that means something has gone very, very wrong."

"So dull is good, then."

"Afraid so. Well, the town and hospital aren't too far away. How's the arm and leg holding up?"

"Pretty good. Pain patch is doing its job, but I can feel some throbbing in both. Not painful, more like a feeling of pressure."

"That's a good sign. Now, brace yourself. I'll try to move as smoothly as I can."

To Celcilia's surprise and relief, Bob managed to do a very good job of walking without jarring her. They got out of the grove and onto the main highway. Bob walked on the pavement, moving onto the shoulder only when a vehicle passed by. No-one bothered to slow down as they whizzed by.

"Why were those crows bothering you so?"

"What? Oh, the ones on my world, you mean."

"Yah."

"They weren't there when we arrived. Which means that someone brought them when they arrived to hunt us. Or, to be accurate, hunt me." He paused but looked as if holding back something.

"There's more. I can read you like a book. Well, not really, but a bit. There's something else."

Bob smiled and nodded. "Ah, you know me so well. But, yes, there's something else. My Uncle Sid mentioned that just before his home planet was attacked they detected crows. Never had any before. Then there's those new traps. Something is going on there that needs investigating."

"So go. Leave me here and I'll catch a ride. Done that before."

"Don't be daft, Cecilia. I won't leave you here, alone and injured. I'm taking you to the hospital and no argument."

As they squabbled a large car passed them, slowed to a stop, then backed up. As it halted next to them, the driver rolled down the window and said, "Oi. Need some help? Oh, hi, Bob. Didn't think to see you out here."

Bob smiled as he recognized the driver. "Hello, Alun. My friend is injured and needs to get to the hospital. Could you take her?"

"Of course. Hop in."

Bob lowered Celcilia onto her feet and helped her into the car. Her pouch had fallen to the ground and he knelt to pick it up. While kneeling, he fumbled at it for a moment before standing up and handing it to her.

"You're not coming," Celcilia said in a matter-of-fact tone.

"I have to go."

"Yeah, you do. Just be damned careful."

"I always am," he replied. He turned to face Alun and said, "I'm in your debt, sir. Please see her to safety."

Alun nodded as Bob shut the door. Then he turned to face Celcilia and said, "Buckle up, miss. We'll have you at the hospital in just a few minute. You going to be alright until then?"

"Oh, yes, thank you."

"What about Bob?"

"No rest for the wicked," she murmured. Then in a louder voice she said, "He'll be fine. Has places to go and worlds to save."

She watched him in the rear-view mirror as they drove away. Then, as if he had never been there, he was gone.

* * *

Bob arrived back on the training planet via a portal some distance from the one he'd left by. He kept it instantiated while he did a thorough scan of the area with his full sensorium. Detecting nothing untoward, he turned back to the portal and put it into diagnostic mode. He frowned in concentration as he amended the changes made just before his hasty exit. The new instructions restricted use of the gates to himself and his younger sister. After a moment's hesitation he added their father to the list. That would ensure that they could shake off anyone forcing them to make the transit. However, he set it up so that only he was allowed to authorize a guest traveller. A quick test proved that the modifications were functional, so he had them transmitted to all the other portals on the planet before dismissing this one. With access to the planet locked down and secure he was free to deal with the ones hunting him.

Choosing a bearing that would lead him roughly towards his exit portal, he set forth taking care to stay beneath the cover of the trees. There were aerial predators to worry about, as well as the human hunters. The planet's ground-based predators were a lesser worry, but something he kept an eye out for. His location was in a buffer zone between the level one and level two areas so encountering some of the planet's nastier specimens was a distinct possibility.

As was his father's wont, portals were placed on hilltops with minor tests around them. This particular test was a variation of the one he and Celcilia had encountered but with the potential for far more dangerous falls. Every time Bob had run this level his father insisted that he pass through the test faster than the time before. It had been some years since he'd been here, but his muscle memory made the correct moves at the correct times without fail. Once safely at the bottom, Bob turned and smiled. It felt good to be back in a place he thought of as a second home.

Bob kept his pace to a brisk trot as he climbed a hill and approached the boundary to the first level. The path here was little better than a game trail but made for easier travel than forcing his way through the brush. Just before reaching the crest, he stooped and finished the approach on his stomach. He peered through the foliage and could make out a few crows scouring the area where he and Celcilia had been. Then he noticed another set of them were flying a carefully coordinated spiral pattern that would take them over his position in the not-too-distant future. That left the question was who they were working for.

He pondered how best to determine that when he saw several figures appear in the sky. They would float up, hover for a few seconds, then float down. A few seconds later they would do the same thing but some distance away. The pattern of their movements covered the area previously scanned by the crows. All in all, Bob saw five people in the hunting party.

Bob smiled as he watched them at work. It was all the familiar pattern of a childhood game—a variant of hide and seek. The difference here was the presence of the crows, which were obviously being used as scouts looking for visual traces. The people were doing a cursory ground search combined with an aerial scan for use of the alternate energies, such as those used by apporting or levitation. It brought back childhood memories—some of them even happy ones. As he watched, he developed a strategy and a predatory grin replaced the smile. He looked at the position of the sun and decided there was time for everyone to get introduced.

He slithered back the way he came until he was out of sight of the observers. Rising to his feet, Bob trotted around the hill towards the location of his prey. They'd be getting tired and hungry after all that usage of the alternate energies. As children, sundown had been a signal to rush to the supper table. On this planet it was the time the blood-kites came out. Most of them were nocturnal, but some packs preferred the daylight. All of them enjoyed the twilight hours.

After a short dash through the brush he came upon the official trail through the area. As he traversed it he scanned the area with care, but could find no evidence of it being used in a very long time. The trail was a body-length wide and consisted of switchbacks around the low hills and streams. The trees, although not dense, created a thick canopy preventing attacks from the air, at least in this section. It was also thick enough to impede apporting, so anyone chasing him would have to follow on foot. He had selected this area because there was a pair of trip-traps that would cause a landslide of rocks upon the unwary. Bob set the trigger on those and added some small-diameter logs across the trail to add more opportunities to stumble.

Continuing on to a stream he came across a pair of snufflers and killed them. He next caught a handful of fish, being very particular about the species. He trotted on until he came to the edge of the forested area and entered the meadow. Bob could hear the sounds of the crows in the distance, cawing periodically to each other. There were also other sounds in the air, sounds that brought a smile to his face.

He cut the bellies of the snufflers, taking care not to break all the way through the skin, and threw them with some force so they landed in the treetops between himself and the crows. As the carcasses hit, each released a spray of blood and viscera onto the trees and into the air. He cut the fish in a similar manner but left them on the ground. From the excited cries of the crows, his movements had caught their attention and he could hear them getting closer. When the first of them came into view, just above the treetops, he tossed one of the fish and hit the crow. The bird tumbled, shrieked loudly, but managed to regain control. It landed at the top of a tree and began to scream in strident tones as it shook fish viscera off its feathers. As its brethren showed up, Bob tossed fish at them—sometimes hitting, sometimes missing. They began to circle the meadow just out of range of his throws, trumpeting their success at finding the quarry.

Their sounds of triumph turned into shrill cries of terror as large shapes slammed into them from above and below. The crows began wheeling about madly as the blood-kites tore through them. At the first sign of the blood-kites, Bob dashed into the forest and dove under a log that shielded him from view. A series of thuds and shrieks signalled the end of the crows. "Never bring a crow to a blood-kite battle," he muttered as he burrowed deeper into the forest debris.

Bob heard human shouts coming from the meadow. Very soon thereafter came a human scream and the sound of a weapon being fired. A different human voice yelled for the firing to stop and to head for the trees. Bob smiled at that—it would seem that at least one of their number had taken his father's level-one course. Still, that was a signal that it was time for him to move.

Bob listened carefully but the sounds of battle were still some distance from him. Extricating himself from under the log with care, he headed for the official trail and trotted to the stream. There he carefully scrubbed his hands and knife in the coarse sand before continuing on his way. He paused to listen to the sounds of pursuit and shook his head when it appeared that they were heading in a different direction. He sent a low-power ranging pulse towards them and was rewarded by the sounds of a hurried discussion and the sound of amateurish stealthy movements heading in his direction.

He trotted up the trail, being careful to leave tracks that were plainly visible, as if made by someone running in terror. He passed by the first and second traps before pausing to listen for sounds of pursuit. The sounds of several pairs of feet greeted him and he tamped down a grin by force of will. Training and experience had taught him the bitter lessons of premature celebration.

A few minutes later his patience was rewarded as he heard the first trap being tripped. The shouts of his battered pursuers had barely settled when the second trap was set off, yielding its own cacophony of screams. There were no sounds of pursuit after that so Bob continued on in full stealth mode to put some distance between himself and his pursuers. Given their injuries, not to mention the sustained effort of their earlier searches, he was certain they'd stop for the night to recuperate. Whatever else they might be, these were not well-trained soldiers.

The next day offered Bob another opportunity to lead his pursuers through a few of his father's tests. The blood-kites forced the pursuers to keep any levitating to a minimum. Bob knew, from bitter experience, that once aroused those packs would follow anything perceived as a threat or prey for a considerable distance. It was that tenacity and fearlessness that caused his father to decree that no-one could harm his favourite birds without severe repercussions from him.

That night Bob crept up to their camp when they stopped for the night. There were, indeed, five of them—several of whom he recognized as from a younger cohort than himself. A couple of them were unfamiliar, which was strange. Their less-than-sure movements led him to suspect that they'd had one of Set's unauthorized aspect changes. What puzzled him were the signs of physical damage still evident from the day's exertions. It was always startling to be reminded that not everyone was as proficient at using their healing factors as he was. It was also another indication that his brother wasn't recruiting the best and brightest. Still, they could be dangerous if not handled correctly.

After spending a small amount of time to rest and recuperate, he prepared a few of the old tests for them. When that was done he looped around to a hidden cranny to wait. To his surprise they waited until after sunrise to resume the hunt. From their groans and comments he gathered that not everyone was ready to face the day. As they trooped below him he saw that most of the complaining came from the two he didn't recognize.

Their unpreparedness and overall amateur approach gave him an idea for a strategy to try. After giving them a suitable head start, he emerged from his hiding place and followed their trail. Their bush craft was so bad that he could actually hear their individual steps as they walked along the trail. Gathering up supplies as he walked, he waited until they were almost at the next test before he attacked.

Bob snapped off a series of stones that bounced off the heads of each of them. That took them completely by surprise, as did the twirling sticks that flew at and clubbed them when they turned around to face their attacker. Predatory hunting cries from the creatures of a dozen worlds greeted them as they faced an ongoing cascade of stones, sticks, and fish that were thrown at them. A couple of them had energy weapons, but those were knocked out of their grasp after the first wild shots. Others fired energy blasts from their embedded tech, but stones thrown at barely subsonic velocities bruised those extremities into pained uselessness. Within a handful of seconds they beat a hasty retreat that bordered on panic.

That retreat took them into the trap itself. Rocks and logs rained upon and around them. What didn't hit them made their footing so treacherous that they fell to the ground where they became a stationary target not only for the trap's debris but also precision throws by Bob. Those that tried to levitate away were caught in cloud of projectiles and fell to the ground. They were all screaming in fear as much as from injury.

As they lay in the dust bleeding and moaning, Bob casually walked towards them. The sun was at his back and they had to adjust their vision to compensate and shield their eyes with their hands.

"Had enough to call it quits?" he asked without a trace of humour.

One of his opponents, a young man with a large human aspect that dwarfed Bob, tried to bring one of his weapons to bear. Bob's hand snapped out and a dagger-like piece of rock embedded itself in his opponent's shoulder. A split second later a portion of Bob's sensorium popped out and emitted a blast that rippled the air. The embedded rock exploded, shattering the shoulder. The young man screamed and fainted.

Two more moved slightly and found themselves the recipients of a dagger of rock embedded in their chests. They gasped in shock and made to pull the daggers out.

"Leave it or I'll explode them," said Bob in a quiet voice of deadly menace. "Anyone else want to continue this game? No? Excellent. Let's have a little talk, shall we?" He pointed at the two with stone daggers in their chest and said, "Remove it. Slowly or it'll bleed too much. Fine. Now drop 'em on the ground. Now everyone sit and make themselves comfortable."

His opponents were soon sitting upright, with the exception of the one with the blasted shoulder who was still unconscious. His wound had stopped bleeding and was slowly scabbing over. Bob looked at them more in sorrow than in anger while shaking his head.

"Idiots. I've been training on this planet since I was old enough to walk. What made you think you could take me on here, of all places? No, wait. Let me guess. Mind-gems for everyone who volunteered?"

He was rewarded with slow nods from everyone. It was the answer he was expecting, but it still disgusted him.

"Figures. So how are they working out for you now?"

One of the youths answered him in a sullen voice, "We tried doing without them. Got sick."

Bob nodded. "Withdrawal sickness. Remember that from your medical history classes? Let me guess, there's a drop or two of something white inside each of those mind-gems, right?"

They all nodded.

"That stuff is called pure quill. That's what makes you sick when you remove the mind-gems. Nasty stuff. Got a whiff of it myself, once."

That got their shocked attention. "You?" asked one.

"Not by choice, no, but caught a whiff of it. Laid me low and made me sick for days."

"Couldn't handle it?" sneered one of the men, bolder than the rest. "Set told us you were weak. We've heard the stories about how crippled you are."

Bob surprised them by laughing. "Did he now? Good to know that he remembers his younger brother so fondly. But as for weak ..."

He gestured towards the group. "Who caught and defeated whom? Multiple times, I might add."

"Fine. You beat us. So what now?" asked another in a sulky tones.

Without a pause, Bob said, "Declare truce. Give me your word."

They were beaten but resistant to the suggestion, which pleased Bob. "I'm not asking for surrender, and you'd be correct in refusing that. All I'm asking is a cessation of hostilities. No victory, no defeat. A truce between equals, as the Precepts prescribe."

It took nearly a minute of sullen silence before the first one accepted the truce. The others followed soon thereafter. The only exception was the young man with the severely injured shoulder.

"What about him?" asked one of his friends. "He can't offer truce."

Bob nodded. "That's true. But right now he's a non-combatant and I'll accept him on those terms. He's safe from me, but he needs medical attention. You all do, if it comes to that. Weren't you taught how to use your healing factors properly?"

As expected, they all shrugged and looked sheepish. Exercising a supreme effort of will, Bob stopped himself from sighing and lecturing them on the importance of paying attention to their studies. Then they surprised him when one said, "We can't use the regular facilities" and the others nodded in agreement.

"What? Oh. The mind-gems." They gave embarrassed nods.

Bob sighed. "Right. Your parents will tear strips off you for that ... possibly literally." He paused for a moment in thought.

"Wait. Set has his own private medical facility. Why not go there?"

The snorts of derision told him all he needed to know about that option.

"Alright," he said, "let's do it this way. You all remember Aunt Freida and Uncle Sid, right?"

"They're lost, aren't they? Killed when their planet was destroyed?" answered one.

"Nah, you idiot," said another. "Aunt Freida showed up a while back when we were kids. Uncle Sid was lost."

"Shut up, both of you," snapped Bob. "They're both alive and well. Aunt Freida is on one of my dad's planets. She helped stop a series of plagues there." That got their attention. "That's right; I said a series of plagues. Manufactured by someone just after her planet, and family, were destroyed. I found Uncle Sid on a distant world. He found and stopped another manufactured plague that came from off-world. Along the way he found a cure for that pure quill withdrawal you've experienced. Between them they can help you get rid of those mind-gems for good."

"What then?" asked one, and the others nodded their agreement.

"That's up to you, isn't it?" answered Bob. "You're all adults. Your path is your own. However, I would point out that Set's path is a poor one to follow. He's lied to you about a lot of things. Offered you pleasures that come with a terrible price. Aunt Freida and some of the older ones have come up something new, a Philosophy of Change. If you're smart you'll take the time to listen to what she has to say."

"And if we don't? What Set's been saying about how we've lost our way makes a lot of sense. He has lots of powerful allies, none of whom like you very much."

"Uh huh. Seen Kydos around recently? Or Freddy? What about Set's plans of interstellar conquest that seem to have fallen apart rather suddenly? He's on a path of destruction and failure, not creation."

"Set told us that you killed Freddy. In an ambush," came the accusation from one.

"He's alive, or at least he was the last time I saw him. He issued a formal challenge, witnessed by Aunt Freida, and I won. Left him with her to get healed."

That got them thinking, and several exchanged looks and nods. A couple still looked sullen. "What if we stay on Set's path?"

Bob shrugged. "Your choice. But next time I won't be so gentle. Or so forgiving."

One of the more agreeable lads looked up and asked in a plaintive voice, "How do we get off this world?"

"Excuse me? Set didn't give you the exit codes?" asked Bob, his tone mirroring his surprise.

"No. Said he'd be back to check on us in couple of days. Told us to enjoy the peace and quiet for a few days after we ... well, you know."

Another piped in, "And the portals are locked. We tried a couple before we started hunting you."

Bob rolled his eyes and once again stopped himself from berating them any further. "Fine. Open up a communication channel in passive mode. Ready? Here's the key and exit codes for the portal over there." He pointed in the direction of the portal he and Celcilia had used. "Use the key when you instantiate the portal, and the code when you set the address. Oh, it's a one-time code so get it correct the first time. Here's the address and guest codes for Aunt Freida's planet. It's another one of my dad's private portals and exits above an active volcano. Everyone ready to levitate or apport? Better be sure." No-one admitted to any problems. "Alright, your unconscious friend is your responsibility. Aunt Freida will be able to fix him, and the rest of you, as good as new. Oh, and tell them that Kydos is severely injured and may require medical assistance ... that bootleg aspect of hers is light on healing factors. Uncle Sid knows where to find her." He paused for a moment before adding, "I know that truce has been declared, but anyone want to volunteer any information about Set's plans?"

They were slow to get to their feet, their lack of willingness to cooperate made plain by the look on their faces.

Shrugging to indicate he wasn't surprised, Bob asked, "How did those crows get here?"

They looked at each other, exchanging looks. Finally one blurted, "Set told us to bring them along with us. Said they'd help us find you."

Bob didn't bother to hold back a sneer. "Ah. And that worked out so very well, didn't it? Okay, off with you."

There was a series of soft *plops* as they apported away. He waited until he felt the portal activate, then he spun on his heels and jogged towards another portal. It was a fine day for a run. Or perhaps a picnic ... he'd worked up quite an appetite and felt that he'd earned a reward.

CHAPTER SEVEN
Blast From the Past

Bob spent the next couple of days resting and thinking. He'd been acquiring a lot of information in the past while, while his actions were mostly reacting and trying to survive. Although already set to block all but a select few, for ease of mind he programmed the portals to alert him if anyone transited in. When he needed a break he went around to the various test areas to check for unexpected traps. To his relief the only ones he found were in the easier sections of the first training level.

Although it was nice to see more people taking an interest in acquiring training relating to the Precepts of Survival, that could only make his own operations more difficult. However, judging by the dumb kids (for so he thought of them) whom he'd just defeated, the quality of his opposition was less than stellar. That happy thought lasted all of a second until he thought of Kydos and Freddy. In his estimation either could have taken on that entire squad with no problem. Well, Freddy would have had to work at it, but would probably have prevailed.

That thought gave him pause. Many of the older generations could have taken on those young fools, but considerably fewer in his own generation. Even some in the older generations, like Sid and his family, paid scant attention to the Precepts of Survival. When he began tabulating what he knew of the various capabilities throughout the Family, there was a real dearth of solid battle training. The more he thought about that, the more he believed it might explain some of Set's allure. Their culture was steeped in traditions of battle and survival, but only a few had extensive training in those skills. Yes, everyone had powers and abilities but that was a far cry from being trained to use them to their fullest extent. Whatever Bob might have thought about his brother, Set was a skilled fighter. That combined with the social manipulation skills of their mother made for a potent force.

However, that only explained a portion of what he'd come across. Set was an egotistical bully, which explained the temples on the low-tech worlds. The Five Stars Empire operation, on the other hand, spoke to a whole new level of organizational skills. Skills which his brother—everyone in his family if truth be told—lacked. That meant someone else was involved. Someone playing a long game over many worlds, yet content to stay in the shadows. Well, more or less. There were the plagues on Celcilia's and Aunt Freida's planets. Then there was that substantial planetary assault force that took out Sid's family.

Those were all major plays, but such plays rarely came out of nowhere. Racking his brains to think of any other attack vector, he recalled the mind-gems. The misuse of those began shortly after the end of the Great Wars before abating some time later. Yet recently there was a resurgence of their use, now combined with pure quill. That gave him pause ... Uncle Sid had mentioned the use of pure quill to create fanatical troops. Which in turn sounded a lot like what Kydos was doing in her initiation ceremonies.

All that begged the question of how this hypothetical shadow group was moving around. Set and his forces made open use of the portal system. It might be instructive to check out the range of operations of the shadow group. The best way to do that was to use the resources built into the portals, so Bob headed off to the nearest one.

He instantiated the portal and put it into query mode. It was a matter of a few minutes to enter the locations of the shadow group's probable activities. Comparing those to portal locations revealed an interesting pattern. The planets attacked by plagues and the planets where the mercenary corps suffered inexplicable losses all had very old types of portals. The only planet that did not have a portal of that vintage was Sid's planet, which had the next generation after those older ones. Another planet hosting an old portal was Celcilia's planet, and he had detailed logs from that.

The suspicious transits were all logged using a generic human code rather than one associated with a specific family. His first thought was that someone was masking their familial association—something uncommon but not unknown. A moment later a far more chilling thought came to him as a fragment of an old history lesson tickled his memory. Those old-style portals were set up at the end of the Great Wars, when possessing a human genome was considered enough of a security measure. That was later tightened up to filter out anyone not of the known families, supposedly on general security grounds.

That left the question of who the unknown humans might be. The only ones he could think of were those associated with the Refuser Faction. They might be passed by those old portals, but that begged the question of how they had managed to travel to planets that had portals. It also didn't explain why the Refusers would bother doing such a thing. They were somewhat longer-lived compared to the younger races, but that was still a fraction of the expected lifetime for any of the Family. This all assumed, of course, that any of the Refusers still existed.

Of more pressing concern, Bob felt, was the need to

upgrade his resources. He had new allies in Freida and Sid, but they had their own tasks and were far away. Something more immediate and heavy-duty was needed. Something along the lines of a forgotten military station. Bob smiled as he thought of the possibilities that could offer. Assuming, of course, that the old station even still existed.

He set up the local portal to confirm the existence of a portal at the address Sid had given him and initiated a test query. As the seconds passed, Bob grew increasingly impatient. Lying in wait like a predator on the hunt was one thing, but this sort of research just made him eager for immediate results. When a minute had passed with no reply, he grew puzzled. Any portal should have responded to the test query, something he confirmed several times with other portals while waiting. It took nearly ten minutes before he got a response—the mystery portal said it had been in a hibernation state.

Any unused portal would enter a resting state, where it would be ready for access within seconds. After some period of time—which could vary but was typically several millennia—it would enter a sleeping state from which it was accessible within a minute or so. Eventually a sleeping portal would enter a hibernation state, which meant that it had all but powered down to conserve its mechanisms. When Bob was younger, his father had told him in hushed tones about the time he'd found a public portal in the sleeping state. That was almost unheard of, and indicated a site of ancient historic interest or an abandoned family world. For a portal to go into hibernation meant it hadn't been used in a time period so long that Bob had never heard of it happening. But a portal unused since the time of the Great Wars would certainly fall into that category.

With growing excitement Bob sent out another query. This one added a status request and the reply came in under a minute. The remote portal was attempting to emerge from hibernation mode and its power levels were very low. So low, in fact, that it would take nearly a day to allow an emergency low-mass transition, and at least two for a person. That startled Bob, as that meant the portal had been all but depleted. He sent out a query for more details and soon had his answer. The power core for the base associated with the portal was offline, and the portal was using its own energy reserves to keep the base going at a minimal level. The timestamp for the last transit was very, very long ago. That left a lot of questions that could only be answered by a visit. Although monitoring was not necessary, Bob indulged his excitement and instructed the remote portal to send back hourly status reports.

Bob spent the time accumulating a store of supplies for his trip. He caught and dried various types of food, not expecting to find anything edible on the base. For containers he prepared lengths of hollowed-out logs which would serve equally well for water or food. Those preparations helped to keep him busy, but Bob's mind was racing at the possibilities of what he might find. This was not just an historical moment; it was a childhood dream of exploration come true.

It took closer to three days than the estimated two, but at last the remote portal signalled that its power accumulation was both stable and sufficient for him to transit with safety. He assembled his gear on an improvised sled, set up the address, and watched as the portal created the transit film. Not knowing the state of the atmosphere on the other side, he toughened his skin and took several deep breaths to charge his lungs and body with all the oxygen they could hold. Pulling the sled with vine ropes, he walked into the blackness and felt the usual tug of forces.

He emerged into a dimly-lit room and dragged the sled into the middle of it. The transit film wobbled, wavered, and vanished before he could dismiss it. Like all such military portals of the era, this one was a permanent facility that didn't get sent into hyperspace after use. The construction of the portal was stark and simple compared to the ones Bob was familiar with. The patterns playing over its surface were faint and slow-moving.

Bob sent a query to the portal and received a quick response. It turned out that the portal's energy levels had been sufficient for a single transit and would take several hours, perhaps a day, to recharge. Bob frowned. Modern systems would have stated explicitly the power levels were sufficient only for a single transit.

The ambient temperature was very low--not enough to freeze atmospheric gases but chilly nonetheless. Speaking of atmosphere, there was very little in the room, which could be a problem. He could minimize his oxygen use to last for an hour and the containers he'd brought had some air that might extend that for another hour. A hurried query of the portal gave him access to the stations environmental controls, which were displayed on one of the walls. The language was unknown yet had a hint of familiarity. The schematic was, in the nature of such things, sufficient to understand the layout well enough. The station was trying to bring the entire facility up to a human-compatible environment. Bob changed the controls to focus the efforts to just the room he was in.

After a minute he could feel the temperature and air pressure increasing. Satisfied that he'd soon be able to breathe, Bob shifted his attention to trying to understand the overall operation of the base's environmental and control systems. It didn't take too long to determine that power was being supplied from the portal because the base's main power was non-functioning. According to the diagrams, the latter was a planetary core tap supplemented by off-line auxiliary units of some indeterminate type. The core tap power room was not too far from his current location, but just outside the zone currently being warmed up.

Bob pondered his options then decided to take a chance

on a quick look at the power room. Core taps were extremely reliable, but he'd never heard of any this old. If he could get it working, even partially, the extra power would help the base become habitable much more quickly. On the other hand the movement involved would deplete his limited reserves of oxygen. He decided that overall the rewards outweighed the risks.

He took a moment to study the control board and control his body systems before setting out. There was supposed to be a doorway to the section where his destination lay, so he set off to find it. As expected, the control schematics weren't to scale and it took Bob a few minutes to find the doorway he required. It was off of one of the many small rooms, but was plainly marked with the same symbols from the control schematic. The problem was that there was enough air pressure differential to make opening the door impossible.

Bob would have sighed except that he couldn't afford to waste the oxygen. Instead, he sealed the room then fired a blast of energy from his sensorium at the wall sufficient to punch a hole in the material. There was a *whoosh* as the minimal atmosphere rushed to equalize the pressure between the two sections. In a matter of a few seconds Bob was able to wrench the door open. It was much colder in this new section and he could feel the residual moisture on his skin freeze. The air pressure was now less than that found on a high mountain, forcing Bob to blink frequently enough to prevent his eyeballs from freezing.

He found the core tap control room without much problem and took a quick look around. The room had lost temperature slowly enough that ice had formed on the ceiling. A large block of it had fallen across some high-power terminals causing arcing severe enough to sever the linkage. Bob spied several bars of metal along the wall. He removed them and twisted them to form a single multi-conductor wire. Looking at the controls, he saw that the circuit breaker associated with the linkage had been forced open. In theory the circuit would be unpowered, but that wasn't something he was willing to bet his life on.

While his healing factors began sending warnings of damage caused by the near vacuum and low temperatures, Bob forced his improvised cable into one end of the broken linkage. Looking around he found what looked to be a plastic rod which a quick scan revealed to be nonconducting. He used that as a hammer to fasten the other end of the cable to form a bypass of the broken section. It all looked to be mechanically secure, so he went to the control panel and reset the circuit breaker. There was a brief flash as sections of his cable equalized the voltage differentials, but after that everything behaved in a normal fashion. The warning lights on the control panel changed colour, which Bob took to mean that the power tap was now operational. A quick query of the portal indicated that its power was no longer required by the station. Heaving a mental sigh of relief, Bob made his way back to the portal room. Along the way he patched the hole he'd burned in the wall and made sure that the door was shut.

The influx of extra power was speeding the station's regeneration by a significant amount. Bob could feel a strong breeze as the ventilation systems worked to re-pressurize the station, and the temperature was much warmer than it had been even a couple of minutes ago. This gave Bob's healing factors a chance to repair the damage sustained by his hands when he'd handled the various items in the power room.

By the time he returned to the portal room the air pressure was equivalent to that at the top of a tall mountain. While adjusting his body to the rapid changes, he examined the control panel in an attempt to see if the new atmosphere was suitable to sustain life. It turned out that the station had protocols in place for a low-pressure event, and oxygen levels were elevated to compensate. Bob was very grateful to be able to replenish his oxygen stores, although it took many deep breaths to do so. Within a few minutes he was able to breathe at something approaching a normal rate. In less than half an hour the station was back to normal atmospheric pressure. It would take somewhat longer for the temperatures to regain normal levels due to the extreme cold soaked into the structure. Still, it was survivable and Bob took advantage of that to look around while his healing factors finished dealing with the injuries caused by the extreme cold and low pressures.

Bob moved around with great care ... any structure this old was bound to be somewhat fragile. There were three mysteries that stood out from his wanderings. The first was the minimal amount of time-related damage. There was dust everywhere and some of the furniture and equipment crumbled at his touch, but by no means all of it. Anything that was integral to the station structure appeared to be fully intact. The second was that there wasn't much to the station, aside from power and portal rooms. The third was that much—perhaps the majority—of the station was hidden behind some form of energy field.

Returning to the portal room, he told the portal to begin recharging itself in preparation for a transit. Freed from the burden of keeping the station alive, the portal said it would be able to perform a two-way transit within a day. Bob wasn't planning on leaving but it was always a good idea to have options. Studying the controls indicated that the areas within the energy field had some form of functionality which wasn't detailed on the control board. That meant that the local control board was only a secondary maintenance panel, and that the important parts of the station were locked away. It took some time but he finally determined that the energy field was actually a primitive stasis field. Finding the controls for it took rather more time and cursing of the station designers. Bob grumbled at the primitive nature of everything, then caught himself and had a good laugh.

Within a few hours he found the stasis field controls. It turned out to be an all-or-nothing control, meaning he'd have to restore everything at once. A query of the control system indicated that the station was ready to deal with the appearance of that larger volume. Taking a deep breath he set the controls to disable the stasis field. There was a deep-felt thrumming that came from all around, lasting for a few seconds before vanishing. He felt the environmental systems kick into higher activity, but nowhere near the levels used when he first arrived.

A thrill of excitement caused him to laugh out loud. This was something out of the entertainment fictions he had read as a boy—finding lost worlds and exploring the unknown. He knew full well that new worlds often offered new ways to suffer and die, but he refused to let reality dampen the fun. So, full of an optimism and joy that he hadn't felt in years he set out to explore.

The reality of what he found sobered his mood in short order. The ancient facility a well-supplied military research base with bodies scattered throughout. They all wore uniforms vaguely reminiscent of the several styles used during the Great Wars. The people, though, had not died clean deaths. In fact, they looked to have died in great discomfort, if not outright pain. Many of them were laid out in precise order in the larger rooms, but some gave the appearance of having died at their duty stations.

A stasis field couldn't stop the inevitable march of entropy, just slow it down. That meant that the corpses were no longer fresh, but not quite mummified. Bob estimated that they looked to be a century or two old. Based on the rate of decay in a modern stasis field, and increasing that due to the primitive tech used, he estimated that the station dated from the early to middle of the Great Wars. That jibed with the tech he'd seen so far, which made this an important historical find.

The first problem to solve, though, was getting access to the main control system. As he'd deduced, the portal room's control panel was a secondary panel. The main one was not accessible from the portal's systems and required direct physical access. That proved to be easy to find and he had no problem in deciphering the system schematics, if not the language.

After ascertaining that there were no obvious problems, he decided to focus his attentions on the corpses. For one thing, now free of the stasis field they would begin to decay at a normal rate. For another, there were at least several dozen of them scattered about. The first task was to determine what had killed them. The second was to hold a proper funeral of some sort. These were ancestors, and as such deserved the utmost respect.

Ancestors or no, though, the bodies needed to be examined in detail. There were maps of the facility that indicated the location of a medical block. Upon arriving there he found it full of bodies on the beds and floors. People in the uniform of the medical speciality lay strewn around. Some were draped across other bodies in beds, and some looked as if they had simply collapsed and died.

He was pondering how to access the data system when he came across several handwritten journals. He overlooked the language, as that would take time to decipher, but instead concentrated on the graphs and drawings. The graphs appeared to chart the number of deaths over time. If he was reading it correctly, the carnage took place over just a couple of weeks, perhaps less. The hand-drawn sketches looked to be observations from autopsies, along with notes. Bob could see that the various organs had been affected—some enlarged and others atrophied.

Bob looked around, almost overwhelmed by the carnage before him. The fictions had primed him to expect an empty station with a mystery to solve. This was a charnel house--the horrible aftermath of a terrible accident or an attack.

He began a detailed examination of the bodies in the medical room. Each one had a blacked and protruding tongue, pustule-type sores on their hands and face, and a swollen neck. There was a lot of powdery residue around, which Bob concluded were the dried remains of bodily fluids. He also found a medical stasis facility meant to store dead crew, which proved to contain another dozen bodies.

He selected one of the bodies at random, took one of the surgical knives, and proceeded to dissect it. What he found was a close match to the sketches. Repeating the process with another body, he got the same results. The sadness of the situation sat like a great weight upon his shoulders. He decided to return to the main control centre, on the assumption that getting access to the station's records would help to solve the mystery.

Bob trudged along the corridor, noting each body as he passed it. There was nothing he could do to help them but he could at least acknowledge that they had once lived and were worthy of respect. He was halfway to the control centre when he sneezed. This was not entirely unexpected given the amount of dust he was kicking up, but then it repeated shortly thereafter.

He paused to confer with his healing factors and discovered that they were in a state of mild alert. There were any number of things that could account for this, but he decided to press them for details. It took several minutes, but the conclusion was that there was a viral agent involved. It wasn't anything that couldn't be handled, but something to keep an eye on.

Given how hard he'd been working, Bob decided that it was time for a break. He returned to the portal room where he had left the supplies. By the time he got there he was feeling somewhat worse, and his healing factors confirmed that the viral agents were becoming more of a problem. As with most problems, Bob decided that a meal was in order and felt somewhat better after consuming it. The only oddity was that he was beginning to feel somewhat feverish and tired, so he decided to have some more water.

After checking the supplies he had brought, Bob decided it might be a good idea to see what supplies the station could offer. There was a mess hall shown on the station layout, which he decided would be a promising place to start. Arriving there he found it to be full of bodies arranged in a tidy fashion on mattresses laid on the floor. Ignoring those, he poked around and found a food preparation area. It offered various devices to prepare raw foods, which was interesting. Nearby he found a storage area for raw foods, the contents of which had long since decayed to dust or lumps of solid matter. Of more immediate interest were the various dispensers of water. He tried a few but none were functioning.

Continuing his exploration turned up a molecular food printer, which seemed to be functional. He selected several items on the menu at random and was rewarded with the creation of a meal, of sorts. A sniff-test deemed it all to be non-poisonous, so he sampled a very small portion of each. His body accepted it as usable food, but the taste left a lot to be desired. He suspected that the subjective decades within the stasis field had left the delicate systems in a less-than-optimal state. Getting the food printer working would be a great help in returning the base to self-sufficiency.

There was a smaller, simpler molecular printer nearby, and it proved to be designed for water. It was a handy, but very inefficient, way of getting water. Normally a large facility would tap into an underground source, so that was one more thing he'd have to look into. When activated the unit generated a quantity of cool water in a simple container, which Bob gratefully drank.

The water both refreshed him and helped wash the foul taste of the synthetic food out of his mouth. That, plus the demands made on his healing factors, had made him realize that he was again very hungry. Bob hurried back to the portal room, doing his best to ignore all the bodies. He arrived at his cache of supplies and settled on the ground. The effort of sitting forced an exhausted grunt of effort from him. Something was not right, but all his healing factors could tell him was that they were working flat out to combat an infection.

Bob chewed on some of the dried meat and herbs, and within a few minutes his appetite was sated. He washed that down with some water, then sat back against the sled and closed his eyes. Although tired, he forced himself to stay awake. To pass the time he enumerated the idiotic blunders he had made in coming here. First and foremost, of course, was the lack of proper equipment ... more specifically, an environmental suit. The small portal on the training planet wouldn't have been able to provide one, but he should have obtained one from somewhere. It was luck, and the rugged engineering practises of his ancestors, that had saved his life.

In the spirit of honesty Bob was forced to admit that his unmatched skills and brilliant thinking had allowed him to make the most of the situation. The memory of the last time he'd tried that line of reasoning on his father sprang unbidden to mind. The drubbing he'd received for being such an ass still brought a shudder, although that was leavened by a wry smile. The old taskmaster was nothing if not fair, Bob had to allow. Not to mention, far too often correct in his evaluations of his youngest son.

Bob found it reassuring to have his father guarding his younger sister. She was a truly amazing person—so smart and good and fun. One of the few rays of sunshine in his life.

The memory of her caused Bob to smile and remember the good times. Such good times when everything was soft and easy, like lying back on a warm summer day and watching the clouds drift by. Such good times. Easy times. So very easy just to drift along without any cares.

With a start Bob jumped to his feet and stood there panting as if after a great physical effort. He wiped his brow and was surprised to find himself sweating and beginning to shiver. A quick interrogation of his healing factors revealed that he'd been burning through energy reserves to keep them powered up. He quickly ate more of his dried meat, washing it down with more water. That made him feel a lot better, and left his mind clear enough to worry. This viral assault on his systems was unlike anything he'd ever heard about, much less experienced. Nothing should have affected his healing factors in this way. Somehow, they weren't sensing the virus as something dangerous.

He sat down and entered a meditative state. This allowed him to interact with his healing factors at a deeper level, a talent he'd developed in his youth. Most people were content to let their healing factors work in their default states, using artificial healing methods when required. Bob, however, had developed his skills to a high level that few were capable of. Healing quickly helped him keep up with his peers, not to mention survive the vicious attacks that had come his way. His father had encouraged his son's talent, and had given Bob access to details of the healing factors that few knew about or how to control.

Bob used this information to dig deeply into the workings of his body infrastructure. As he had deduced, his healing factors had become partially blind to the effects of the virus. The virus had binding agents which, in effect, numbed the natural defences. The healing factors normally built upon those defences, fortifying and enhancing them.

After studying the situation, Bob triggered several specific allergic responses to counteract the stealth effect of the virus. That would kick his healing factors into a heightened level of awareness and allow them to purge the virus. The only negative was that for a day or so he'd have the sniffles. A minor drawback and something he'd not experienced since his childhood training had him experience something called "the common cold".

Within seconds he could feel his body defences ramping up as the virus was finally being recognized as dangerous. A few minutes later several waves of nausea passed through him, and he expelled clots of encapsulated virus material. This was repeated a number of times over the next hour, and each time Bob drank a large amount of water to help with the flushing. Two hours later he was feeling nearly back to his old self, aside from a runny nose. Smiling as he used a sleeve to wipe his nose, he added towels to the list of things to look for.

* * *

He spent the next few hours re-filling his water containers and re-exploring the facility. It was eye-opening, and humbling, to see how many of the details he'd missed while under the influence of the virus. Examining his actions, and the detailed logs of his healing factors, the effects probably began shortly after he arrived. Perhaps stirred up when the environmental systems regenerated the station's life support, or possibly when he encountered the bodies.

During his explorations Bob came across the main environmental control area. There were several bodies on the floor and a number of active displays. He studied the displays while taking care not to touch any of the controls. As expected, the system had a number of devices to scrub the air of anything toxic. However, those had been overridden when the station powered back up and restored the atmospheric pressure. The displays indicated that the scrubbers were somewhat clogged ... a not unexpected development after dealing with so much kicked-up dust. Cleaning those got added to his growing list of chores.

Of great interest were the displays showing the outside conditions. From the local gravity he'd estimated that he was on a large-ish planetoid or small planet. That was borne out by the indicators, as well as the absence of any significant atmosphere. Water and other substances were apparently obtained from large deposits of frozen material. Bob knew that this was not uncommon for military bases during the Great Wars. Although this base was beginning to seem less and less like one used for strictly military purposes.

From the displays he got indications of further unexplored areas, so he went off in search of those. In short order he came across a well-stocked armoury, with weapons ranging from knives to nuclear grenades and everything in between, many of which he recognized. What struck him was that it was all gear for combat troops. Aside from propulsion packs there were no vehicles of any sort that he could see. There were several different styles of environmental suits, ranging from skin-tight suits for maximum flexibility, to armoured suits up to and including powered armour.

Bob snorted at the sight of the powered armour and found himself sneering. In his experience powered armour made the operator overly confident. It was terribly effective until some unkind soul turned it into a coffin using any number of techniques. It was something he'd gotten rather good at, over the years. His personal favourites were sprinkling ground glass inside the suit and putting purgative agents into the drinking water.

In spite of that, he spent some time checking out one of each type of suit. From what he could determine, each was in working order needing only a recharge of energy and supplies. There was a clearly-marked service facility for each type of suit, so he plugged them in to be made ready. Just in case.

A little further on he found airlock doors to the outside, and next to those a hangar with two small space vessels. Bob made happy sounds at the sight of those—he'd loved space vessels since he was a young lad. Such things were very rarely used these days as people were content to use portals. Some of the younger races made use of them, of course, and had developed some splendid craft. But for function and speed none could compare to the vessels his people used during the Great Wars. No new ones had been made for generations, and few of the old craft remained operational.

The hangar was pressurized so he went inside and examined the craft with great care. Both had maintenance panels open, with gaping holes where components should have been. The airlocks were open so he went inside. The craft, not all that large as such things went, was cramped on the inside with only a modest amount of living space. Bob's grin grew larger, if possible. If his guess was correct, these were of the scout ship class. That class were lightly armed, but tended to be the fastest ships in their fleets. In addition, they typically had the best sensors and stealth capabilities available. They had been used as courier vessels and probes behind enemy lines. To Bob's mind, it was the stuff of legends.

With regret he left the vessels, and promised himself to fix at least one of them. Aside from the sheer joy of it, they would offer him a way to bypass the portal network. That would give him a tremendous operational advantage. If, that is, he could repair what was an obvious attempt to render them non-operational. Given the plague, that might have been an effort to keep everyone contained.

Next to the hangar there was a well-equipped repair shop. The mystery there consisted of several locked cabinets, a couple of which were fairly large. Bob added those to his list as a priority item. Anything locked up had the potential to be useful or at least interesting.

Beyond the repair shop was a featureless corridor that led into a series of rooms that proved to be living quarters. Unlike the barracks he'd seen earlier these appeared to be private quarters, probably for the officers. Only one had a body, and he or she had been killed or committed suicide with a knife to the heart.

He performed a cursory check of each room, but found nothing of immediate use or interest. When he got to the end of the corridor, there was another short corridor branching off at right angles which led to a single room. It proved to be larger than the others, and unlike the others was split into an office and sleeping area. The office area featured a desk and several chairs, which would have allowed it to be used for small meetings. Bob guessed that this might have been used by the facility's commanding officer.

Bob examined the desk with great interest and discovered an interesting mix of old and new tech. On the top were hard-copy pictures showing laughing people, implements for handwriting, and a terminal. Inside the drawers were the usual mix of office supplies and knick-knacks. The surprise was discovering several journals which had been used to make handwritten notes. Although the material of the journals felt robust, Bob turned the pages with care. The person writing in them had a neat, precise script. The language looked tantalizingly familiar, but he didn't worry about that ... he was just trying to get an overall impression.

The journals were numbered. The earliest ones had many lengthy entries, and the later ones many short entries. All were written in the same precise script. It was only the last journal that showed a change. Towards the end the handwriting became hurried, even sloppy. There were periodic lists of what looked like names. Those lists became more frequent and longer. That changed with the last entry. That appeared to be written by someone struggling to make the writing legible, and ended with what looked to be a signature.

* * *

After several weeks of hard work Bob made the facility a usable base of operations. His first action had been to deal with the bodies. Using the energy weapons in the armoury, he had carved a tomb into the rock and carefully placed each body within it. A cairn of stones was placed in front, then melted to seal the opening. Once the bodies were dealt with, he cleaned the air scrubbers and ran the system through decontamination mode several times. That, and a large amount of manual labour, returned the station to a state of proper cleanliness.

Decrypting the language had taken him over a week. The Great Wars had forced the standardization of the language, and after that people saw no reason to change it very much. However, the station dated from just before the middle of the Wars so the language had enough differences to make it hard to decipher. The handwritten journals still eluded him, but he was sure that he'd be able to read them in time.

Learning the language allowed him to access the station records. One of the first things he looked up were the personnel records of the people stationed here. After he'd learned their names, he returned to the tomb and recited the names of each one and promised that their sacrifice would not be in vain.

The history of the station proved to be fascinating. It had been designed for small-scale reconnaissance and covert actions behind enemy lines. Later it became host to a small, secret research project. The results of that project had fractured the social cohesion of the base and caused a serious rift to develop. Then a team had made first contact with an alien species. When the team returned to the base, the plague had broken out. There had been arguments as to how to proceed, but the virulence of the plague had been so great that most of the personnel died within a few days. The remainder, including the commander, did what they could but in end decided to destroy the base. However, one of the dissenting factions had made that impossible, so the commander evacuated the air and sealed the bulk of the base within a stasis field. For some reason, no communication of the station's status was ever sent out and the station was lost to history in the fog of war.

Bob then turned his attention to the mystery of the secret research project. There were very few locked areas in the facility. The locked areas in the hangar had housed parts that had been removed the scout ships, which he was happy to find. There was only one locked room with no markings to indicate its function. The station logs indicated that it was assigned to the exclusive use of the research group, but had no other details.

Whatever was inside was drawing no power, so it didn't appear to offer any danger. To be on the safe side, though, Bob donned an armoured suit before he forced the door open. Even with that protection, he slid a sensor probe inside the room to confirm that it was safe before entering. It proved to be a room of modest size, housing a large empty cylinder in the middle of it. There was equipment bulging from the walls, which could be extended towards the cylinder to perform various functions. Display screens—now unpowered—festooned the walls.

Bob stood in the research area that had caused such a problem and shook his head. So much trouble caused by something that looked bland and utilitarian. To be on the safe side he kept the suit on and the sensor wand active as he made a thorough examination of the room and its equipment. To his relief, everything was in a powered-down state. He discovered no written notes, but there were several data systems that were independent of the station's systems. In short order he had those powered up and spent the next couple of hours skimming through the records.

What he found both fascinated and horrified him. The goal of the project had been to create a fully-functional adult human body within a few weeks. Such research had been long been abandoned by his people as a moral and technical abomination. Judging by what he had found, this was one of the first attempts to develop such technology. It had not, of course, been the last.

For although the technology could create was a body, the mind was blank. Or, at best, a poorly-performing meat robot. The hope had been to create a perfect soldier, or a soldier-body that a mind could somehow be transferred into. There had been a number of spectacular failures, and any number of less-spectacular ones, and the technology was shelved before the end of the Great Wars. After the Wars, the process was abandoned as it could not be used to incorporate the advanced tech the survivors required. All that remained was the revulsion for the technology.

Bob tried hard to understand the mindset of the people stationed here, but found it difficult. To him, it was just a failed technology. To them, it was new and full of promise—but no-one was sure if that promise was of heaven or hell. There had been two factions: those who were desperate to use it as a tool to help humanity survive the onslaught of genocidal horror, and purists who saw it as the literal end of humanity.

Perhaps it was the strain of the never-ending war, or perhaps the isolation of the base had played a role. In any case, the two sides had all but stopped talking to each other, agreeing only that the project should be kept secret. In the midst of this came the first contact with a new species. Bob had found only a modest amount of information about them, but they sounded very much like the Ravens. They were a secretive race and little was known about them, but he recalled that they'd been discovered sometime during the Great Wars. In any event, the scouting team discovering them had returned to the base and the plague had broken out. The end came soon after that.

Bob sighed as he examined the equipment. It was a technical marvel, and quite unique so far as he was aware. It could create a functional adult body within the span of a few weeks, complete with well-exercised musculature. But once removed from the machine it was incapable of volition to the point of being unable to feed itself. A mindless, helpless, sack of organs. He thought that modern tech might be able to do something about the mind issue, but there was little point ... the body would be merely human. A well-optimized human body, to be sure, but still inferior to what was available these days. The technology, although amazing, was of no practical use.

Learning about the pettiness and foolishness of the ancestors he'd been raised to revere was disheartening. Shaking his head as he took a final look around, he left the room to return to the hangar. At least there he could work on something useful. Within a few days he managed to get one of the scout ships powered up and began a full systems checkout.

After that, Bob spent his time learning how to operate the small craft and fixing any problems that came up. Those issues were minor, and for the most part a result of hasty attempts to render the craft unusable. The power source, although advanced for its day, worked but not to the level that he had hoped for. Of course, improving its output would strain other systems, which would necessitate upgrading those, necessitating changes in the control systems, and so forth. In the interests of getting a working vessel up and running as quickly as possible, he decided to resist the urge to improve things. As his father had often told him, "Perfection is the enemy of good enough. If it isn't broken, don't fix it."

After a week's work the craft was space-worthy, and his mood had greatly improved. Even in its current state, the ship appeared capable of speeds just over one thousand times the speed of light. Fully tuned up, the specifications indicated that it should be capable of nearly twice that. Even that lower speed would get him to two planets on the portal network in just over a month.

There was a mysterious third portal within a two-week journey, one that he had found in the station records. He managed to verify its existence by sending a series of low-level queries to it. It wasn't on the portal network, that he was aware of, which meant that there was a possibility that it was another lost base. There were a few other portals in the records but that was the only one he could establish contact with. All the bases in the records were military bases, which wasn't surprising. Any potential enemy incursion from a fallen military base could only reach another military base, thus maintaining the integrity of the main portal network.

For similar reasons there was little information that wasn't related to military operations. Certainly nothing that would give an enemy any insight into the civilization that built the base. For Bob, that was the biggest single disappointment about the facility.

After a hearty meal from the food synthesizers—which could now create tolerable food—Bob settled himself for an evening of study. He was attempting to understand the handwritten journals that he'd found and was beginning to make some headway. The writing in the journals found in the medical section was, as was customary for medical professionals, unreadable. The ones found in the quarters of the commanding officer were more promising, and he was making progress on those.

The entries were, for the most part, unremarkable. They tended to give personal comments to events that happened, or sometimes notes on items that required administrative action. There was little description of the missions being run, other than tantalizing hints when talking about their status. Given those hints, and what he'd found in the armoury, it appeared that the base specialized in hit-and-run attacks rather than all-out battles. Most of those were accomplished via the now-lost military portals, with only a few using space vessels. Given the scale of the conflict, that made a lot of sense. The humans had faster ships, but far fewer of them. Their alien adversaries had armadas, but their speeds were orders of magnitude slower.

That thought caused Bob to inhale sharply. Sid's planet had been attacked by just such an armada, but there weren't any suitable planetary systems nearby. That meant it came from far away, meaning that whoever had launched it had done so at least several decades, or even centuries, prior. That, combined with the precision of the attack that spoke of detailed knowledge, meant that the unknown opponent was playing a very long game.

Long games were mandatory in interstellar conflicts, but portals added another dimension. They offered a way for rapid deployment of small forces and intelligence gathering. On the other hand, space-based attacks could take a long time to come to fruition especially if the target was a long way away. That meant it was possible for strategies and tactics to change before some types of attacks could be completed. It was that dynamic tension offered by the portals that had provided humanity's slim advantage in the Great Wars, allowing them to change tactics faster than their adversaries could adjust.

Bob had begun to follow the example of his ancestors in the base and write things down. There were plenty of paper-like materials, of various sizes, and writing implements. He used the mess hall as his office, and had several walls covered with lists and diagrams. After so many years of travelling light, he found it somewhat intoxicating to have a fixed base of operations where he could spread out and keep proper notes.

One thing that had concerned him was security and the possibility than an enemy would find the base and his research. Computer systems could be more easily encrypted than hand-written notes, after all. His mind eased on that score after giving the matter some thought. For one thing, he wasn't yet familiar enough with the ancient computer system to be fully trusting of it. For another, it was often just handier to write things out, if only in the form of rough notes. The most important thing, of course, was that if an enemy found this base he'd have even bigger problems than worrying about someone reading his notes.

So Bob added his thoughts about the attack on Sid's planet to the "Big List of Mysteries", as he liked to call it. Next to the list was a large, rough drawing of the galaxy. Some of the list items had strings attached to their location in the galaxy. The known portal network was marked in blue to indicate the locations. Known private portals were marked in yellow, with his family's indicated by pressing a little harder on the paper. It was a handy graphical summary of what he knew, and something that he spent time every day looking at. There were no legends to indicate what was meant by the representations, and Bob's own handwriting was unreadable by nearly everyone. Any adversary attempting to gain information from the notes would find it very tough going.

Between worrying about strategy and intelligence analysis, Bob spent some time in the armoury. He drilled with the weapons, with and without the various environmental suits, until he was comfortable with them all. The propulsion units that clamped to the back of the suits were challenging to learn how to use, but great fun. They provided him with the ability to zip around as if levitating, but with much greater speed and endurance than any but the larger battle aspects.

In theory he could use the units to reach or descend from orbit, if he cared to operate them to the point of burnout.

As an experiment he tried apporting while wearing a skin-suit and propulsion unit, and managed to do it without collapsing from the effort. It was a near thing, though, and certainly not something to be tried while tired. Still, it would be a useful ability to have if he ever had to operate in an environment with toxic or no atmosphere.

After weeks of effort there came a time when everything was cleaned and ready for use. Given that Set's main operation had been neutralized, Bob felt it was safe enough to do some exploring. He decided to use the scout ship to check out the other lost base. There was little information about it, which meant that it was another classified facility. The portal there appeared to be operational, but the scout craft would give him a safe base of operations if the facility was damaged. Bob had no desire to repeat the experience he'd endured when arriving at the current facility.

Bob spent a day ensuring that the base would function in his absence, and that the portal would restrict entrance to only himself. The ship had enough provisions to last six months, far longer than he was expecting to be out. He added an assortment of weapons and environmental suits from the armoury, and included a collection of military clothing to complete the ensemble. It felt as if he were going off on one of those secret military missions his ancestors used to perform.

After taking a final look around the hanger, he boarded the ship and prepared to leave. The air from the hangar was evacuated, the doors opened, and he eased the ship out on its belly repulsors. Once clear of the facility, he watched as the doors closed and waited until all systems indicated the base was sealed. Then he slowly applied power and lifted off into the "deep black" as his childhood fictions had called it.

CHAPTER EIGHT

Secrets in the Deep Black

It didn't take Bob long to learn that space travel on a fully-automated vessel was incredibly boring. It took a few days for the initial thrill to wear off, but after that it was a long journey in a small enclosure. It had all been so much more glamorous in the fictions he had read as a boy.

Still, one thing those fictions—and many historical accounts--had were numerous tales of small craft such as this. What every story had emphasized was the skill of the ship's operators. That made him realize that he'd been so focused on getting the ship operational that he'd neglected to study the tactical aspects of its use. If nothing else, working on that would help to pass the time.

Working on those skills turned out to be a fascinating study. The old stories gave him a rough idea, and his own training and experiences added more. The craft was lightly armed, but it turned out that many of its systems could be used as weapons. The propulsion systems could cause considerable damage at short ranges, and interfere with sensors at longer ones. Active sensors used at high powers were potent weapons when focused on a target. Most interesting of all was the ability to link the controls of the ship and environmental suits to form a formidable multiple-component fighting system. After he spent a couple of weeks learning how much there was yet to learn, Bob began to appreciate why many of the stories praised the skills of those ancient fighters.

It was only when he began to work on tactics that Bob stopped feeling like a backward student. He was very experienced in ways of sneaking about, and the ship offered yet another tool to do just that. From a reconnaissance point of view it was a way to approach a planet that was totally unexpected in this day and age. In addition, the cloaking technologies made it all but invisible. The variety of sensors available, although somewhat crude by modern standards, was functionally superior to any but those available to the larger battle aspects.

It was with some regret, then, that Bob realized he was approaching his destination. To minimize the resultant energy wake he eased slowly out of FTL while still well outside of the planetary system. Then he spent several days studying and mapping the system, charting the planets, their satellites, as well as any major bodies of interest. His target was the fourth planet from the sun, and he used his new-found knowledge to mask his approach by occulting his ship behind other planets, comets, and asteroids. That took a week of careful piloting, but by this time Bob was in full-on hunting mindset and didn't worry about the time. Approaching a potentially hostile target was a process that took as long as it took, something he was very experienced with.

In time, Bob was almost to the target world, hiding behind a comet. He timed his approach so that he could emerge from cover while the target planet's large natural satellite was occulting him from view. That last sprint got him to the far side of the moon, where he landed to make preparations for the final approach. The first thing, though, was to relax for a bit, so he did some light exercising and ate a hearty meal. Then he made sure that everything was packed away securely in the event violent manoeuvres became necessary. He donned a skin-suit in case the cabin lost air pressure, and racked the helmet next to his seat. A belt for weapons and supplies was stored nearby for fast access, as were an assortment of hand weapons. With his ship and supplies prepared, he decided to take a brief nap.

A half-hour later, Bob was awake and ready to go. He gave the impellers a touch of power--just enough to raise him above the ground--and proceeded to traverse towards the side nearest the planet. It took him several hours to complete the trip, and he had the passive sensors scanning for anything anomalous. Just before he reached the terminator he enabled all the stealth systems before proceeding. Bob had left that to the last minute because while the cloaking minimized heat radiation, it caused the ship to get rather toasty after a while.

Then he emerged to face the planet. He paused the ship, hovering just above the ground, while he scanned the planet with his passive sensors. It proved to be nothing special, as planets went, and the side he was facing was in local night. The sensors detected nothing of note, so he applied power and headed towards the planet. The portal was located on the other side of the planet, but he didn't know exactly where. Sometimes, Bob thought to himself, military secrecy could be most annoying.

It was just a matter of a few hours before he was in an equatorial orbit around the planet, allowing the rotation to overtake his position. The other alternative was to do a polar orbit, which would allow him to do a complete scan of the planet in a single day. The former offered a higher chance of quick success and he didn't want to keep the stealth systems running any longer than he needed to.

An hour later the side of the planet with the portal began coming into view, and several hours later Bob found the installation he was looking for. It was unshielded and easily seen by eye when he knew where to look. There was something odd about the shape, but he held off worrying about it until it had passed beyond the horizon. At that point he descended and landed in a mountainous area. The landing site was hidden by the terrain from anyone not airborne, and trees offered some protection from that. There was evidence of wildlife, and the possibility of fresh food brought a smile to Bob's face. The ship had a small stasis unit for food and samples, so that idea got put on his to-do list for later.

The first thing he did, though, was to deploy a few portable sensor pods throughout the area as a protective measure. Each was less sophisticated than his own sensorium, but as a grid could both scan a larger area and pinpoint signals of interest. While doing this he kept the skin-suit on despite the friendly environment, as it was designed to allow for easy carrying of equipment. It also had some passive stealth tech, which he thought might be an advantage.

The pods weren't near the target facility, but were useful to check for extended operations out of there. Bob spent the rest of the day watching the sensor readouts and trying to get a feel for the rhythms of the ecosystem during both the day and night. It wasn't as good, perhaps, as being in the middle of it all, but allowed him to get a lot of information in a short time. He also studied the orbital images of the facility. As suspected, there was something odd about the shape but the terrain obscured much of it.

The next morning Bob set out carrying a full load of sensor pods to plant around the target. As before, he wore the skin-suit but this time added one of the propulsion packs. He used that at a very low power setting to partially offset the weight of his load, and kept to low-lying areas to minimize the chance of being detected either visually or by the small amount of energy emitted. The use of the propulsion pack posed a risk of detection, but Bob felt the chance to deploy the maximum number of sensors outweighed the risk.

Several hours of careful movement brought him to a ridge that was just beyond the facility. The closer he got to the ridge, the less power he applied to the propulsion pack. By the time Bob arrived, the unit was powered off and he struggled to maintain a quiet approach with his load. He halted in a gully and shrugged off the load of sensor pods. Then he made a careful approach to the top of the ridge, and extended a surveillance wand to sneak a peek. It fed into his suit via an optical fibre to prevent stray leakage of signals, with information shown on a display in his helmet.

Once again, he was struck by the odd contours of the facility but reminded himself that this was only the visible portion. Still, what he could see resembled a truncated wedge. There was a large semi-enclosed open area at the rear, and the structure tapered from there until it disappeared into the hill. The open area was shallow—roughly a body-length—and inside there were doors that in all likelihood led to the interior. There was a low-level fear field, with enough intensity to keep out the local fauna and insects.

Bob lay there observing the area for over an hour. He saw two people come out and walk around, but they stayed close to the facility doors and were content to mill around for a few minutes before returning inside. Their attitude resembled that of someone taking a break. There were no guards of any sort that he could detect, nor any security mechanisms. Satisfied by the results of the quick look, he deployed the sensor pods in a rough circle with the facility at the centre. Some were deployed behind the ridge with only their wands extended, while others were set up on the ridge to allow their entire suite of sensors to view the area. Once satisfied that they were all working, he headed back to his ship.

The trip back took far less time than the trip out, and Bob arrived back before sunset. A quick check of the ship's sensors showed that they were receiving information from the new stations as well as the old. The shape of the facility still puzzled him but he decided to put that problem on hold for the time being. He had passed some tasty-looking local fauna and decided that he deserved a treat.

By the time he got back from the hunt and had prepared a hearty meal, night had fallen. From what he could determine from the sensors there was still no efforts made regarding security. As he watched the images he realized what the structure reminded him of ... the aft end of an early post-War transport vessel. With that theory in mind, he examined the surrounding terrain. It was just possible that the terrain had been moulded by a ship making a heavy landing. The ridge might be the weathered result of ground pushed aside, with the bulk of the ship buried under debris. As interesting as that hypothesis was, though, it didn't explain the presence of a mid-War military portal.

Bob leaned back in the chair, a happy expression writ large on his face. Mysteries upon mysteries, and it was obvious that coming by scout ship had been a good decision. Then he frowned as he remembered the status queries he'd been sending out. It was barely possible that someone might have noticed those ... a low probability, but within the realm of possibility. Still, there was no sign of anything other than casual activity.

Then the display flashed an alert ... it had detected the use of the alternate energies. That was quickly refined to show the use of a portal with incoming traffic. The confirmation of the presence of a portal brought the smile back to his face. He examined the energy signatures more closely and was pleased to see that they correlated with those expected from a mid-War portal. To make a positive identification would require access to the unit itself, but he had little doubt that this was his target. That left the not-so-minor question of what to do about it.

There was also the question of who these people were. The use of the portal indicated that his own people were involved. A chill went along his spine as he recalled the mysterious Others that he'd ruminated about not so long ago. Which still left the question of what was going on here. Bob narrowed his eyes and huffed once in irritation. Then he forced himself to calmness and sat back to watch. Information was the key to understanding, and his sensor network gave him an excellent vantage view of what was happening.

As Bob waited for something to happen, he reviewed the images of the people he'd seen earlier. Their faces didn't seem familiar, so he switched from visible light to full-spectrum mode. There was little in the way of information to be gleaned from the non-visible energies, which was strange. Any of his people would have given off at least hints of the alternate energies even when not making use of them. The most probable answer was that these weren't his people, but were merely human. This whole setup was getting stranger and stranger.

The next day served only to deepen the mystery. Shortly after sunrise, a series of energy readings emanated from the structure. At the beginning they were electromagnetic in nature but then added some of the alternate energies. All of them were highly structured in format, but not something that he recognized. It went on for several hours before diminishing in volume and tempo, eventually ceasing altogether. Almost an hour later, a similar but somewhat different sequence of energies was detected. Again it went on for several hours before terminating. During this time no-one came out of the facility. Just at sunset, however, three individuals came out to walk about as a group, apparently having a discussion. From their energy signatures they were merely human. As the sun set they went back inside.

Nothing happened until mid-morning of the next day. A group of eight individuals came out, a couple of them not moving very well. The sensors indicated that some of the group were emitting low-levels of the alternate energies. Bob nodded at that—at least some of them were his people. They were too close together to determine which ones, but that question was soon answered.

The two who were unsteady on their feet moved away from the group and began moving around with movements suggestive of exercising. They were both using the alternate energies, as was someone else in the group that was standing off to one side. Then two of the group moved towards the ones who appeared to be injured and began examining them with extended sensoriums. Those four seemed to be the only ones emitting the alternate energies.

Then the four began to levitate until they were barely above the ground. They held that position for a few seconds before floating back to the ground. This was repeated several times, followed by a short break. After the break the injured ones moved around for a time before heading back into the facility. By the end of the training session—or whatever it had been—the injured ones were moving with much improved ease and control. There was no more detectable activity for the rest of the day.

Bob had watched until sunset without trying to think too much upon what he'd seen. When there was no more detectable activity, he got up, stretched the kinks out, and got something to eat. Pacing within the narrow confines of the scout ship was unsatisfying so he went outside to listen to the night sounds as he pondered. Those injured individuals were his people, that much was plain. And yet they moved as if recovering from a severe injury. Such things were rare, but not unknown. Still, to have two people recovering at the same time was very strange. Bob wondered if this was some sort of medical facility.

That was an interesting thought, so he pursued it further. Medical facilities were well known, and this was most certainly not one of those. On the other hand, Set was known to have an off-the-books medical facility. There couldn't be too many of those around, so it was possible—even probable—that he'd stumbled onto his brother's little secret. Even so, that left the question of who the merely humans were. Set never treated the younger races as anything other than playthings, which meant these were in some way special. The only way he could see to find out anything more was to enter the facility and check things out. A secondary goal had to be getting tissue samples from everyone there, to try and figure out who was using it. Having several of his own kind there certainly made things more challenging. A predatory grin came to his face as Bob settled back in the chair ... it was time to make a plan for some direct action.

* * *

An hour later Bob set out towards the mysterious facility. He wore a layer of removable armour over a skin-suit as the best balance between protection and stealth. The armour also offered the chance to carry more weapons plus bio-sampling kits and several sensor pods. As before, he wore a propulsion pack since it gave him more options for fast movement. Given the level of his opposition, he wanted all the advantages he could get.

Flying low to the ground over the now-familiar terrain allowed him to make the trip in just over an hour. His sensor array detected no outside activity so he approached the facility from the side, moving along the wall to the open area. He extended a sensor wand around the corner but the coast was clear and there were still no signs of any security apparatus.

Emboldened by that, Bob moved into the sheltered area and took a good look around. What he could see only deepened the mystery. The construction was, for the most part, very solid as if expected to hold up to enormous forces. The doorway, by contrast, looked to be a feature that was added on as an afterthought. He put any further analysis on hold, but recorded everything for later examination.

The door had a lever that looked like a latch. Bob moved it with care, then cracked the door open a wee bit and extended a sensor wand inside. There were no people or obvious threats so he ducked inside and closed the door. The inside proved to be a barren room of moderate size that had another door on the far wall. Bob examined the new door before opening it a crack to look for threats. On the on the other side were empty corridors, so he entered and closed the door behind him.

There was a pair of narrow corridors branching off, running some distance each way, terminating in solid-looking doors. Along each path were a series of archways that protruded slightly from the walls. Everything was made of a metallic substance. He chose the left-hand corridor and walked along it. The archway proved to be similar to a standard emergency bulkhead mechanism. It reminded Bob of the interior of a large space vessel.

As he walked he kept close tabs on the sensors in his suit but detected nothing untoward. The metallic construction absorbed all forms of radiation, so he focused on listening. The soles of his boots were designed to be silent as possible, so his own movements were all but noiseless. The more he explored the stronger became the sense that he was on a space vessel of some sort.

Bob decided to accept that as a working hypothesis. If the design was at all similar to warships of the post-War era, the upper levels were used to transport goods and offer some protection for the critical inner levels. Assuming he had entered from the aft section and was walking along an upper-level corridor, the bridge was in the centre of the forward section. The engines would be below him, buried below ground level. Access to those lower levels would be varied along any outer corridor. Given that the ship was occupied by a few people who went outside, it was unlikely they'd have walked as far as he had to access the outside doors. That implied that he was in a seldom-used corridor.

There was a sharp bend up ahead which he approached with caution. A quick peek detected no activity but he could see an access door. That opened into a vertical access tube that traversed the interior of the ship, so he followed it down. The lack of any security was making him nervous ... it was too good to be true, but he continued on regardless. In short order he had reached a level that was in the middle of the access tube's path. Exercising caution, he exited to find himself at a T-intersection of corridors. His sensors were picking up faint electromagnetic activity up ahead, so he chose that corridor.

The indications got stronger as he walked along, peaking in front of a broad, sealed door. There were no signs of life that he could detect through the metal, so he cracked open the door the smallest amount and inserted a sensor wand. The readings became stronger but there were no signs of life. He entered the room and shut the door before looking around.

It was a large room, containing three vats, each three times Bob's height in width and length and almost twice his height. Each vat was surrounded by an array of equipment and displays. Bob's heart raced as recognition came to him. This was a metamorphosis chamber, of the sort his people used to modify their aspects. By the looks of things, it had been used not too long ago.

After taking a deep breath to calm himself, he made a quick examination of the area. The equipment was, for the most part, of an old style of design. He couldn't place it exactly, but it was definitely of a similar era as the rest of the ship. There were some anomalous tech that was definitely newer attached to the main controls for each vat. Not wanting to risk alerting anyone, Bob touched nothing but took care to make a record of everything using only passive sensors.

His tour finished at one end of the room where he noticed a stasis facility similar to that in the medical wing of his own base. The indicators showed that several of the pods were in use, but that the occupants were dead. There was no indication of the alternate energies within the pods, which meant that the occupants were merely human. That begged the question of why Set would be storing human cadavers, but Bob simply added that to the growing list and moved on.

The other end of the room appeared to have more controls of some sort, so he headed towards it. Along the way he paused to attach a sensor pod to each vat's control system. He kept them inactive, since the probability was very high that accessing the controls would get noticed or even set off alarms. On the other hand, activating them after he left the ship might serve as a good distraction. He also took a small sample from the fluids in each tank, stowing them in pockets of his suit.

It turned out that the room's control section had no easily discernible functions, but did include a schematic of the ship. As he had guessed, it had the shape of a transport vessel. The bridge was about where he had expected it to be and not too far from his location. He slipped one of his few remaining sensor pods next to the controls, just in case he could find something interesting once he activated it.

Bob exited the room and made his way to the bridge. The lack of security and absence of people were making him more than a little nervous. Even if the entire compliment consisted of the people he'd seen, he would have expected better operational security even from the incompetents that Set tended to recruit. Even so, he reached the bridge without incident and found it empty but active.

It looked like a bridge from an old warship. Bob took a quick look around to get a sense of things. Despite the danger, he felt a thrill at being able to see and touch a piece of history. If this ship was as old as he thought it was, it was something unique. To his knowledge, no operational ships of this type had ever been found. He placed a sensor pod in an out-of-the-way nook, linked it to his ship, and set it begin downloading the ship's records after being activated. A second pod was placed and set to do the same thing—his ship would operate them in parallel to make the job go faster.

Bob searched for, and found, the security controls. Its displays showed him in the bridge, but also nine other persons in another part of the ship, further forward and two levels down. If memory served, that was typically the recreational area. That brought a smile to his lips, and he searched the control panel and pressed controls that would let him monitor that area. A small screen burst into life showing eight people gathered around a table and drinking something. The audio picked up their conversation clearly.

"Hey, Virgil, how ya doing? New aspect feeling like home, yet?" asked a man whom Bob recognized as one of his people he'd seen earlier.

"Just about. The mechanics feel good, but the alternate energy controls still need work," spoke one of the ones who had appeared to be injured. That was a name that Bob recognized as someone from Set's generation, but not in that aspect.

"And you, Applo, how does your new aspect feel? Does it take long to adapt?" asked one of the merely humans, in a thick accent that Bob couldn't place. Again, he recognized the name as someone from Set's cohort.

Applo answered, "It takes time to adjust, Micpence. Set

explained the process to you, did he not? It gets easier the more you use it, though. Don't worry. Your time will come soon enough."

"Time. You and Set speak about how soon it will come, but still we wait. The experiments have not been successful," growled one of the other merely human men, again in that strange accent.

That got Bob's interest. It was one thing to be running an off-the-books aspect modification site, but quite another to be upgrading the merely human. To his knowledge, that had never been done. That meant yet another mystery, and he grinned in spite of himself.

In tactical terms, he was faced with four of his own kind, two of whom were still adjusting to their new aspects. Those latter two would be dangerous, but not much more so than a well-trained merely human. Then there were the four merely human who looked to be unarmed. That accounted for eight hostiles, but the security sensors had shown nine life signatures. Where was the ninth?

As if to answer his question one of the newly-altered turned to face the camera and waved. "Hi, Dotrump. Sorry you're on duty and missing the party."

Micpence said, "Dotrump is here, gathering food for himself. Everyone is here."

"Then who's that monitoring us from the bridge? The tell-tale light is on," one of the others said, pointing at the camera.

Displays on the security board flashed for a moment. Virgil said, "Security system shows someone in the bridge."

Bob decided that he had overstayed his welcome and that it was time to go. He activated a sensor wand and left it on top of the security station to broadcast the audio to him. He also activated the two pods in the control room. A quick glance at the display revealed that his opponents were splitting up into groups and heading his way.

Heading back the way he had come, he reached the access tube and headed up. There were sounds coming from below so he activated his propulsion unit and flew up to the door he used to enter the tube. After exiting, he closed the door and used a handgun to fuse it shut. He paused to tell the sensor pods into the metamorphosis room to activate and download whatever data they could find.

He'd taken but a few steps when he heard someone hammering on the door. Without pausing he primed a proximity bomb and slapped it on the wall. As he approached the convergence point of the two main corridors he began to pick up indications of the use of the alternate energies. Still running, he tossed an impact grenade ahead and was rewarded with a scream when it exploded.

The wand in the bridge was picking up sounds that indicated that someone had entered and was at the security console. "Intruder in unused upper corridor heading towards exit. Quintlen, Pharm and Saund, follow in that corridor to stop him from doubling back. Virgil and Applo, intercept at the exit. Chaugnar and Xiclot, fly outside in case he breaks out. Micpence and I will coordinate from the bridge."

Still running, Bob approached the intersection point and pondered what he'd heard. The merely humans were coordinating the attack, and his people were actually taking orders from them. That was unheard of. A blast from behind him put an end to extraneous thoughts, and he slapped on another proximity bomb. Then he tossed another impact grenade towards the intersection, but its blast invoked no screams.

Approaching the intersection, Bob crouched as he slid into it. He fired a pistol with one hand and tossed a pair of bouncing grenades with the other. A series of energy beams emerged out of the smoke and dust, and a couple struck him. The armour dissipated the brunt of the blasts and the minor wounds were quickly healed.

Bob heard a yell of fear, followed an explosion as one of the bouncing grenades hit a target. A flurry of energy blasts flew at him, but were all high and wide. He had now skidded to a halt so he slapped the last of his proximity bombs on a wall, threw the last two grenades into the corridor, and fired until his pistol was drained. When the grenades exploded, he got to his feet and ran to the exit as he switched guns. There were no more energy blasts, but he did hear one of his earlier proximity bombs go off. He'd just reached the exit door when the proximity bomb he'd left at the intersection blew, and the force of the explosion flung him outside.

Sensor readings indicated use of the alternate energies in bearings that indicated someone in flight and someone on the ground, one to either side of the ship. Bob ran in a broken pattern along the ground. He headed towards the ridge and the cover offered by the boulders and trees. He could hear the voice of Dotrump vectoring in the two attackers to his position.

Bob reached the ridge and dropped behind a grouping of large rocks. That shielded him from ground attack from all directions except the rear. A sensor pod signalled that an attacker was very near it, so Bob instructed it to self-destruct. The screams of pain and curses were music to his ears.

"Xiclot, attention. Chaugnar is injured. In Set's name I command you to eliminate the intruder. Coordinates follow."

Bob frowned as he ran to a new position. The sensor pods in the control room hadn't finished downloading all the data, but it would seem that time had run out. With some reluctance he instructed them to begin transmitting jamming signals that would interfere with both communications and ship operations. That jamming would be far more effective, at least in the short term, than any mere explosion the pods could create.

A blast of energy seared the area that Bob had just left. It would seem that Xiclot had arrived to do battle. Bob decided to stay on the ground, and dash from cover to cover. His own sensor network, although slightly degraded by the loss of one pod, worked well enough to give him a good idea of where his opponent was. After executing a series of dashes and snap turns to confuse his opponent, Bob did a flip and managed to fire a shot from the battle rifle at Xiclot. The shot missed, but was close enough to force Xiclot to spin away and spoil his own aim.

That established the pattern for the next several minutes, with Bob running on the ground and taking snap shots that forced Xiclot to veer away. Finally Xiclot worked up enough speed to overcome Bob's running and dodging and managed to fire off several close shots of his own. Bob snapped on his propulsion unit and made a sharp turn skyward. He'd been keeping his rifle on maximum power and single shots, but now used it at continuous beam mode and sliced it towards his opponent. Xiclot was taken by surprise by Bob's aerial manoeuvring, and despite skillful flying was slashed across the torso by the energy beam.

As he manoeuvred away he fired several energy bursts that hit Bob, shattering the armour and searing flesh where they hit. Fighting the pain, Bob returned fire and slashed a beam across Xiclot's face. There was a soft *plop* sound as Xiclot apported away to the ground at the far end of the ship. Even as his own wounds were healing, a short blast of energy hit Bob in the chest catching him unawares. The armour absorbed the hit with minimal damage, allowing Bob to fly to the ground and into cover. It appeared that Chaugnar was still a force to be reckoned with.

On the ground, Bob struggled to catch his breath as his wounds healed and he took stock of the situation. Xiclot was some distance away, and Chaugnar's energy signature had gone silent after his attack. The battle rifle was nearly drained, leaving Bob with only a handgun to fight off his attackers. There was a lull in the fighting, so he took the opportunity to eat a snack and drink some water. As a precaution he also told his ship to prep for immediate flight.

Without any warning Bob sensed the destruction of the sensor pods he'd left in the bridge. Their last signal burst indicated that they'd self-destructed to prevent tampering. There was a burst of static followed by some unintelligible talking. Then Bob heard a wide-beam broadcast on the alternate energy bands.

"Chaugnar. Chaugnar, get inside to the portal right away. Those idiots have rigged the engines and power core to self-destruct. We need to leave right away."

"I can't. I'm pinned down. My injuries prevent apporting for a few more minutes."

"We don't have a few minutes."

Bob considered the exchange for a moment before chiming in. "Feel free to leave at any time, gentlemen. I have no issue with any of you. I will honour a truce that allows you to leave."

There was silence for a moment. Then he heard, "Who are you to declare and honour a truce?"

"Oh, Set knows me well enough. I'm his younger brother."

"Bob? You? That's you attacking us? Why?" came a pair of voices talking over each other.

Bob sighed. His sensor network was showing a rapid buildup of energies within the ship. "Xiclot, Chaugnar, stop being idiots and leave. Hurry. You don't have much time. Oh, and pick up Applo and Virgil along the way ... they're in the right-hand corridor, and probably not in good shape. Uncle Sid and Aunt Freida have a proper clinic set up if you don't want to go to the official ones. Here's their address and guest access codes. It exits above a volcano, so be prepared to apport or levitate right away."

"What about you?"

"I'm fine, thanks. Be sure to tell Set that I said hello, would you?"

"But ..."

"Shut up and go. My sensors indicate you've got perhaps a minute, maybe less. Run."

He saw a figure scamper down the hillside and run into the ship. The figure paused at the door only long enough to make a brief wave before going inside. His sensor network indicated that both his adversaries had vanished, which meant they'd entered the ship. That left only himself to worry about.

Bob commanded the ship to lift off and fly towards him at maximum speed, preparing for a mid-air pickup. Then he triggered the propulsion unit for full power and shot skyward. The sudden acceleration strained his partially-healed wounds, but his attention was focused on meeting his ship. It was an interesting mathematical problem, all things considered. He needed to meet his ship and get out of range before the ship below exploded with what promised to be a very large boom.

He was moving at such-and-such an acceleration, his ship at a thus-and-thus acceleration, and they needed to meet at a net zero velocity so that rendezvous could take place. From what he could tell, he might make the rendezvous but not in time to escape the blast. A pretty little problem indeed, to pass the time as he raced towards his ship.

The heart of the problem was that his propulsion unit was insufficient to the task. The ship, on the other hand, could move into orbit in the time required. Bob thought that it was rather ironic that he'd be down here with escape in plain sight, far above. Then he laughed as a possible solution came to him. A quick calculation indicated that it just might be possible. He contacted the ship and had it adjust its course and speed slightly. It would now fly high above him, towards orbit, but with zero relative velocity at the peak.

The trick of any rendezvous was to match speeds, Bob recalled from his elementary math classes. Time grew short as sensors indicated that the overload-driven explosion was only a few seconds away. Bob turned off the propulsion unit and shrugged it off. The wind tore it out of his grasp and its passing slashed a gash in his leg. The weapons followed without incident.

Then time ran out as the ship far below exploded, and Bob's time frame for action shrank to seconds. He took a deep breath and apported to the limits of his ability, up range of his ship's path. That would buy him a small measure of time that might be enough for the scout ship to meet him at an appropriate speed. The wave of radiation from the blast surged forth, and it became a three-way race with no obvious winner.

Soon, Bob saw the profile of the ship as it approached. However, he also saw that the front of the shock wave was approaching and that they'd all meet at the same moment. It was time for desperate measures.

Bob commanded the ship to open the airlock and roll such that the airlock presented itself to him. Their relative velocity was still too high for safety, so he knew that this was going to hurt rather a lot. He relaxed, instructed his ship to close the airlock after one second and leave orbit thereafter. After making a synchronistic pairing on the inside of the airlock, he apported. The velocity differential slammed him against the inside of the airlock with enough force to shatter both armour, bones, and flesh. The airlock slid shut and the ship flew into the deep night of space.

It took less than a minute to master the pain, but considerably longer to heal the damage sufficiently well to stagger out of the airlock into his cramped quarters. There he began the painful process of removing his suit and the pieces of it that were embedded into him. He paused often to drink water or eat something as the healing factors required, but within an hour he was well enough to take a shower and collapse on his bed for a well-deserved rest.

Bob was awoken by the insistent trilling of an alarm. His mouth tasted quite foul and his eyes wouldn't focus, so without moving he transmitted a query to the ship's controls. The problem turned out to be that it was now several planetary diameters away and required a more detailed destination than "up and away". His brain was still was a bit fuzzy, so he told to ship to return home. The response sounded like a happy electronic mumble, but at least the alarm went away, so Bob returned to his nap.

He awoke several hours later sore but healed, more or less. At the very least he was able to stand and stretch to test the state of his body. One wall was reflective enough to serve as a mirror, so he used that to examine the parts of his body he couldn't see directly. There were quite a few angry-looking scars where armour fragments had pierced him, and his bones weren't quite fully healed, but all in all he was in reasonable shape. He put on an undress uniform and headed for the bridge by way of the galley.

His healing factors were demanding specific elements, notably calcium, so he chose foods high in that. With the essentials out of the way, he selected a tisane for sipping and headed to the bridge. Once there, he confirmed that there were no ship-related issues before settling down to examine the data the sensor pods had downloaded from the now-destroyed facility.

To Bob's pleased surprise, one of the bridge units had downloaded from most recent to earliest and the other from earliest to more recent. Between them they'd managed to download more than half the data. Even the pods in the metamorphosis chamber had managed to snag some data. There was lots of information to sort through, which helped to mitigate the feeling of loss he felt at the destruction of the facility. There were so many mysteries left to solve, and any information at this point would be useful.

That reminded him of the bio-samples he'd taken from the vats, and he hurried back to retrieve them from the remains of the suit. To his relief two of the three vials were undamaged, and he put them into a stasis chamber for analysis back at the station. Then he returned to the bridge to look at the retrieved data. It was a long way back to the base and he wanted something to do other than sit around and heal.

CHAPTER NINE
The Best Laid Plans

By the time he returned to the base, Bob was fully healed and had learned enough to solve a few of the mysteries. The crashed ship was, or had been, a medical ship. It had run into difficulties and was forced to make an emergency landing at an abandoned military base. There had been problems on landing and the ship had slid into the facility. Only the lower levels of the base, which included the portal, had remained intact. The surviving crew had used the portal to leave the planet.

The ship had sat there in station-keeping mode for many years, unused and unvisited. For many centuries the logs consisted only of local environmental conditions and the status of the ship's systems. Then came a gap of millennia in the records, where Bob's sensor pods had been interrupted in their downloading. When the records began again, there were centuries of minimal events until some centuries ago when someone came through the portal and began a partial power-up of the ship. In absolute terms, Bob figured that would correspond roughly to just before Set had set out on his idiotic scheme of conquest, so the timeline was consistent.

There was no direct link between the ship and the portal, but the ship's sensors noted uses of the alternate energies consistent with portal transfers. Those indicated modest usage with the occasional spike, building to a plateau. That plateau indicated steady use for the most part, except for a few spikes and dips. It appeared that Set had done a constant business in aspect modifications.

That part puzzled Bob, since changing aspects using the regular facilities was not something that raised red flags. On the other hand, changing an aspect was considered a major event and not something to be undergone on a whim. That could interfere with the plans of someone like Kydos, who'd run a series of god-scams over a number of worlds and needed to adjust aspects to match the local's expectations. Others, like Freddy, liked to try on different imposing aspects to make themselves feel powerful.

Bob added all the information to the timeline next to his Big List of Mysteries. He also began a list of Set's known associates, including where he'd run across them. Stepping back, he realized that it was all getting rather crowded and messy. "Just like real life," he muttered.

Still, he felt good about destroying Set's bootleg aspect facility. Despite his own preference to keep the aspect he had, during his dating years he'd enjoyed the possibilities new aspects could offer. But the idea of changing aspects like one changed clothes bothered him. It took a lot of time to gain proficiency with a new aspect, and becoming the best one could be was just the right and proper thing to do. The memory of the gang of fools who'd tried to assassinate him came to mind—posers and incompetents, the lot of them.

It came as something of a shock when Bob realized that was one of the things that offended him most about Set's plans was its divergence from the Precepts of Survival. He exhaled so quickly that his cheeks puffed out, and he wondered if this dismissal of the younger generation meant that he was getting old and set in his ways. That caused him to laugh for a few seconds until he remembered that there were a number of the older generations attracted to Set's path as well.

Thinking along those lines got him so depressed that he decided to have an early supper. While sitting in the mess hall eating, Bob realized that his curmudgeonly ruminations had caused him to forget about the strange humans at the facility. Gulping down the remainder of his meal, he hurried to the scout ship and removed the biological samples he'd taken from the metamorphosis tanks. He took the samples to the medical wing and set the equipment to analyzing it.

While that was being done, Bob went to the portal room. He queried the portal's diagnostics to determine how the security procedures made use of genome-detection. In the early days of the Great Wars, the portals would pass anyone possessing a human DNA structure. Some of the Enemy had gimmicked that by the simple expedient of wearing a human skin obtained from victims or clones thereof. To counteract that threat, the portals began performing a deep-tissue, full-body probe of the DNA. This also led to the genetic sampling of every human, with emphasis on those in the military. Over time every portal became a repository of the genetic sequence of every authorized human. In the early days, such as when the base was constructed, authorization was limited to specific people. By the end of the Wars it was simply every one of the few surviving humans.

The next step was to have the local portal update its authorization list from the current portal network. With the two sets of genetic databases in hand, Bob returned to the medical wing and obtained the genetic information of everyone in the base. Comparing the information was instructive. Some of the people on the base were ancestors with whom he shared DNA. Many of the other personnel shared DNA with others in the Family of Humanity. It came as something of a surprise to find a few who were not part of the Family. They were, however, listed as authorized for portal travel as part of the humanity-as-a-whole protocol that was established at the end of the Wars. That protocol was used only by older portals; newer ones had a slightly modified version. Another interesting thing, as far as Bob was concerned, was that each of those human-but-not-ancestors were part of the Purity faction that had been opposed to the research into body-growing.

The results of the analysis of the metamorphosis tanks was interesting as well. It had managed to tease out the DNA from a dozen different humans, with the hint of more that couldn't be fully sequenced due to degradation. Seven of the sequences had matches in the Family database. Of the remaining five, three were unknown but two were descendants of the Purity faction.

Bob sat back in the chair and steepled his fingers, tapping them against his nose. Set was trying to use metamorphosis technology upon non-Family humans. Not the merely human from the younger races, but someone related to ancestors who weren't of the Family. From the biotechnology point of view it was a foolish thing to try, and bound to fail. The ancestors had modified themselves to utilize the technology as part of the blending of genomes. These strange humans, descended from the Purists, were nearly identical to the younger races. That was confirmed from the overheard conversations that mentioned a continuing failure to give them new aspects. Still, Set was getting something in return for making the effort.

That led to the political side of things. What was it that Set was getting in return that was so valuable that he'd treat these Purist-descendants as equals? The only things that Bob could think of were mind-gems and pure quill. Still, the one was just tech and the other just a drug. On the other hand, that drug could bypass the healing factors and cause addiction in his own kind. Set needed loyalty and dedication—the pure quill would certainly ensure that.

Those young toughs he'd encountered on his training world seemed to obey because they had no choice. Perhaps Set lured people in with fancy promises, keeping them loyal with mind-gems and pure quill. Which sounded a lot like how he treated the younger races.

Snorting in disgust, Bob leapt to his feet and began pacing back and forth. So many tantalizing hints and theories, but still many questions. He stopped, took a deep breath, and calmed himself. This was getting too big for just himself—it was time to pass along this information to Sid, if he could. Sid had training and contacts that could prove useful.

The other question was how best to put an end to the obscene alliance that Set had forged. In the worst case, the pure quill could be distributed like a bio-weapon that could affect everyone. The fact that it bypassed the healing factors was what made it so dangerous to his kind. Bob stopped in his tracks. He realized that there was something else that bypassed the healing factors ... the plague that had infested the station when he arrived. It had shown up right after the ancestors had contacted the Ravens. He didn't know much about them—no-one did—but he recalled that they were an avian-descendant species. That made him think about the feather Sid had found, and how it oozed pure quill.

That chain of reasoning decided his course of action. It essential to make a copy of everything he found and pass it on to Sid, and as quickly as possible. The only trick was how to do it. Transiting to the planet Sid and Freida were on was not the wisest course of action. For one thing, he wouldn't be able to carry much with him given his limited apporting abilities. For another, there was a good chance of finding injured and angry enemies there getting treatment.

Bob pondered his options as he bustled about making copies of his research. The best way, he decided, was to send a message to Sid to get his thoughts. To do that he'd have to transit back to the training planet to use that portal. If he was going there, he might as well take along some supplies to set up a secondary cache. In fact, he could do that while the station took care of making the copies of the data. There was rather a lot of it: logs from the two different stations, the diagnostic dumps from the portals, the handwritten logs, and his own notes.

He set the station to making the copies, then went to the armoury and selected a suitable array of weapons. To that he added a couple of environmental suits, medical supplies, and a toolkit. The armoury was set up for field operations of this sort, so it didn't take long to assemble everything. There was even a nice anti-grav sled that held it all.

Bob went to the portal room and transited to the training planet. A quick check of the logs confirmed that no-one had arrived on the planet since he had left. The first thing he did was to send a message to Sid via the volcano portal, rather than the public portal on that planet. He didn't go into detail, just asked if it was safe to send a dawn boat with physical supplies.

While waiting for a reply he distributed the equipment. There was enough gear to make two good-sized caches. The first location he chose was the hidden cave that he and Celcilia had used. The second was a similar cave in the third level training area. He left a handwritten note with each, saying that it was equipment from a wartime base plus the date he'd left it there.

By the time he finished and went back to the portal there was a message from Sid waiting for him. It was short and to the point. "Yes, send anything you want by dawn boat. Address it to both Freida and myself. Under no circumstances should you come here in person. We're still treating some of the people you sent here, and they are very cross with you. Also frightened of you. A bad combination, in my experience. We're getting dawn boats with supplies quite often these days, so one more won't arouse suspicion. It is getting very busy here. Freida and her friends are studying and teaching philosophy classes, and I'm struggling to learn more about it. Fascinating stuff, especially the new teachings from the Eldest Ones. This could be the catalyst for change we are looking for. We've had a couple dozen people show up for the lessons! Oh, be careful of where you go. Set is on the warpath about some of your recent exploits. No-one seems to know exactly what those are, but it certainly seems to have made him angry. That's losing him followers, by the way. The ones you've sent here are fed up with him and word is spreading. The only safe refuge hosting a public portal that I can suggest is your Aunt Gertrude. She's in touch with Freida about this philosophy thing, and has assured us that you'll be safe with her. So, carry on, nephew. And please be as careful as circumstances allow. Both of us send our love."

Bob had to swallow several times to get the lump out of his throat. It was a good feeling not to be alone in his fight. With that thought in mind, he returned to the base (which he was beginning to think of as home) and prepared the shipment for Sid. He added his own observations and conclusions in both data and handwritten form. It didn't take very long to finish putting everything together, and he put it all on the anti-grav sled.

When he caught himself grinning with excitement, he decided it would be best to take a short break. It was far too easy to start making mistakes when carried along in the emotions of the moment. So he forced himself to have a hearty meal, eaten slowly, while contemplating what to do next. After staring at his maps and notes, he decided it was time to check out his theory about the anomalous humans. The Purity-descendants, as he thought of them. From what he knew now there was a good chance that they were Refuser-descendants, given the similarity in positions and philosophies.

Whoever they were, though, he needed to find out more

about how they fit into Set's organization. If nothing else they posed a real threat to everyone, and their operations needed to be neutralized. To that end, Bob decided to check out a few of Set's temples. He would take along a genome analyzer that could quickly check for Family or Refuser affiliation. It would be a simple series of fast scouting operations: a quick look-around, acquisition of bio-samples, and exit to the next world. This sort of peek-and-run mission was different enough from his usual style that it should surprise any opposition looking for him. Easy peasy. What could go wrong?

He face twisted into a grimace. As his father and Precepts of Survival were fond of saying, "Overconfidence is the creator of failure and death." In truth, infiltrating a temple was never something to undertake lightly. Each had a different layout, many layers of security, and lots of armed guards. On the other hand, he was not without resources and experience in such things. Bob leaned back in his chair with his hands steepled together as he pondered this interesting problem.

* * *

It took the better part of a day to create a detailed plan and several more days to organize the logistics. Normally he would have chaffed at the delay, but the importance and complexity of the mission kept him focused on getting things organized. There were a number of issues that needed addressing before he could even think of heading out.

The first issue was the location of the temples. He knew of a few deserted ones—he grinned at the memory of seeing them conquered—but knew the probable location of only two intact ones. The only easy way to find their locations was to access portal logs, but that would alert his targets of his interest. Locating temples and shrines without accessing portal logs was an exercise in sifting through sparse clues and following up leads that seldom amounted to anything. Still, two probable locations was a good start. With any luck, he'd be able to get more information about others from them.

Thinking along those lines brought up the issue of how to maximize the information acquired in a short visit. Fortunately his base supplied the answer to that in the form of the sensor pods and wands that he'd used to such good effect recently. The base had a limited supply of each but could manufacture more on demand, which Bob instructed it to do. The wands were small enough that they could be shot into a facility, like an arrow, but had limited capabilities. The pods were larger but had a wider range of capabilities, including hacking into control systems and checking for use of the alternate energies. Bob decided to configure the wands to emphasize chemical detection ... he needed to track how pure quill was being distributed.

A secondary use of the sensor pods and wands was as a distraction. As he'd seen at Set's medical facility, their self-destruct and jamming capabilities offered a most satisfactory way of focusing the opposition's attentions away from himself. He debated leaving them in place as long-term intelligence assets, but decided that it was probably better to keep their existence a secret for as long as possible. Besides, he'd need all the distractions he could get on a mission like this.

That happy thought made him realize another use for exploding sensor wands might to help determine information about a structure. A quick search of the base's database showed that same idea had occurred to his ancestors. A wand could be set up to emit a sharp pulse of energy as it exploded. A properly set up pod could interpret those signals to create a map of a structure, with more explosions enhancing the map's details. That was just the sort of information needed for a subsequent visit, so he made sure his pods and wands were capable of that.

The portable genome analyzers required a fluid sample, preferably blood. Acquiring those samples would require direct action on his part. The trick would be to get the maximum number of samples in the least amount of time. Given that his targets would be unlikely to cooperate, Bob decided the best technique would be to slash with a needle, store each needle in a sealed pouch, then input the samples after he'd exited through the portal.

Of course, to do that meant that he would need to get inside the structure and run around slashing everyone in sight. Running around inside the structure would be greatly assisted by having maps of the layout, which would require the sensor wands to explode, which in turn would make everyone very upset with him. Better to sneak in and do a quick run-through, even if that meant overlooking some of the more interesting areas.

On the other hand sneaking in and out quickly meant apporting, which would seriously limit the amount of equipment he could carry with him. The list of equipment required for even a single mission, much less a series of them, was getting rather large. A propulsion pack plus armour and weapons was a tempting option, but the weight would prevent apporting.

Bob heaved a large sigh and scrubbed at his face with his hands. Large-scale campaign logistics were the sort of puzzle that he'd never enjoyed. Then he raised his head and laughed at himself. Here he was complaining about having too many resources, when for so long he'd been satisfied with what little he could carry or purchase along the way.

One solution would be to transit back to the base after each mission for resupply. Unfortunately that would leave a record that would reveal the existence of the base, something he'd very much like to avoid. The only other secure site he had access to was the training planet. Although it was well known, he'd locked down all the portals that were on it. Still, it was accessible by ship if anyone had access to one. All things considered, though, it was the best place for staging and resupply for each mission. On top of that, he could afford to take an excessive amount of gear on each sortie, destroying unused equipment when he left. He could even use a propulsion pack when entering a new world and use or destroy it as required.

He briefly considered using one of his scout craft as a base of operations, but decided against it. Although it could carry a lot of equipment and offered a unique way to approach a planet, it would take many weeks to move between target worlds. After he hit the first one, word would spread instantly via the portal network. The only way for his scheme to work was to hit as many temples in as short a time period as possible. The ship would be useful for follow-up visits, but not for a rapid series of scouting sorties.

All in all, Bob was quite pleased with his plan. It offered the chance to acquire a lot of new information in a short amount of time. The next few days would be busy ones. The first step was to send the results of his research to Sid—something he'd forgotten to do in the excitement of planning a new mission. It was very nice to have allies, but after so long on his own it was sometimes difficult to remember to include them.

Getting the dawn boat would require a small detour. From the training planet he'd have to go to a public portal on a waystation world, as only those could be used to summon a dawn boat. Once such a transfer was initiated it was inviolate and secure until received by the addressee. The public portal would also allow him to check up on the latest news.

Once back on the training world, he could spend the time checking out good spots to cache all the gear he'd be using. After that he'd make up sets of gear for each sortie and store them in the staging areas. He expected that to take a solid two days of effort, perhaps three. After the staging was completed he'd rest for a day, then set off on what promised to be a fun adventure.

CHAPTER TEN
The Tables are Turned

Bob was breathing heavily as he ran through the dark forest. His enhanced vision allowed him to see perfectly well in the near darkness. That allowed him to run at the best possible speed—not his best speed, as the forest floor was littered with things to catch and trip the unwary. Still, it was faster than the half-dozen thugs chasing him, and their cries were far behind him. If there were any others waiting near the portal his extra speed would get him there before they expected him.

He had no wish to harm any of them, but they were a nuisance. Armed as they were with cudgels and knives they were no real threat to him. Still, any scuffle might damage the contents of his knapsack and that wouldn't do at all.

As he approached the portal he began to slow and soon came to a halt. Trying to keep the sound of his panting to a minimum, he examined the area carefully. Judging from their shouts, the pack of thugs was several minutes behind him. Bob moved forward, keeping to the shadows and making use of available cover. A minute later he was satisfied that he'd found all the guards. There were only two of them, on opposite sides of the only easy entrance to the portal grove. It was the matter of seconds to disable and leave them unconscious on the ground.

Upon reaching the portal Bob paused to collect his thoughts and his breath. This was his sixth world in two days and he was getting tired, hungry, and his energy reserves were low. His mission of quick scouting missions was not going to plan, more so than was normal.

The first sortie had been a test where he'd gone to an abandoned. On the tactical side, it had allowed him to hone his techniques for infiltrating such structures. As a bonus, he'd detected traces of pure quill and found an undiscovered data cache. The data offered a rich source of details, even if it was somewhat out of date. It confirmed the locations of the two temples he knew about plus one more. After that he had transited back to the training planet to re-equip and store a copy of the new data.

That had been the only sortie that had gone to plan. The problems had started after transiting to the first real target. The infiltration had gone as planned, aside from a higher-than-expected level of security. Exploding the sensor wands and pods had dampened their enthusiasm, and they offered little opposition to his escape.

When he had tried to leave, however, he found that the portal had been hardened against him and the choice of destinations severely limited. There was a note from his elder sister that read, "Not so smart now are you, Bob?" It would seem that she had heard about his little jibe left on the portals of the training world. He sighed. After all these years—and his selfless coaching—she still hadn't managed to develop a sense of humour.

The available destinations were places he had wanted to go, which was puzzling but acceptable. The real problem was that he was unable to restock his supplies from his caches on the training planet.

To complicate matters, he discovered that each of his destinations had squads of goons ready to give chase as soon as he left the portal grove. Still, he'd managed to find out rather a lot at the cost of rapidly using up his equipment. For one, the Refuser-descendants were all high up in the temple hierarchy, overseeing the dispensation of mind-gems and pure quill. For another, he began to recognize some of the strange symbols on the temples as variants of the family sigils of members of the Purity group that had been on his base.

After each transit the list of available destinations had been reduced. It was obvious that the portal-loop was set up as a trap of diminishing size. He'd managed to gather his bio-samples and other intelligence, but he was being herded in a fashion that was most annoying. Another worry was the impression that the objective was to harass rather than capture him. It all seemed part of a plan of attrition rather than incompetence on the part of his pursuers. That impression was reinforced by the lack of opportunities to eat or rest, which impeded his ability to apport. Still, there had been nothing he could do but carry on. His initial impressive load of equipment had been reduced to the knapsack, the bio-samples and collected data, and a gift for a favourite aunt.

Bob's attention returned to the here-and-now as his breathing finally returned to normal. With calmness achieved, he instantiated the portal. The structure began as a hint of an outline, becoming a ghostly but translucent form, and finally an opaque but still insubstantial form of smoke. The cries of his pursuers were getting closer, which meant that they were somehow able to breach the portal glade. Bob shook his head and resisted the urge to fidget; these older portals took their own sweet time. Within seconds the building changed from a smoky apparition to something solid. The structure didn't appear to be anything special. It was just an open cube with hexagonal columns and featureless floor and ceiling, slightly over three body-lengths along each side. The open interior suddenly held a darkness that hurt the eyes to look at. It was time to go.

Bob narrowed his eyes in concentration and picked a destination from the short list available to him. Symbols describing his destination danced in the air within the film of darkness. The symbols flickered for a handful of seconds before solidifying and becoming a bright red colour that slowly began to fade. As Bob strode towards the centre of the cube he could hear the baying of his pursuers. They were close, but too far away to affect the transfer.

Stepping through, Bob felt a familiar prickling of his skin followed by the warmth of the sun of a new world. There was no point in requesting a précis of the planet from the portal, as all such information was now blocked to him. Still, there was an inviolate storage locker here which Bob used to cache his hard won samples and data so they wouldn't slow him down. He did keep, however, his knapsack containing the gift. Bob dismissed the portal and found its slow disappearance somewhat disconcerting. Now that he thought of it, all the portals in the portal-loop were quite old and slow in operation.

The sunshine and fresh air of this world felt good. Bob paused to appreciate his surroundings as he looked around. It had been some time since he'd been here, and was eager to see what changes had been made. The most obvious change was the modest, but well-maintained, path that lay ahead of him. Checking his bearings, the path headed towards a nearby village. It used to have establishments that served excellent food and beer, and he hoped that was still the case. All the recent exercise had left him quite peckish. It looked to be mid-afternoon local time, so there should be food available.

It was but a matter of few minutes to reach the edge of the woods. Bob frowned ... the woods around the portal should have been much larger. Its psychic defences were normally enough to keep people from being too interested in the area. Passing out of the forest, he saw what might be an answer.

To either side of the path, and as far as the eye could see, were fields of what looked like grain. Given that large fields like this were tended infrequently, that might serve to keep the portal's defences minimized. Strange that the initial encroachment had been allowed, though. Even stranger, this wasn't the first world where he'd seen this type of thing. Unique to this world, however, was the tall, thick hedge of spiked vines surrounding the glade and to either side of the path for some distance beyond.

An hour's leisurely—for Bob at any rate—walk along the meandering path brought him to the outskirts of the remembered village. He frowned, as it was more run down than he remembered, with fewer and cruftier-looking people. However, a few minutes later he turned a corner and was pleased to find that the tenor of the place improving almost with each step he took. The general traffic of people seemed to indicate something of significance ahead, so he allowed himself to be drawn along with the flow.

His curiosity was rewarded by the discovery that his destination was a large open public square. This was new, which meant the village had grown enough that the older areas were no longer the prime real estate that they once were. The smells reaching his nose also revealed the presence of food hawkers, and he quickly made his way over to the area of the square that was reserved for them. The gold coins he used to purchase food and beer got some strange looks, but were accepted after a thorough examination. Interestingly, he received far less change than he expected. It appeared that inflation was the price of progress.

He bought some cheese, a small loaf of bread, a couple skewers of roasted meats, and a tankard of dark beer. As he ate, Bob wandered about the square, blending in with the crowd. Different areas of the square were dedicated to different types of products, and he enjoyed watching the interplay among the people.

Another new aspect of this town was the appearance of glass windows. Once a rarity, they were now common. There were two reasons why this pleased Bob. The first was the prosperity and technological advancement it indicated. The second was that it made it easier to check if anyone was following him by using reflections. Over the course of his stroll around the square he had spotted several people tailing him and several stationary souls who were surreptitiously signalling the mobile tails. His stroll had taken him back to the food vendor area, so Bob drained his mug and returned it to the vendor who nodded his thanks.

With his basic needs taken care of, it was time to figure out the motives of the various tails.

None of the ones he'd seen looked like heavies or thugs, despite their sketchy appearance. Perhaps his tails were just curious about a stranger, although a town this size should have a goodly number of those passing through. Maybe they were criminals looking for an easy mark—although criminals tended to take one look at Bob's size and physical condition and leave him alone. Or, given that there were stationary watchers as well as mobile ones, perhaps something larger was in play.

While pondering this pretty puzzle, he kept walking. Passing by the last booth in the food area he noticed they sold distilled spirits. It proved to be a potent, if young and raw, whiskey. Bob bought two large bottles of it and placed each into a separate pocket of his coat. His followers were becoming less careful about being spotted so he considered it a good time to move away from innocent bystanders. Given that his presence on this world was compromised, another portal transit was in order. It would be recharged by the time he got back to it.

Bob headed back by the way he had arrived. It was the fastest way back to the forest and the portal within it. He kept his speed to a normal brisk walk until several turns had put the town, and its population, behind him. He paused for a moment and listened intently—he could hear the faint sounds of pursuit. He trotted at a good clip and those sounds began to fade into the distance when he heard another sound join them—the sound of hooves beating rapidly and getting closer. That meant he needed a new plan.

One plan would be to stick to the path and run to the forest. The good part of that plan was that he could match the speed of most horses and maintain that pace for longer than they could. The second plan was to cut into the fields and make a straight line run to the forest. The disadvantage of that was that the uneven ground wouldn't support his top speed, but would disadvantage the horses at least as badly if not worse. This pause to plan had taken but a moment in real time, and Bob leapt into the field to his right and made a bee-line for the forest. There was no point in obfuscating his path, as it was obvious what his destination would be. He just needed to reach it a couple of minutes before the others.

Thanks to his unerring sense of direction, Bob was fully confident that he was heading the right way. The roughness of the ground and the need to press through the head-high grain slowed his progress. That progress, however, was better than that of his pursuers, judging from what he could hear. He estimated himself to be about a minute ahead of them and they were slowly losing ground. There was a slight rise coming up and that would allow him to confirm his location.

Bob adjusted his stride so that he'd hit the top of the rise on a down step, which would save him a precious second. He approached the rise, and as he cleared it was heartened to see that not only was he on course but only a few minutes away. That put a smile on his face until he heard a sharp retort and felt a sudden tugging at his shoulder. The tugging and the pain the followed caused him to stumble and it took him several steps to get his rhythm back. The blood dribbling out of the hole in the front of his jacket confirmed that he'd been shot through his right shoulder. A happy shout from behind him confirmed that his pursuers had seen the result of the shot.

As he ran, Bob pinched the exit wound shut to aid with the healing. The entrance wound didn't feel too bad, although it was too numb to properly evaluate its state by how it felt. Worse, it was out of reach without some serious contortions, which would require stopping.

Bob evaluated his position. His pursuers had greater numbers, weren't very far behind, and had projectile weapons that they were proficient at using. On the plus side, he was still ahead although the stumbling had cost him some of that lead. On the bad side, he wouldn't reach the portal with enough of a lead to activate it and leave. Worse, the effort of running and dialling up his healing factors was beginning to eat into his minimal reserves. On top of that steaming pile of 'worse', his damaged shoulder was affecting his running and not in a good way.

First things first, he angled his direction to be slightly to the right of the path's entrance into the forest, towards the thorny hedge. The rough ground and grain prevented him from going faster with any degree of safety, so he'd have to depend on near-perfect timing. Removing his left hand from his right shoulder, he was heartened to see that the blood had stopped seeping out and that the pain had diminished to a slight ache. He tensed his right shoulder and arm slightly as he ran, preparing them for what lay ahead. As he neared the thorn barrier, he spun on the ball of his foot and pivoted towards the path's entrance into the forest. A chorus of shouts and a few scattered shots greeted that move. Fortunately, all the shots missed.

Just before he reached the path and the entrance Bob dialled back his healing factors to preserve energy for what was to come. As his foot hit the path, he bounced back into the grain, and was rewarded when a pair of shots flew by where he had been. Risking a burst of speed he bounced back onto the path, went through the entrance and immediately bounced to the right to roll behind a large pair of trees. A fusillade of shots answered those manoeuvres but the trees protected him.

He jammed both hands into the pockets of his coat and withdrew the two bottles of whiskey. Briefly breaking cover he tossed each bottle at the hedge, one to either side of the forest entrance, before leaping back behind the trees. A series of shots rained out, but the brief look had been enough for him to gauge the timing of the next move. Bob took a deep breath, extended his sensorium, and focused intently on constructing the appropriate subetheric forms. Another part of his mind was marking time, and at the appropriate moment he stepped out from cover and unleashed his carefully crafted forms. The air rippled with their passage so quickly as to seem instantaneous. The instantiated forms struck the shattered bottles of alcohol and created a fog of the fluid. The pursuing riders charged into the gap and through the fog, firing their guns.

Bob had always found fuel-air reactions interesting, and was fascinated at how difficult it was to get them just right. All that practise paid off with a satisfying explosion. Less satisfying—incredibly disturbing in fact—were the screams of pain and terror that followed. Keeping a firm check on his feelings, Bob sprang towards his stunned, and still armed, opponents. Using his dagger he quickly dispatched the men and their injured mounts.

That took care of the immediate threat, but he could see men approaching on foot about a minute or two away. He grabbed a rifle, knelt, and fired at the distant men. The shot had the desired effect, which was to force them to stop and scatter into the fields to either side of the path. With luck that would delay them long enough.

After grabbing another rifle, he ducked to one side. He poked the expended rifle through the hedge at about shoulder height. He set the other rifle up at about the height of a kneeling man. Then he ducked behind the trees just in time to avoid a series of bullets whizzing by. Shielded by the trees, Bob rushed towards the portal. He instantiated it and waited impatiently for it to form. As soon as the transit film was created he concentrated on creating the symbology for his destination.

However, his weakened condition and the stress of being forced to kill ruined his concentration. Shaking his head to clear it, he heard the sounds of armed men approaching the entrance to the forest. He was out of time and options. Taking a deep breath he took the one course of action open to him. He formed the emergency symbol that was drilled into every child and activated the portal. It would send him to the nearest sanctuary planet. Not ideal, but right now it was his only alternative.

The sounds of men approaching became louder, and Bob ran into the blackness and safety.

The transit was surprisingly rough and lengthy. Upon exiting, the difference in gravity fields caused Bob to stumble. The rough ground, and his weakened condition, turned the stumble into a fall and tumble. He got to his feet as quickly as he was able and looked around. Something wasn't right—then he remembered that the portal was still active. He turned to focus his attention on it, and the effort to close it was far greater than it should have been. The portal dimmed and faded into a smoke-like structure. There was a soundless sigh, felt rather than heard, as the smoke became solid and collapsed into an amorphous heap upon the ground. Something was very wrong.

Bob stood there panting as he extended his sensorium and probed at the remains of the portal with all his passive sensors. Despite the apparent destruction, he could detect traces of the alternate energies stored in the portal's accumulators. However, when he sent out a query the portal remained unresponsive. Further probes with beams of focused energy showed that the core portal mechanisms were intact but all the control mechanisms were destroyed. In theory it might be possible to access those core mechanisms, but it would require energy far in excess of what he could generate even when healthy.

Repressing the urge to sigh, he did a slow scan of his surroundings using all his passive sensors. There was no trace of tech of any sort other than the damaged portal. With very few options left to him—none of them good—Bob decided to focus on basic survival for the moment.

The first order of business was to get away from the unusable portal since that was the obvious place for whoever had set this trap to find him. He needed to survey the area to find shelter and nourishment. Panting as he looked around once more, he sniffed at the air. The surroundings consisted of sand and weathered rocks. There was a scattering of grayish vegetation that proved to be dead and desiccated. The air was bone dry with an odd metallic tang, and proved to be not very rich in oxygen. The gravity was somewhat higher than the planet he had just left. The temperature was unpleasantly hot. That wasn't surprising given the large size and reddish colour of the sun.

There were a series of low hills not too far in the distance, so Bob headed towards those at a measured pace. As he walked away he broke off one of the dead branches and used it to hide his tracks. A little further on he hopped off the sand and onto an outcropping of rocks, being careful not to leave any smudges. So far he'd not seen any indications of water or living vegetation. That could become a problem, if only because it would slow the healing of his wounds and regeneration of his energy reserves. Thinking of that reminded him of the dull ache in his partially-healed shoulder. Stopping to check the exit wound on his front, he saw that it was oozing slightly, no doubt caused by his clumsy entry into this world. Suppressing the urge to sigh, he allocated an extra trickle of energy to healing his wounds as he resumed his march.

* * *

It took Bob longer than expected to reach the base of the hills. Part of that was due to the efforts made in hiding his tracks. Part of it was due to the confirmation of a lower-than-expected level of oxygen in the air. Finally, part of it was due to weariness. He'd been through an awful lot in a very short length of time and needed to recuperate. Unfortunately, the universe seemed disinclined to grant him that recuperation, so he trudged up the hillside being careful to look all around as he climbed. Along the way he found scraps of lichen on some of the rocks, which he tore off and put into the pockets of his tattered coat.

He took his time going up the hill, so by the time he got the top he wasn't too badly winded. Crouching so as to minimize his profile against the horizon, he moved slowly until in the shade of a large boulder. He settled on the ground with a soft grunt, and sat trying to catch his breath. The low oxygen content of the air made that a challenge and the metallic tang left a nasty taste on his tongue. There wasn't even a hint of a breeze to take the edge off the heat.

Waiting until he'd stopped panting, Bob leaned back and activated his full sensorium. Setting it to passive mode he scanned the area around him, from ground to sky, from his feet upward to the limits of its resolution. For all the good it did him he could have used his organic eyes. He could detect nothing technological in sight between here and the horizon. Also, no obvious signs of vegetation or water. That reminded him of the lichen in his pockets and he grimaced. Eating that without water would be a grim business.

Steeling himself, he set his sensorium to include the active modes at their lowest power. Another careful scan revealed nothing of interest, so he increased the power by a fraction and repeated the process. That scan revealed the presence of water, of some sort, roughly ten kilometres from his current location. Bob pondered his options. He glanced at the sun, factored in how far it had moved since he'd arrived, and estimated that he had about eight or nine more hours of daylight. Which meant that the days were thirty to forty hours long. There was another cluster of hills ahead of him, and the source of water was between here and those hills. Stifling a grunt he got to his feet and began walking towards the water. He could only hope it would be easily accessible.

A couple of weary hours later, Bob lay on his stomach at the edge of steep cliff. His sensorium insisted that there was water in the canyon below. Unfortunately there was no obvious way down and it was too far to jump. His weakened condition precluded the use of his limited levitation or apportation abilities. This was like one of his father's tests, with the old man going on and on about "spare the trauma and spoil the child". A soft grunt of laughter bubbled from Bob. This situation had trauma a-plenty, for sure. A worn-out, low-oxygen planet, with heavy metals in the air. To top it off, the sun was heavy in the ultraviolet judging from the dryness of his eyes and the developing sunburn on his exposed skin. Oh, and his injured shoulder still ached. Just the sort of survival scenario the old bugger loved.

Thinking of some of those old trials brought a smile to Bob's face. Numerous times spent cheating death while pissing off his father by finding unexpected ways around the traps. Ah, good times. Thinking of those brought to mind one of his adventures not too dissimilar from his current predicament. Good old dad had expected him to crawl down a sheer cliff, but Bob had spotted a talus slope and surfed down. Ruined his boots but ended on the bottom intact and whooping with exhilaration—until his father had caught up with him.

A scan of the area found several potential slopes, but they were on the other side of the canyon. Still, that encouraged him to scout around on his own side, and within a few minutes he found a suitable slope. Loose sand and rock wasn't as surf-friendly as talus, but one took what one could.

Bob hopped onto the slope and began running until the ground began sliding beneath him. At that point he assumed a stable pose, with his arms extended and hoped that he didn't hit anything on the way down. Luck, punctuated by a few close calls and fast hopping over boulders, was with him and he reached the bottom without wiping out. Of course his forward velocity was still very impressive, so he had to work feverishly to shed it by running while keeping his balance. Soon enough he came to a halt and began whooping with glee.

As the echoes of his yells died out, he grinned and headed towards where his sensors had indicated the presence of water. The outcropping of the first living vegetation he'd seen marked the location more precisely. No running water was evident, but he'd not been expecting that. Using some nearby sticks, he began digging. The ground was loose sand that became harder the deeper he dug. The stick proved sufficient to the task of breaking through the soil, and within a few seconds he could smell water. When the hole was as deep as the length of his hand, he encountered a dark band of moisture. At that point he widened the hole and sat back to wait. If necessary he could have simply sucked the wet soil but he wasn't that desperate.

While waiting for the water to accumulate Bob brushed himself off and examined the nearby plants. He cautiously bit a small piece of a leaf and immediately spat it out. The sharp metallic taste indicated that they were saturated with the heavy metals that were common on this planet. The inner part of the stalk was somewhat less metallic, but still not something he wanted to eat. Pulling out some of the roots, he found them to have almost no metallic taste, so he pulled up a handful for a meal. They'd go well with the lichen in his pockets.

A quick look at the hole revealed that a small amount of water had accumulated. Bob created a straw from one of the stalks and knelt to sip up the water. There were only a couple mouthfuls but it tasted wonderful. Well, actually it was on the brackish side but by this time he didn't much care. For his meal, he scraped the dirt off the roots and lichen, and munched on those while waiting for more water to accumulate. Soon, there was enough water for a mouthful that washed down the last of his meal.

By this time the sun had set and it had grown very dark. Despite everything that had happened, Bob was feeling content. He'd had a sip of water, a bite of food, and some boyish fun ... what more could a man want? A fire would have been nice, but was out of the question since it might draw unwanted attention. Despite the coolness that came with nighttime in a desert, he was surrounded by rocks that had absorbed enough heat to keep the area comfortably warm.

He decided to risk a brief probing of the ground with active sensors, and confirmed that there were no living organisms around. So he lay back and looked up at the night sky, but saw only a handful of stars. That meant that he was probably a good distance from the centre of the galaxy, suggesting that this planet and its sun were very, very old.

Although he could see in the dark Bob decided to wait until dawn before travelling on. For one thing, that would give time for a goodly amount of water to accumulate. For another, he needed the rest.

Normally a light sleeper, Bob decided to play it safe by enabling his passive sensors and setting them to wake him at the first sign of dawn. With that he relaxed and allowed himself to sleep. He actually slept until his sensors woke him up. That was highly unusual but not unexpected given his recent exertions. He dug up a couple handfuls of roots for a meal and combined that with the remains of the lichen. There was enough accumulated water for him to be able to drink his fill, wash his face, and clean off his wounds. The wounds had healed nicely and the shoulder had only a slight bit of stiffness.

The canyon led off in the direction he needed to go, so he decided not to waste time or energy climbing back up until he had to. Besides, there was a little shade for most of the day which helped take the edge of the oppressive heat. He was refreshed enough to walk at his normal distance-eating speed, so by the time dusk came he was approaching his destination. He could see that the canyon ended not too far ahead, but there was another oasis where he was so he decided to spend the night there and reap the bounty of the land, such as it was.

Bob arose the next morning just before dawn after a refreshing sleep. He made a quick meal of roots and water, then exited the canyon. The base of the hills was about a kilometre away. The sun was just starting to rise and the temperature wasn't terribly hot, so Bob decided to jog the distance. It felt good to stretch himself again. His powers weren't fully recharged—he'd need to find a better source of food for that—but were a lot stronger than when he'd arrived. He strode easily up the incline to the top. Standing with his back to a boulder, he once again activated his full sensorium in passive mode and scanned the area. Finding nothing of interest he repeated the scan with the active sensors at their lowest power. At that point all Hell broke loose.

The ground shook so badly that Bob was forced to squat low with legs apart. Off to one side and down-slope a crack in the ground began to form. A grinding roar filled the air as it opened up quickly and in less than a minute it became a gaping hole into the planet that glowed a dull red from deep within. Surprisingly there was little in the way of dust or debris flying out of the hole, despite emitting strong blasts of hot, stagnant wind. Once the hole achieved its full size the trembling ceased, as did the blasts of wind. The silence was startling after the short-lived but intense roar that greeted its arrival. Bob had reflexively disabled and withdrawn his sensorium, but not before catching the faint echo of a portal and the *slash* of a teleporter. There was a feeling of expectation in the air.

While waiting for the stage show to play itself out, he focused on the faint 'taste' of the new portal. It was different from most he'd encountered, with overtones of a private type used by an elderly uncle—the name Virgil came to mind—who fancied himself quite the portal engineer. Judging by the echoes it was located far away. In any case it was shielded beyond his ability to access it.

A series of gouts of flame, accompanied by deep roars, arose from the pit and flew high into the air. Each gout of flame was topped by a large deep-red orb. The orbs slowly settled back to the surface. There were too many of them, scattered in every direction, for Bob to track accurately. Fortunately the speed of descent of the orbs was slow enough to give him time to get at least rough bearings on them, and the situation was not good. Whatever those orbs were, they had him surrounded. There was another eerie silence as the orbs finished their descent—he counted a dozen of them. Within seconds all of the orbs were on the ground and throbbing with an angry red glow.

The silence was broken by a deep-pitched hum from the pit as another orb, larger than the others, slowly rose up. Bob watched this new arrival while attempting to keep an eye on the others. It rose up about ten body-lengths above the ground, then floated to one side and landed softly. All was quiet for a few seconds, then all the orbs began to brighten in luminosity, although their colour remained an angry red. Brighter and brighter they glowed, forcing Bob to slit his eyes. He sneered as he stood up, recognizing the show for what it was.

The brightness of the orbs reached a zenith and then dimmed rapidly to reveal a figure where each of the orbs had been. Every figure was his size or somewhat larger, clad in impressive armour, each different from the other as were the weapons they held. The figure revealed by the largest orb was, of course, the most impressive of all. It was the largest of the group, fully two heads taller than Bob and proportionally broader at the shoulders. Its armour was more ornate and had a subtle inner glow. There was no weapon evident as the figure spread its arms wide and called out, "Hello, little brother."

Bob descended towards the figure, picking his path with care to avoid stumbling. That, he knew, would be fatal. When he reached the bottom, he walked at a measured pace towards his elder brother until they were separated by three body lengths.

"Hello, Set. Fancy meeting you here. Come here often? Sorry you can't stay."

Set grinned and shook his head with exaggerated sadness. "Oh, little brother. Is that any way to greet me? It's been so long."

"Not long enough."

"Really? Are you still upset about that little contretemps on our training planet? We're family. Forgive and forget."

"Uh huh. That why you brought your thugs with you?" Bob looked around at Set's entourage and snorted with derision. "Still recruiting from the shallow end of the gene pool I see."

That got an angry muttering from the others which Set silenced with a glare. Despite his brave front, Bob recognized the figures for what they were—Set's top-drawer cadre of warriors. The self-proclaimed "Elites" that he had first heard about when he visited the Five Stars Empire. Subsequent information had confirmed that they were very powerful, very nasty, and very dangerous. One on one, none were a match for him provided he didn't make any mistakes. He could probably handle any two of them, maybe three. As dangerous as they were, they were just conventional humans with advanced training and weaponry. Set was the real danger. This was too much like the no-win situations that his father used to enjoy throwing him into.

"Now, now, little brother. Let's not be calling anyone names. Who knows ... perhaps you'll be wanting to join me and be working alongside these fine fellows."

Bob gave a derisive snort as he shook his head. "Not going to happen."

Set looked at Bob, the very model of a concerned elder sibling. "Please, little brother, don't be like that. We are family and you belong with me. Or, if not with me then at least back home with the others. Youngest sister misses you terribly, you know. It's her Naming Day soon and you don't want to miss that."

Bob cut him off with a brusque wave of a hand. "Had this same speech from Mom not too long ago. Said 'no' to her. Saying 'no' to you."

That startled Set, who gaped at him for several seconds before finding his voice. "Have you lost your mind? I figured you might refuse me, but to disobey Mom? And she let you live?"

Bob chuckled at the memory of that encounter. "Well, I didn't exactly stick around after that. And I made sure that she was ... distracted."

Set jerked his head back and gaped for a moment. Then he regained his composure and began to chuckle. "Yeah, you always did have a knack for trickery and distraction. Would have loved to see her face when you pulled that on her. From a distance, of course."

Bob gave a brief nod of his head to acknowledge the compliment.

Set regained his stern look. "But you're dealing with me now, little brother. Take a look around—you'll not be pulling any nonsense like that with me." Set's wave encompassed his Elites. "Not if you expect to survive."

The two stared at each other in silence for a time. Finally Set said, "Look here, little brother ... Bob. Be reasonable. You can't beat me. In fact, you can't even leave here without my help. The public portal is shattered, and the private one we used is hardened against you. Without me, you're trapped here."

"Where is here, by the way?" Bob enquired in a calm tone. "Or is that a secret?"

"Nah, you'd have figured it out soon enough. It's an old prison planet. Very old and forgotten. It's got the bare minimum for survival, perhaps, but not much in the way of food or water. You'll burn out your body's systems just trying to eke out nourishment from the soil. Then you'll die. Alone and forgotten. Not a pleasant way to go."

That piqued Bob's interest—he'd found more resources here than Set knew about. Which meant that he was in better shape than expected. Not much of an advantage, but right now he'd take anything he could get.

"So, those thugs chasing me on those other worlds were yours?"

"Yes, indeed. Didn't expect them to succeed, of course, but they did blood you and wear you down. Between that and the travel--courtesy of your elder sister's efforts by the way—you've got to be feeling a bit tired, eh? So listen to me just this once, eh?

Bob shrugged. "So talk. What is this wonderfulness you're offering?"

Set arranged his face into an expression of earnestness. "Times are changing, little brother. You can be a part of it. We've been sitting back too long, withdrawing from the galaxy, content to sit idle on a handful of worlds."

"More than a handful," murmured Bob.

Ignoring the comment Set continued, "I'm setting up an organized expansion to bring order to chaos."

"An empire," came another murmur from Bob.

Set glared. "Call it what you will. This time it'll be done right so that it will last. It will give us—all the families—back the power we should never have given up. There's enough for everyone, little brother. You want to coddle the primitives? Fine, take a few worlds for yourself and do whatever you wish. There's lots of worlds for the taking, filled with grubby primitives for you to uplift and do whatever with."

"And what do you need me for, exactly?"

"Ah, you're beginning to see the possibilities, aren't you?" Set leaned forward, his face becoming animated. "I've been working out a system and proving that it works. You've seen bits and pieces of it, but not the whole thing. I need to grow it, though, and for that I need Family members. After a few more of us are on-board, we can create a critical mass of change that will be unstoppable."

"This, ah, system of yours, Set. That's the temples you've set up?"

"Yes, among other things. I've got over a dozen of them set up on ..."

"Fifteen, actually. With twelve minor shrines."

Set looked taken aback. "Well ..."

Bob smiled broadly. "You might want to check on them to get a more recent count. Most of the shrines are gone ... with some minor assistance from me, I'm happy to say. Along with a third of those temples you worked so hard to set up. Did some social tinkering here and there to inoculate those populations from ever falling for your scams again, too.

239

Worked so well that I planted those memes on all those other worlds where your temples are. As well as on a number of other planets in the area. I think you'll find those temples to be rather less active than what you're hoping."

Set's sudden inhalation of breath through clenched teeth was like a hiss. Bob moved back and forth as if lecturing, but his overall path was towards the gaping chasm. He kept his sensorium powered off, of course, but could feel the heat from the pit on his skin. That heat meant power of some sort was being generated, and making use of scraps of power was something he was very good at.

"What did you do, little brother? It took me centuries to set those up."

"Nothing much, really. Didn't have to—your tactics saw to that. Do you have any idea how much you are feared and hated?"

"Their fear is the whole point," said Set through gritted teeth. "It ensures obedience."

"Yes, well, that approach creates enemies. And over time, a lot of enemies. Give 'em a workable plan and some training, and soon they're a determined cadre of revolutionaries."

Set was breathing heavily, but growled out, "Those temples were impervious to anything the primitives could have done. Those structures were meant to last for eternity."

"Meh, not so much. Some of those 'primitive' planets have some good tech, and it's easily transported through a portal. Good enough to weaken the structure, or at least accelerate the ageing of their surfaces. Nobody likes to worship at a grotty-looking temple, you know."

"You ..." Set growled through clenched teeth.

"Yep, me. I admit to helping out just a smidge." Bob got a faraway look on his face as he smiled and said, "Ah, good times, good times."

Getting himself under control with difficulty, Set waved a dismissive hand as his face assumed a look of stern forbearance. "Annoying, but they have served their purpose in the Grand Plan. It is almost time to unleash the full weight of my might."

"Again, meh. You're referring to the Five Stars Empire and those accumulated legions of mercenaries? Gone. I convinced them to start a revolution against the Empire. Which, thanks to you, was a hair's breadth away from collapsing anyway."

Set's face was beginning to flush as his self-control slipped. "I will go there and set things right, personally. The troops will rally to my banner when I start making a few examples of the trouble-makers. Oh, it may take a little time as I noticed the portal there isn't responding. What did you do? Set it into a deep diagnostics mode? That'll only buy a delay of a couple of months at most."

"The portal is gone. I set it to self-destruct. They're free of you, for all time."

"What?" The revelation stunned Set, and all he could do for several seconds was to open and close his mouth noiselessly. Then he ground out, "Not even you would commit such a sacrilege, such an obscenity."

Bob shrugged. "Did it, nonetheless. And not for the first time. Your dreams of empire are over, Set. You'll never be able to gather that many troops together again. And, by the way, you might want to pop in and see how Kydos is doing. The poor dear has taken a turn for the worse, I fear. So sad."

Set growled and made inarticulate sounds. "So, you're the reason she turned feral, are you? Do you know how many people she slaughtered at the temple before she was driven off? After that, the townspeople executed most of my troops there."

Bob shrugged. "You mean killed the ones who didn't self-destruct or die because of withdrawal symptoms when the pure quill ran out? As for Kydos, she tried to kill me. Several times. Those bootleg aspects of yours just aren't very good, you know. At least that won't be a problem anymore."

The look on Set's face brought a warm glow to Bob's heart. "Oh, wait ... you haven't heard? My, my, my. So busy delegating that you lost track of so many important details. All your trusted confederates seem to be keeping information from you, if not outright abandoning you. I can't imagine why."

The rage-infused look on Set's face brought a glow of happiness to Bob's dire situation.

"Oh, speaking of confederates, Elder Brother, whoever was it that helped you make the leap from a handful of temples to dreams of empire? I know you always yearned for something grand, but you lack the organizational skills for it. You needed those skills plus something special to offer people. Something that only you could supply them. That's where the Refusers came in, isn't it, with their mind-gems infused with pure quill?"

Set had by this point gone beyond red-faced fury and into white-faced incandescence.

Bob continued to press his point, playing for time. Ever since the new private portal had been used, he could once again sense the faint presence of the damaged portal. It wasn't functional, but the energies it controlled were still viable. A desperate plan began to form. "What will you your allies, the Refusers and the Ravens, think of you now? Or has the power behind the throne outwitted you in a long game and is now your employer? Have you fallen victim to a dagger of eons?"

That got Set ranting so hard that spittle came out of his mouth as he spoke. Ignoring the diatribe, Bob snuck a peak over the edge of the pit. There was lava accumulating some distance down. He couldn't sense any obvious signs of Set's portal or any other technology, but didn't dare take the time to actively probe for it. Heat energy was diffuse, but lava was very hot and there was a lot of it. The big question was, was there enough of it to be useful?

Set finally regained control of himself. "I've heard enough, little brother. I'll let the Family know that your last words were to spit on them and the memories of our ancestors." With that, Set raised both hands to waist level and used them to indicate that his Elites should start moving forward.

"That would be just more of your lies, Set. I love them all—even you—enough to speak the truth. I have never offered serious violence to any of them—even you, Elder Brother."

Set's face contorted with hate. He hands were clenched with rage and a low growl arose in his throat. He took a stiff-legged step forward as the growl turned into a snarl. Bob just laughed and stepped backwards over the edge of the pit.

As he fell Bob assumed a starfish stance to stabilize his descent. He drew a deep breath and began to prepare himself for the upcoming ordeal. Timing was critical and there were only scant seconds to set everything in motion. With one part of his mind he gathered his powers for an apportation, with another he defined the coordinates for a portal transit, and with another he prepared to absorb the energy of the lava to power the whole process. A small fraction of his mind was aware that Set was on the edge of the pit looking down.

Bob could feel the apportation field building within him. He folded the flickering energies of the damaged portal into the apportation and modulated the merging energy fields with the destination address. Uncle Sid had told him—it seemed so long ago—that Aunt Gertrude would offer him safe haven. Given that he'd not be able to mask his destination, that seemed the best bet.

The rapidly increasing heat was boosting the process, allowing him to reserve his own powers for the tricky task of matching intrinsic velocities between here and the target planet. He didn't have enough energy to do a perfect job of that, but it should suffice. To the destination address he added the command to perform an emergency bounce-jump as soon as he arrived. That'd force the destination portal to send him to a random location on the planet, making it harder for Set to find him.

He felt the *rasp* of Set's active sensors but rebuffed the attempt to establish a communications link. Then he hit the molten rock and within microseconds had extracted much of its energy. As the molten rock became solid, Bob's body was enveloped by a churning blackness that was impossible to look at. Then in an instant it, and he, were gone.

CHAPTER ELEVEN
Family Matters

An indeterminate time later Bob felt the familiar lessening of transit forces that signalled his arrival. As quickly as it began, though, they were replaced with a harsh series of forces that seemed to twist through him. This was the hand-off moment between portals, except that this time he was acting as a portal controller. Time seemed to stand still as he focused on the energies ripping at him. With an effort of will he emitted subtle bursts of energy to force the wild forces to envelop but not touch him. At the same time he began to align his energies with those of the receiving portal. It was like trying to achieve simularity for apporting from the viewpoint of himself and his destination at the same time.

It seemed like a hopeless task but he managed to get the alignments close enough for the receiving portal to work with. He felt a moment of clarity as he popped out into the new world, then he felt another twist of energies that signalled the bounce-jump. This time he appeared at a considerable height above the ground, dropping with a bit of sideways velocity. It appeared that the receiving portal hadn't managed to fully cancel the intrinsic velocity difference between the two planets.

With a grunt of effort he flipped himself to face the ground he was falling into. It was the shoreline of a large body of water, possibly an ocean, and his trajectory looked to terminate on sand rather than water. From this height, though, one was as deadly as the other. He took the time to take several deep breaths and still his mind. Focusing his attention on the rapidly-approaching beach, he managed to achieve a simularity lock and apported.

He managed to shed most of the excess velocity, but still hit an area of soft sand with enough force to knock the wind out of him and leave him momentarily stunned. Bob fought to regain full consciousness and control but struggled against a debilitating lassitude. All his reserves of strength and power felt depleted. A groan escaped from him as he forced himself to move. It took several attempts to roll over onto his side. That hurt rather a lot so he took an inventory of his status.

He felt tired and sore, but there were no bones broken. All internal organs were functioning, although his spleen and liver had some minor bleeding. His healing factors were sluggish but sufficient to deal with the internal bleeding. Every gram of fat was gone from his body, consumed in the effort required by the combined transit-apportation, giving him an almost cadaverous look. He could hear the lapping of the waves not too far away and decided that getting some water was of primary importance.

After a couple of painful false starts he managed to get to his feet. From there he staggered the dozen metres to the water and fell to his knees to drink greedily. It was brackish sea water, but sufficient to his needs. He drank his fill, ate a few strands of seaweed that floated by, then got to his feet and scanned the area. There was a large boulder, slightly taller than he was, a short distance along the beach. That was the only defensible spot in sight, so he headed there. Along the way he picked up a stick to use as a cane. It took a painful eternity, but he finally managed to reach the boulder.

Not daring to sit down, he leaned against the sun-warmed stone, grateful for its solidity. He allowed himself a few seconds of relaxation and appreciation of the scenery before getting down to the matter at hand. As the Precepts of Survival said, "Enjoy every moment. It might be your last."

Remembering that piece of wisdom got a small, but heartfelt, chuckle out of him. He'd managed to make Set look foolish—again—and accomplished an amazing feat of manipulation of the alternate energies. All in all, a good day. Then he gave his head a shake to remind himself that the day was not yet over. And was highly unlikely to remain "good."

The first step was to somehow contact Aunt Gertrude. She'd have detected the arrival at her portal and would sooner or later figure out that there had been a bounce-jump on exit. That would get her actively looking for him. That meant it was up to him to get her attention. Given his all-but-exhausted energy reserves, it would have to be something simple. That problem was complicated by the fact that the highest level of tech he had on him was the stick. Then he paused. The stick was the best tech on him, but not in him.

With a grin he began sketching out a complex set of interlocking symbols in the sand. After several minutes of careful work he stood up to examine his efforts. It was larger than he would have liked, but as small as he dared make it given the mechanical properties of the sand. He frowned as he focused his attention on his left wrist. A wound opened up and he allowed a portion of his blood to drip into the symbols, making sure that the blood coated all parts of the pattern. With that done, he pinched the wound and forced it to heal. The healing took longer than he would have liked, so he walked to the water's edge to take a drink and eat some more seaweed.

Returning to his boulder, he saw that his blood had soaked in and dried nicely. Extending a section of his sensorium, he focused a beam of energy at the symbol and was rewarded with a flash of blue light. His makeshift subspace amplifier was now primed and ready for use. All that remained was for him to rebuild his energy levels sufficiently to make use of it. Even emitting that modest beam of energy had tired him quite a bit.

Bob allowed himself a satisfied smile at his handiwork, but that was soon replaced by a frown. He'd forgotten that Set was on his way, if he hadn't arrived already. If he arrived before Aunt Gertrude could be contacted, he might recognize the crude subspace device and destroy it. What was needed was a distraction, and that was something Bob was good at.

With a groan he heaved himself away from the boulder and got to work. He drew a circle around the boulder, with a radius of about twice his height. At regular intervals he drew smaller circles, and within those he carved intricate designs. It was all nonsense, of course, but it certainly looked as if it could be a makeshift subspace something-or-other. For good measure he added some of the symbols that Celcilia had used to contact Kydos plus some from Uncle Sid's old alternate energies detector.

He hobbled off the water's edge for another drink and some seaweed. He'd arrived before local noon, been working for a couple of hours, and had several more hours before sunset. Groaning as he forced himself erect, Bob hobbled back to his boulder and allowed himself to sit. His physical strength was returning, at the cost of nearly depleting his healing factors, but it would still be a while before his energy reserves became sufficient to activate the crude subspace amplifier.

To pass the time he did stretching exercises to keep his muscles from seizing up. Every so often he would walk to the water's edge for a drink. To his relief, walking was no longer a chore. He didn't dare fall asleep, or even nap, so he engaged in some deep meditation and relaxation exercises. The sun was about an hour from setting. It was almost time to start the next phase.

Without warning he felt the *slash* of a teleporter. The sky above him was shattered with flickering lights that coalesced into a swirling darkness that swelled from the size of an egg to a circle of nearly four metres diameter. Twelve glowing red orbs emerged, followed by a single larger orb. There was an audible *snap* as the swirling darkness shrank and vanished. The orbs landed in a circle around Bob, with the largest one settling within the perimeter established by the others. With a final hellish glow the orbs vanished to reveal Set and his Elites.

"Hello, little brother."

Bob could only nod, not trusting himself to say anything. He rose, took two steps away from the boulder, but remained well within the circle.

Set moved forward slowly. "I'm actually impressed with that stunt of yours, little brother. Very impressed. Oh, it was an incredibly foolish thing to do, combining an apportation with a portal transit. And to power it using a diffuse external energy source. The whole effort was nothing short of masterful. Something for the histories, in fact."

Bob tilted his head to acknowledge the compliment, watching Set walk slowly towards him.

"A truly magnificent effort. But, in the end, a wasted one. You can't run from me, little brother. You can't hide. There's nothing that you can ..." Set had stepped over the carefully constructed circle and its ancillary symbols, but something stopped him before he smudged any part of it.

"What?" muttered Set as he stepped back away from the circle and its ornamentation. Then in a louder voice he said, "What is this?" as he moved his head to make a careful survey of the symbols. After a few moments he sneered and said. "Fah. Nonsense." Yet there was an element of uncertainty in his voice.

Still smiling, Bob put several fingers into his mouth and

whistled a shrill blast through them.

Set relaxed and grunted with amusement. "You never could get the hang of that. Nice try, though."

Bob removed his fingers and waggled them before reinserting them. Set crossed his arms and sneered. Bob took a deep breath and whistled again. This time the air shimmered as the piercing sound he produced echoed and began coming from all around them. Unseen by the crowd, the original symbol he'd carved into the sand began to glow with a soft blue light. The Elites were all grimacing, and several had their eyes closed in pain. Soon they had all dropped to their knees. Set looked started for a moment, then gave a wry smile. Bob's breath gave out after a minute and he removed the fingers from his mouth to gulp in air. The symbol continued to glow for a second before becoming inert.

Set clapped his hands slowly several times. "Good effort, little brother. Sonically induced subetherics? Didn't think that was possible. You're just full of surprises today. That'd be to call her, wouldn't it? But you lack the power. You always have. No, this is your final mistake. For the sake of our family, I'll count to ten to give you a fighting chance. All right?" The last was said very softly and tenderly.

Bob nodded, feigning more weariness than he felt. He knew that he only a few seconds left, given Set's predilection for lying. He panted to better oxygenate his body for the coming ordeal.

As expected, Set attacked on the count of "four". His speed was faster than Bob had ever seen and the resultant punch slammed Bob against the boulder and knocked the breath out of him. The damage was minimal, aside from additional bruising, but his muscles were momentarily paralysed. Grinning broadly, Set stepped back beyond the circle and motioned his Elites to move in. "Crippling blows only. If you kill him, you die," he warned them.

The circle of Elites constricted uniformly until it was within about five body-lengths of Bob. The first of the Elites dashed in, hoping to take advantage of Bob's weakened condition. Unfortunately, his victim wasn't as helpless as expected. It was a mistake that cost him his life as Bob spun and slammed the soldier's head into the boulder, crushing it. The remaining Elites paused in their advance. Several heartbeats later, a pair of them shared a glance before moving in together.

Each held a short staff, which they wielded one-handedly. They rushed Bob from either side, but their timing was just a fraction off. Bob blocked a blow from the Elite on his left with his arm, which allowed him time to shift position to dodge the thrust of the Elite on his right. Bob's right hand flashed out and slammed into the throat of that Elite and gripped hard while pulling the Elite along the line of attack and into the path of his companion. The two of them collided and ended up in a tangled heap on the ground. Bob spun on the balls of his feet and dispatched both with kicks to the head. Three hostiles neutralized, but at the cost of a broken and now-useless left arm.

A snarled command from Set sent four Elites towards Bob. They moved in like a well-practised unit, and Bob was hard-pressed to parry their blows. Even so, he was only able to delay the inevitable. A blow against the injured left arm momentarily distracted him, allowing a blow to his right knee that rendered it incapable of bearing his weight. While struggling to maintain his balance another blow struck his left shin. Bob fell to the ground, with shards of bone protruding from his left leg and his right knee shattered. Looking up, he saw Set advancing towards him, his face a study in unrestrained rage. None of them noticed a brief flash of blue light that came from the makeshift subspace amplifier.

Without warning, the sky above them screamed as it was

torn apart and a nightmare creature flew through the resulting rift. It was fully fifteen metres in length, five in diameter at the front, and tapering to one metre at the tail. The gaping mouth was a maw ringed by layers of sharp teeth. Its body had the colour and odour of a rotting corpse. Protuberances varying in size from a few centimetres to several metres were ringed about its body in apparently random fashion. Tendrils of varying sizes festooned the body.

As a unit the Elites turned and attacked the creature. Some threw their staffs, while others grabbed weapons off their armour and fired. Blasts of energy and solid projectiles raked the creature's body with no visible effect. After a moment of absorbing the onslaught in silence, the creature retaliated. The large protuberances began belching fire so hot that it fused the sand as it raked the Elites. Within a handful of seconds the Elites were reduced to bubbling puddles of melted armour and flesh. Then the creature settled its bulk on the ground, just off to the side of Bob and Set.

Though his injuries were severe and causing him tremendous pain, Bob managed to whisper, "Hi, Auntie Gertrude. Sorry to pop in unannounced." For his part, Set stood there with his mouth open, trying to recover from his rage of a moment before.

"Bob. Set. You know I don't allow fighting on my planet. What have you two got to say for yourselves?"

Set took a deep breath, drew himself up, and said in a sharp tone, "See here, Aunt Gertrude. I am not a child and demand that you treat me with the appropriate respect." With that, he waited for a response. When there was none he regained his confidence and continued. "You know full well that the Protocols allow me free travel to any planet with a public portal. And, I'll point out, you destroyed my most elite soldiers. That was very rude and uncalled for. I demand compensation. Significant compensation and ..."

"Silence, boy." The volume of the command was not loud, but the tone of command caused Set to close his mouth with a snap. Then he recovered his poise and said, "No, Aunt, I will not be silent. You owe me ..."

Aunt Gertrude flicked a tendril out like a whip, catching Set across the chest. The impact sounded like a locomotive hitting a wall at moderate speed, and Set was flung high into the air. Despite his own injuries, Bob winced at the sound—that was going to cause injuries that at least equalled his own.

At the peak of Set's arc of travel the air rippled and screamed as a rift opened. Set flew into the opening and vanished. The rift wavered, burped, then closed. Gertrude extended an eye which turned to look balefully towards Bob.

"As for you, young Bob, I ..." Gertrude paused for a moment before continuing. "I say, it is exceptionally rude of you to lay there bleeding when I'm talking to you. I insist that you heal yourself this very instant. Bob? Bob?"

Bob was trying very hard to respond, but only coughed up blood when he tried to speak. Blood was also beginning to flow out along his shattered leg bones. That, combined with the pain from his shattered knee and other injuries, was making it very difficult for him to think clearly. His healing factors were depleted and unable to cope. Despite his best efforts Bob blacked out.

* * *

It was the singing that woke him up. A faint singing that was coming from inside him—throughout his body, in fact. Snapping to the highest level of alertness that he was capable of—a fraction of his normal best—he realized that he was stretched out on his back on the sand. Something inside him was not so much singing as emitting a repetitive series of faint sounds as it did ... something. Bob managed to open his eyes to see Gertrude's face above his, peering anxiously at him.

"All you feeling better, dear boy?"

To his surprise, Bob was. Not very good, but at least not on the brink of death. That was a good beginning. There was a pressure missing from his back, and glancing to one side he saw that his aunt had removed the backpack. Rotating his head to look at her, he cleared his throat. It took a couple of failed attempts, but Bob managed to croak out, "Yes, thank you, ma'am. Ah, I don't mean to sound ungrateful, but doesn't transfusing me with some of your healing factors transgress the Precepts of Survival?"

"Very true, and reflects well on you and your training that you bring that up. But what is the First Addendum? Hmm?"

Despite his pain Bob smiled as he replied, "I was taught it as 'don't be an asshole'."

"Harrumph. Well, yes, that's the colloquial version that seems to be all they teach these days." Bob could hear a distinct smile behind the stern voice.

"Sorry, Auntie. I believe the formal verse goes something like 'don't put undue emphasis on the letter of the Precepts to cause injury to the spirit of others'."

"Well done, young Bob. Now speaking of injuries, I'm afraid my healing factors can't do much about that leg of yours. The knee is repairable in situ, but not those bones."

Glancing towards his left leg, Bob saw what she was talking about. The broken ends of the tibia were sticking out several centimetres. It looked ugly and felt worse. "I see what you mean. From the angle of the broken ends, I'll have to apply traction until it is healed. How long will it take for your healing factors to repair it? My own could do it in a minute or two, but I'm afraid they'll be of no use."

"Quite so, Bob. Your healing factors are all but destroyed—you're going to need a complete transfusion. We're sufficiently related for my own to be able to help you, but dissimilar enough that it will be somewhat painful when they are fully activated. Not a good long-term solution for you, I'm afraid. As for how long it will take, I'm really not sure. It'll depend on your own energy levels. The Precepts can be stretched to allow me to supply new healing factors, but the rest is up to you."

"Of course, Auntie, and thank you again for the gift. Uhm, I'm going to need something to clamp my foot against as I pull. Would it be a breach of the Precepts if I lodged my foot in one of your scales and used it as a brace?"

"Not at all, dear. But you realize that I can't help in any way. The choices, and the successful mastering of the challenge, are yours alone."

"Understood, ma'am." Bob was so focused on moving closer to his Aunt, and not passing out, that he failed notice when she scuttled a ridged limb closer. She watching silently as he lodged his foot amongst the scales, then used his arms to heave himself back. The ends of the bone slowly slid back into his leg as Bob applied pressure. The strain of the effort forced him to shut his eyes in concentration and his arms to quiver—but he held.

Unfortunately, the same could not be said of his foot, which began to slowly slide back towards him. Taking care to check that Bob's full attention was occupied, Gertrude carefully wrapped a tendril around the foot and held it firmly, even pulling it back enough to equalize the forces acting on the bone. When the ends of the bones were lined up, Bob grunted softly with the effort required to hold the pose. Gertrude aimed a small protuberance at the leg and beamed a focused set of energies at it and to his damaged knee. She knew it was unlikely that Bob was capable of reshaping his own energies to supply her healing factors with what they required. And, Precepts be damned, Bob was her favourite nephew.

After nearly five minutes the repairs were all but complete and Bob was beginning to breathe more easily. Gertrude aimed a brief energy burst towards Bob's torso while softly retracting the tendril that was holding the foot. Shortly after she did that Bob took a deep breath, dislodged his foot from her scales, and slowly pulled his leg back.

"Best be getting some water now, dear. And perhaps a bite to eat if you can manage it."

"Yes, Auntie," murmured Bob. He looked around and gauged the distance to the water's edge—it looked to be a good ten metres. Without allowing any emotion to show, he began the process of arranging himself to crawl the distance.

"Just one second, dear." Gertrude swivelled her body and one of her longer protrusions carved a channel from the water to almost where Bob lay. He looked at her and quirked an eyebrow. "I'm very grateful, Auntie, but is this quite proper?"

"It is more than one body length away from you," was the prim reply. "That is the well-established minimum distance."

That wasn't a rule that Bob had ever heard of, but he wasn't about to argue. He managed to roll over to the now-filled channel and drank his fill. A few strands of seaweed floated by so he ate those and realized that he was actually rather hungry. A few more strands drifted by, with an unseen assist from Gertrude, and he made short work of those. He uttered a contented sigh that stopped short as he realized that there was a strange craving for something else. Bob tilted his head and listened intently—his new healing factors were trying to tell him something. He swallowed several handfuls of sand, washing them down with some of the brackish water.

"It'll be interesting to see how your silicon-based healing factors integrate with mine," he said. "They seem to have healed things well enough, at least in the short term."

Gertrude seemed a bit flustered. "I do hope that it will work out. You'll be able to deal with any issues once you get your new transfusion."

Bob frowned at that. "Not sure when that'll be, Auntie. I do a lot of travelling around nowadays and don't think I'll be getting home any time soon."

"Speaking of travelling, dear, how did you get here? The portal was rather confused about that. And doing a bounce-jump upon arrival? Whatever for, dear? Is this some silly new game? I began a search for you, but it wasn't until I heard that subspace transmission that I could locate you."

Bob grimaced as he answered. "I was on the run from Set."

"From where?" came the brisk query.

"Not sure. Set called it an old prison planet. He fried the portal after I went through, so I couldn't make any queries. 'Twas far away, though—only a handful of visible stars from where I was."

"He destroyed the portal you say?"

Bob nodded. "Not entirely, though. I was able to make use of the remains to synchronize with my apportation field and transport here."

Gertrude shook her head, displaying deep sadness. "All the prison planets were abandoned long, long ago. They were designed to be unreachable except by portal, and those were of very limited functionality. How did you survive there, much less find the energy to apport here?" Bob described his experiences there, as he carefully tested the many repairs to his body.

"That was very clever, dear boy. Combining an apport with a portal transit is a rare skill, indeed. Still, that explains how Set and his followers were able to damage you so severely. And yet you were still able to construct a makeshift subspace amplifier. Your father would be very proud of you, Bob. I know you chaffed and suffered under his tutelage ... more so than any of your siblings. Yet here you stand, a testament to the Precepts of Survival." There was obvious pride in her voice.

"Thank you, ma'am," said Bob bowing his head.

Gertrude continued in a stern voice, "But I've been hearing stories about you. You've been gadding about, causing problems for the entire Family, not just your own, and not just Set. Oh, wipe that grin off your face, Bob, this is no minor matter."

"Yes, Auntie," was all Bob could say. The grin grew even larger.

"Why interfere? You always hated the politics of the Family and ran away to escape it, as I recall."

Bob shook his head, took a deep breath, and looked at Gertrude. "It needed doing, it's as simple as that." His tone held a hint of defiance. "Yes, I bummed around for a long time. But I saw things. Things I couldn't overlook." His face took on a faraway look as he talked. "The portal system was being modified—a change here, a tweak there. Some routes were only accessible from specific portals, passkeys were changed, that sort of thing. On one planet the encircling forest had been contracted to almost the minimum, as if being prepared to be enclosed within a structure. Like a temple. Set's been setting those up, you know. Those tweaks to the portals were my elder sister's ham-fisted work."

Gertrude nodded. "That sort of thing happens now and again, you know. One or two of the young ones gets all worked up and try to set up a small empire. It never works out and things go back to the way they were soon enough."

"Not this time, Auntie. Set was changing the game. Those thugs you disposed of? Each of those represented an enormous standing army from a different world. And each of those has even more worlds serving their expansion. He was even making alliances with the Ravens."

His aunt shuddered at the latter. "Well, that might not be entirely bad, you know. No-one has tried to contact them in a very long time. They're just so ... alien." Gertrude shuddered, sending ripples throughout the length of her body.

"He also made an alliance with the Refusers. Was attempting to apply metamorphosis technology to them."

Gertrude stiffened as she flung herself into air while bellowing a curse. She descended until she was directly in front of Bob's face. "Are you sure?" Her voice was low, flat, and dangerous.

Bob nodded. "I stumbled across a bootleg medical facility that Set was running. Found some Refuser-descendants there. Sent all the data logs and biological samples to Uncle Sid and Aunt Freida. Found more traces of them in Set's temples."

His aunt drifted back, settling onto the ground with delicacy the belied her bulk. Then she let out a huff and said, "If I'd known he had done something like that I'd have done worse than send him home slightly injured." Bob felt sure that the inflicted injuries had been more than 'slight'. He looked at her and said, "That's why I didn't tell you. Even injuring him will cause repercussions. Anything more would have caused a serious breach. Or worse."

"I thought you were the one who declared himself to be above Family politics," said Gertrude in a soft voice. Then her voice strengthened. "But don't you go worrying about me, young man. His breach of etiquette deserved no less. Your father will agree with that, I'm sure."

"But not my mother."

"No, of course not. But that won't really change things between her and I. Is she working with Set, do you think?"

Bob nodded. "According to the few messages from my father, she is. She's gotten ... chaotic. Much more so than ever before. As has my eldest sister. Set's certainly put a bug in their ears about something. I've had to neutralize some of their antics to preserve lives."

"And these lives you are saving, nephew—these are the younger races?"

Bob nodded.

"Why? I'd truly like to hear your reasons."

"Because it's not right, Auntie," said Bob with some heat. "The others treat the younger races as toys or trifles—refer to them as 'merely human'. Most of us stick to our home planets—or tread very lightly—but others go out of their way to intrude. Some, like Set, have gone the warlord route."

"Perhaps the younger races need guidance, dear. Someone to instruct them in the ways of the larger universe and raise them up."

"No, Auntie Gertrude, they deserve to be left alone. To make their own mistakes and determine their own fate. To reap the rewards of wisdom or failure, as the Precepts instruct. But whatever their fate, it should be theirs and theirs alone to determine."

"Hmm, and where did you ever get such queer ideas, dear? So terribly old fashioned and out of favour."

Bob gave an exaggerated shrug. "Oh, here and there. Reading the old books. And, just perhaps, hearing a story or two from you. Remember how I used to come here when I was just a boy? We'd come down to the beach to watch the sun set and the stars come out, and you'd sing stories to me for hours until I fell asleep."

"Yes, I do seem to recall something of those days," Gertrude said, a hint of wistfulness in her voice. "You were such an active boy, but you'd always make time to sit with me. Good days, even if they are long gone."

Bob snapped his fingers. "That reminds me—I brought you a gift." He reached towards the knapsack and began opening it.

"A gift for me? Oh, how kind. I scanned the knapsack when I took it off you, but the wrappings are coated in impervium. Thought it best to leave it for you."

"Oh, you'll like this. Did you want to unwrap it?" He held it out to her.

"If you'd be so kind as to do it for me, dear, I'd much

appreciate it. I'm not as lithe as I used to be." In truth, Gertrude wanted to see how well Bob's hands were working. His injuries had been more severe than she suspected he realized.

As he carefully removed the wrappings, Bob talked. "I was on Earth a while back and picked this up for you." He finishing the unwrapping and proudly held up a package.

"Is that tea?" asked Gertrude with genuine eagerness.

"Oolong black dragon. I remember you talking about it."

"Oh, Bob, what a thoughtful gift," exclaimed Gertrude. She was touched by the gift and the thought behind it.

Bob was delighted that he'd managed to both surprise and please the old girl. "I'm afraid that I wasn't able to bring along a tea pot ..." he began.

"Not to worry, dear, I have just the thing. Let me fetch it." The air rippled and tore as a small rift opened up. Gertrude reached inside and brought out an ornate teapot and kettle.

"I remember those," exclaimed Bob. "You'd make tea with them every time I visited."

Gertrude smiled. "Indeed. Then we'd walk to the beach and you'd snuggle up next to me. We'd talk for hours."

Bob smiled broadly in contented recollection. "How about I make us some tea? Oh, that reminds me, I chatted with Aunt Freida not too long ago. She sends her regards and said to remember her to you. Since then, Uncle Sid mentioned that the two of you had been messaging."

"Oh, thank you for that. She and some of our old friends have developed a serious interest in some fascinating philosophical ideas. Very intriguing stuff. However did you come across her? Please tell me how she and Sid are doing. Their letters have been light on personal details, with nothing about how Sid came back."

"Well, she's homesteading in an inland sea on one of Dad's worlds after beating back a mysterious series of plagues and doing a lot of gardening. Sid was on Earth battling plagues of his own, then got settled in. Recently I've been sending them ... uhm ... some injured parties that didn't want to go to the official medical facilities."

"Oh, it sounds like there's something of a story behind all that."

"Indeed there is, Auntie, indeed there is. Will you pour or shall I?"

As the sun set and stars appeared, they talked long into the night.

CHAPTER TWELVE
Old Friends

The tea room's young waitress was enjoying a rest after a busy afternoon. There would be another rush in an hour or so, but for now she was content to sit and read her book. The door's hanging bell jangled to indicate the arrival of another customer. She stifled a groan as she got to her feet, but presented a smile to the customer in the booth. The smile became strained as she got a look at the man sitting there. Except for the well-tailored suit he looked like one of the hard-used homeless men she had seen in London during her last trip there. His skin looked weathered and worn, almost like leather, except for what looked like a dull metallic sheen to it.

"What can I get for you, sir?" she said.

The man looked up into her face and she shivered at the intensity of the gaze that reached right into her. He smiled, but it was the look of a hard man trying to appear less frightening.

"Good day, young miss. Could I trouble you for a pot of oolong black dragon tea, please?" His voice was not unkind but had an edge to it that matched his hard looks.

"Uhm, not sure we carry that, to be honest. Is there something else I could get for ya?"

He shook his head while maintaining the smile. "Really?

Perhaps the proprietor might be the one to ask about it. Memory can be such a tricky thing."

She opened her mouth to speak, then closed it. Without saying another word she turned and hurried into the back room where her mother was.

"Mum, there's an awfully queer-looking gent out front. Asking for oolong black dragon tea. Told him we ain't got none, but he said to ask you." She wrapped her arms around herself and shivered.

The middle-age woman jerked upright. "Queer? How? Did he say or do anything wrong to you?"

"Nah, nothing like that. Just ... looks not right, somehow. Physically, I mean. Talks polite enough, though."

A frown crossed the older woman's face as a long-buried memory teased at her consciousness. She shook her head to focus on the here and now, and said, "Never mind; take yer break and I'll deal with him." With that she walked out to the serving area, wiping her hands on her apron as she went. Her bad arm had been acting up the past few days and her temper was getting frayed. She got to the gentleman's table and found him studying the menu with great interest.

"Sir, we've got none of that oolong ..." Her voice faded away as the man lifted his face to look at her.

"I'm sorry to hear that, Celcilia. Well, whatever you have handy will do nicely, I'm sure."

"You." It came out as a soft exhalation as she put a hand on the table for support.

Bob came quickly to his feet and helped her into the chair opposite his.

"Sorry to barge in on you without notice. But I was in the area." His smile, although faint, was warm and genuine. "But sit and take a load off your feet. You look like you've had a hard day."

"And you look ... Goddess, Bob. You look like you've been dragged through Hell itself. Multiple times."

A wry smile briefly touched his face. "Not far from the truth, I suppose. Not dead yet, though."

She shook her head in amazement and wonder. "All these years and not a word from you. Still, I guess I owe you thanks for setting me up with the funds for this." She waved a hand to encompass the shop.

"I owed you, and I always try to pay my debts." His face had grown serious.

"Where did you go? How have you been?" She held up a hand, turned her head, and called out, "Rhoswen, dear, bring us a pot of tea will ya, love? Anything that's handy." She turned back to face Bob. "My daughter. Met her da at the bank when I first tried accessing the account you set up for me. He was just a clerk then. Manages it now." She was clearly quite proud of her husband's accomplishments.

"I'm very glad to hear that you've done well for yourself, Celcilia. It was something that was of concern to me."

"But not concerning enough to come back sooner, was it?" There was a note of bitterness and echoes of an old hurt in her voice.

"I've been busy."

"Places to go and worlds to save, is that it?"

Rhoswen arrived bearing a pot which she placed in the centre of the table, then placed a china cup in front of each of them. "Will that be all, mum?" She looked as if she wanted to stay.

"Yes, thank you, love. Go back to your break."

The girl moved reluctantly but hurried away at a hard stare from her mother.

"She's a lovely girl." Bob said, but it was obvious that social niceties were now almost foreign to him.

"She is that, all right."

"Does she know about ..." his voice trailed off on a questioning note.

"Nah. What was I going to tell her? Told some of it to her

da, but learned right quick not to tell much." She shook her head. "Wouldn't believe it myself if it weren't for my arm." She rubbed at it in manner that suggested long habit.

Bob sighed softly, though the expression on his face didn't change much. "I am sorry about that."

"Don't be," came the harsh reply. "Weren't none of yer doin'. And you saved my life. From Hell itself, if not worse."

"Worse?"

She snorted a laugh that was almost like real humour. "Back here with no job, no useful education, no prospects, and a bum arm to boot. Not many options for someone in that state." Her gaze turned to look out the window, but focused on something far away in time. "Lay in that hospital for the better part of a day until they fixed me up and discharged me. The homeless get treated last and tossed out as quick as possible. Found a place to sit and went through all the belongings they'd given back to me. Nice bag, by the way. Used it for years."

Her gaze returned to his face. "Anyway. Found the note you left with the banking information. Figured it for a joke, but had nothing to lose so I went to the bank and handed it to them. Worked a treat—just like winning the lottery. Well, not enough to retire and live a life of luxury but certainly for a fresh start." She waved her right hand to indicate the store. "Bought out Eiriana—this used to be her shop, you may recall. She wanted to travel and I needed to earn a living."

"And you stayed here."

She gave a small, amused laugh. "Hadn't planned to. But had to stay for a few days. Wynny put me up at her B and B. Remember her?" Bob nodded. Celcilia continued, "Sake, Rhoswen's da, had some questions about things, there were papers to sign, and it took a while to set things up." She gave Bob a mildly sour look. "Your instructions were less than clear, you know."

Bob attempted to look innocent, but was long out of

practise. "My apologies. I didn't have time to study your planet's financial intricacies in detail."

Celcilia tried to glare at him but ended up laughing instead. Still chuckling, she poured tea for both of them. They spent a minute in companionable silence as they drank.

After a minute, Celcilia spoke. "So, Bob. What happened after you dropped me off here? Did you manage to settle things with your family at all?"

It was Bob's turn for a gaze that looked far away for several seconds before he turned to look at her. "I stepped up my campaign to stop Set. Turned out to be something worse than I ever imagined, so I pressed harder. He pressed back. Caught me a couple of times. We fought."

"And you won?"

He shook his head. "No. Almost, but not quite. He would have killed me—almost did, in fact—except that an aunt of mine interceded. I needed medical treatment but couldn't use the official sites. Aunt Gertrude healed me as best she could." He looked at his hands, then back up to her. "Did a good job, too, for all that our healing factors weren't entirely compatible."

"That caused the ... uhm ... special tan?"

Bob snorted a small laugh. "That and a few other things. Nothing important. Nothing that has stopped me from doing what needed to be done."

"Which was?" she asked softly, guessing what the answer would be.

"I had to put an end to it."

"End to what?"

"All of it. I found out who was behind Set's plans. Put a stop to it once and for all."

She stared hard at him. "What did you do?"

He smiled at the tone in her voice, reminding him as it did of elderly aunts quizzing him when he had been an unruly child. His own voice was mildly dismissive. "Oh, nothing much. I've destroyed most of the portal network and am working on the rest. Oh, and forced the Eldest Ones to step up their planned evolutionary upgrade."

"What? How did you get here? Wait ... what upgrade?"

Bob barked a quick laugh. It had obviously been a long time since he'd had cause to laugh at all and he was out of practise. "Remember I told you about the Eldest Ones?" She nodded and he continued. "They developed a new philosophy—the Philosophy of Change—that actually allows people to progress to a higher type of being, physically as well as mentally. Truly amazing, actually. So I decided to help things along."

"Meaning?"

"I ... persuaded ... people to take training from the Eldest Ones. For their own good, you understand."

"Oh, yes. Of course," she said in a low mocking tone.

His eyes twinkled. "Oh, yes. All sorts of wrong-thinking folks needed some counselling from older and wiser heads. Well, floating balls of coherent energy, but you get the idea."

Celcilia could only nod.

"It all started out rather slowly, but it turns out there was already a groundswell of interest. The desire for a change in the status quo had been brewing for a long, long time. More so than I realized. My own modest efforts only forced things to snowball faster than expected."

"And who did you piss off doing that?"

"Ah, you know me so well. Well, in this case pretty much everyone."

"By everyone you mean ..."

"Everyone," he said firmly. "The ones I encouraged to get re-educated were rather angry. Their relatives and friends were angry at the way I'd done my encouraging. And on it went. The destruction of the portals just added fuel to the fire."

"What about those elevated beings?"

Bob grinned. "Well, I'd fouled up their carefully prepared plans, you see. They weren't prepared for the influx of people and had to rush the training. Many important noses got put out of joint."

Celcilia snorted. "Imagine that."

Bob managed to look hurt. "It was for everyone's good, really. Then, of course, the Eldest Ones were caught totally off guard by the groundswell of interest in the Change. Elevated beings they may be, but they still don't like being made to look silly. And far too many don't have any sense of humour whatsoever."

Celcilia re-filled their cups as she thought about what she'd heard. They sipped in silence for a time before Celcilia blurted out, "Here, now. The portals—why are you destroying them? With everyone becoming an elevated being, why destroy the entire network?"

Bob's face became serious. "To stop anyone from interfering with the younger races ever again. The unmodified of my kind that I told you about—the Refusers—can access some of the portals, and they're a nasty lot. On top of that they're allied with a very manipulative alien species. Stopping everyone from transiting between worlds is the only way to save your people. With my people elevated--or most of them at any rate--there'll be no way to re-create the network. I've left the private portals but destroyed the galaxy-spanning network. Well, mostly. Not quite done, yet."

He shook his head sadly. "There'll never be anything like it again, I shouldn't think. My kind are now too few and spread too thin to recreate it. No-one else has the combination of technologies nor the long-term society." He sighed heavily. "It really was our ancestors' shining achievement ... but it was time to end it."

"Does no-one object to all this re-education business and destruction of portals?"

Bob gave an amused snort. "After fighting Set and his lot I can handle anyone. He'd trained himself and his followers for battle. Now, he and his followers are being re-educated, healed, and trained in the Change. Whether they want to or not. Compared to them, anyone else is just a thug. Dangerous enough, but nothing I can't handle."

"Your brother went willingly? Or after you beat him?"

"Heh. No, I had to trick him into chasing me through a portal." Bob shook his head in wonder. "He'd forgotten how I'd do that when we were children, only this time I knew more tricks. Did a split transit, where I went to one planet and he got dumped in with the Change lot. I chuckled about it for days."

Celcilia chuckled and shook her head. Then she grew serious. "Wait ... do these elevated ones not object to the portals being destroyed? Do they not use them?"

"Not as far as I can tell. Don't much care, actually."

"What do you mean you don't care? What's going to happen when you join up for this change upgrade thing?"

Bob sighed. "That isn't going to happen." He held up a hand to forestall her queries. "There's politics involved, you see. For the first time in a very, very long time my people have been forced to sit down together and figure out what they want to do in life. As a species, I mean. Last time that happened was at the end of the Great Wars and we've been coasting along ever since. Apparently agreement on something small was required to get things moving—turning their backs on me was it."

"Meaning what, exactly?" she asked in a small voice.

"Hmm, best I can describe it is as being 'shunned'. Interaction with me is forbidden. The only exception being if official permission is sought and unbreakable restrictions placed upon them."

"Restrictions?"

"Think of it as a geas ... a binding. In practical terms, they can't speak to me or directly interfere with my actions. Only observe."

"Observe what?"

Bob chuckled. "Turns out they like to watch me encourage people to join them. Well, that and to make sure I don't do more than hurt their feelings as I do it. Which I do. Mostly."

"More or less," she added.

He nodded and they both chuckled at that. Their cups, and the pot, were empty. Celcilia asked, "Another pot?"

Bob shook his head. "I'm sorry, but I have to go."

She shook her head, sadness writ plain on her face. "Where are you off to now?"

"First, to destroy the portal in the forest. Then off to the next planet. Not many left, now."

"What happens to us? To all the other human planets?"

"Whatever you want to have happen. You're on your own."

"What about those others things lurking about? Those unchanged of your kind and the remnants of the other species?"

"They are few in number and stick to their own planets. Don't poke them and they won't poke back. If any wander by, just leave them alone."

"And if they want a fight?"

"Look, don't worry about it. The odds are truly astronomically small that anything will just wander by any time soon. This is an unused part of the galaxy. Not to mention that the Great Wars left swathes of dead worlds and solar systems between the human worlds. It's a big galaxy, and FTL ships don't shrink it by much."

"What about the Elites? You once told me that there were squads of them somewhere out there doing Set's work."

He favoured her with an amused look. "You remember a lot of things. That's surprising, but I'm impressed."

She returned his look with one of her own. "I remember it all. Might not have told much of it to anyone, but wrote it all down to make sure I remembered it cleanly. So answer the question, please."

Once again he was reminded of being questioned by an elderly aunt. "The destruction of the portals trapped them on whatever planet they were on. Some got eliminated by local forces."

"And the rest?"

Bob sighed. "Will have to wait, I'm afraid. Some—hopefully most—are addicted to a drug called pure quill. That's what the smoke was that Kydos used in her ceremonies. Without the drug, they lapse into catatonia and die. Once their supplies are gone, the problem will solve itself."

"What about the damage they'll cause until they die? What about the ones who aren't addicted?" Celcilia asked in low, sharp voice.

"Best I can do, Celcilia. There's only one of me, and taking out the portals and dealing with my own kind has to be my priority."

"What about getting help doing this cleanup business?"

"It's the Change, I'm afraid. It's swept up everyone except myself and those I've yet to convince to join it. Once joined, the shunning is mandatory. The others hate and fear me."

"Goddess, Bob. You've really, really pissed off the great and mighty this time, haven't you?" she sighed in exasperation.

"Heh. It's a gift. A gift honed by much practise."

That got a snort of laughter out of her, but after a moment she grew serious. "Anything nasty left on Earth?"

"Only whatever was created by yourselves." He stood up. "Time to go, I'm afraid."

She stood up as well. "What happens when it's all over and done? When there's no more monsters left to fight or bridges to burn?"

He gave her a wan smile. "Rest, I think. I'm feeling tired to the bone and need a long vacation. But seeing you again has cheered me up more than you realize."

"Will they ever take you back?" she asked in a low voice, fearing what the answer might be.

He shrugged and said in a weary tone, "I just don't know. It's all I can do to focus on the next task and the one after that and the one after that." He paused for a moment then said, "Goodbye, Celcilia. Thank you for surviving." In a more formal tone he added, "You are a credit to your ancestors. May you be a source of pride and inspiration for your descendants." Then he gave a small, formal bow, turned, and walked out of the store.

She stood there and watched as he walked away, then cleaned up the dishes from the table. Carrying them into the small kitchen she placed them into the sink and leaned heavily against it.

"Mum? Anything the matter?"

She turned and smiled at her daughter. "Not a thing, love. Look, why don't we close up early tonight and go for a walk? Like we used to."

Rhoswen smiled as she nodded. "But what about those dishes?"

"They'll keep until morning. Now, let's grab our wraps and head out before someone else comes by."

As they left Rhoswen asked, "Who was that man? You used to know him?"

"Oh, a long, long time ago. Not in the way you mean, though. He got me out of a bad spot. At risk to his own life, I might add. Oh, don't look at me that way, my girl. I had my wild times and adventures when I was your age. I had a somewhat different sort of upbringing, you see, and got sent down a nasty rabbit hole. You interested in hearin' about it? And if you're still set on headin' out to the uni and seein' the world, there's some tricks I should be passin' on to ya. As well as that boot knife of mine you've always fancied."

Her daughter gave her a disbelieving look as she nodded. "Even the weird stuff, mum? The stuff you whispered to da when you thought I was asleep?"

Celcilia chuckled. "All of that and more. Wrote it all down for you to read after I was gone. Seein' my old friend made me think you might want to hear it now."

The two women headed along the street arm in arm, intent on their discussion. The lights of the town were bright enough to mask the brief pulse of soft, pale light that came from the forest several kilometres away.

CHAPTER THIRTEEN
A Gathering of Spirits

The prey unleashed a fusillade of shots, then turned and ran. Bob evaded the energy blasts with slight twists of his body that slowed his progress only a bit. It was enough, though, for the prey to increase the distance between them. That was enough of an edge that the prey managed to evade Bob's sight once again. Rather than charging blindly ahead, Bob slowed to a halt and extended his sensorium. A moment of listening located a brief energy surge that signalled a failed apportation. The location was in the general area where Bob figured it would be.

The two of them had spent much of the day chasing each other in a twisting race through the forest. Bob had allowed himself to become the hunted for a time, which served to deplete the energy reserves and weapons of his target. His own reserves, on the other hand, were barely used. This was a task for which Bob had honed his abilities over many years and many similar chases. He gathered some fist-sized stones, and flung them towards his prey in the manner of a mortar attack. The object wasn't so much to hit his prey—although that often happened—but to keep him in a panicked state. Things went so much easier for all concerned when his prey panicked and allowed themselves to be herded.

The resulting gasps and moans heard a few seconds later

brought a smile to Bob's face. It was a faint smile, but all that his face was capable of these days. The years had not been easy for Bob and those hardships were writ plain upon him for all to see. His healing factors, once awesome in their abilities, were now capable only of healing wounds with little concern for cosmetic niceties. That no longer concerned him, as he never visited the worlds of the younger races any more.

The faint tingle of a familiar energy signature brought him up short. He uttered a soft sigh then turned around. "Wondered when one of you would show up," he said in a whisper.

A luminescent orb floated silently before him. Its edges weren't well defined, but it was roughly ovoid in shape and as tall as he was. There was little colour to it aside from a faint mother-of-pearl tinge.

"Ah. Still giving me the silent treatment, are we? Fine, but stay out of my way. I have prey to deal with."

He turned and began to walk away but the orb moved to block his path. Bob rolled his eyes. "Fine. His name is Virgil. In the past I'd have called him 'uncle', but I don't do polite honorifics any more. I'm going to destroy the portal on this world, and before I do that he needs to leave. As always, I've pre-programmed the portal to stay instantiated and send him to Aunt Gertrude's planet for philosophical re-training. For some reason, he is resisting. With, I might add, lethal force. I, on the other hand, have remained the perfect gentleman and used only minor force to protect myself."

Bob lifted his arms, spun once around, then lowered his arms to face the orb once more. "See? Not even so much as a sensor wand or grenade, as you lot demand. Still, one does what one can." He turned to leave, paused, then turned to face the orb. "Oh, you've probably noticed that I've set the portal to create a jangle field around this area to inhibit apporting or levitating. That's only fair, is it not? Now that the forms have been observed, I'll thank you to get out of my way and let me go about my chore."

The orb hesitated for a moment before moving off to one side. Bob gave a slight bow before hurrying to catch up with his prey. The Changed never interfered much, but they did insist that he at least pretend to treat his prey like humans. He had to allow as they had a good point, as it was far too easy to start dehumanizing them. That path led to madness and was one that he'd managed to avoid ... with increasing difficulty.

As he ran he wondered if this was someone he knew. At first the Changed would often appear in forms similar to their aspects, but now only appeared as orbs. Or perhaps it was the same person each time. Although there were subtle variations between them it was impossible to tell for sure. He understood that most of the people he knew had undergone the training and transformed into their Changed form. Many of the rest had done it voluntarily or retreated to family worlds, but there were still a few holdouts where they shouldn't be. Most of the public portals, such as the one here, were gone. Only a few more to deal with and he would be able to rest. There were days when the thought of that was the only thing that kept him going.

A slight stumble brought his full attention back to the here-and-now. Bob gave his head an annoyed shake as he focused on the task at hand. He could hear his prey—Virgil, as he was supposed to think of him—moving about, but in a somewhat more controlled fashion that drifted away from the portal. That was annoying but not unexpected. On the more positive side, Virgil was heading towards the crest of a hill that rose on the edge of a drop-off that led to a rocky plain. Bob turned to the orb and said, "This could get interesting."

Bob ran, taking advantage of natural cover as he moved towards the drop-off. Once there, he was in a slightly open area and the orb trailed behind bobbing up and down as if trying to warn him about something. A blast of energy rippled the air where Bob had been, but he'd dodged out of the way and into the field of boulders. He skipped among the boulders, bouncing off their sides in a random fashion. Energy blasts rippled the air, missing him by a considerable margin, until he vanished behind a wall of tall boulders. He paused for a moment then sidled amongst them taking care to remain out of Virgil's line of sight.

A shimmer of nearby energy caused him to turn his head. The orb was now by his side. Bob frowned. "Did Virgil see you follow me?"

The orb wobbled from side to side, signalling "no".

"Hmm," said Bob. "You're more talkative than the usual Changed. But thank you for not giving away my position. He's settled into a very nice spot up on that hill. Ready to fend off any assault and got me pinned down." Bob grinned. "And with all that external weaponry, too. Well, let's see if we can get him to expend some more of his ammunition. Time for some active measures."

A slight protrusion extended from Bob's neck which he pointed towards some specific boulders further into the field. The air wavered as he transmitted a short burst of energy. A second later several projectiles came screaming from the top of the hill and exploded into the boulders. Bob repeated the exercise but aimed slightly to one side and further away. Again came a rain of projectiles. He aimed at a third set of boulders but there was no answering fire.

"Well, he's either out of ammunition or he's realized that I'm using the rocks to bounce a false signal at him. Let's move over there just in case he decides to lay a barrage in this direction." Matching action to words Bob moved a dozen metres to one side then squatted to wait. The orb followed, keeping a low profile.

"Oh, that's a nice slither you've got there," commented Bob. "Ever have any combat training?"

The orb remained motionless.

Bob uttered a theatrical sigh. "And here I thought we were getting along so well, too. Well, those first pulses I did were ranging bursts. Between his firing and the backscatter from the bursts, I have a good idea where he is. Now, take a good look at where we are in relation to him. Want to pass me a few of those fist-sized stones? No? Never mind, I'll do it myself."

After collecting a dozen suitable stones, he hefted each one to gauge its weight before putting it down before him in order. "Is it time?" Bob asked. "I think it's time. Let's do this, shall we?"

He turned towards the low hills in the distance and fired off several bursts of energy. The air rippled with each one, but the bright sun made them all but invisible. A volley of hypersonic missiles streaked forth from the hilltop to slam against the far hills. Then another volley, followed quickly by another. As the sound of the explosions reached them, Bob stood up and lobbed his stones like grenades towards the hilltop. He bounded away, angling up the slope, taking care to stay behind cover.

A series of yells from the hilltop, followed by a couple of screams of pain, gave Bob the signal he was waiting for. Unleashing a burst of speed that was almost too fast to follow, he broke cover and bounded up the hill. He entered the bush at the base of the hill and, despite his speed, managed to make a noiseless ascent.

By the time the orb caught up, Bob was chasing his prey through the forest. Any time Virgil paused to fire a weapon, the attempt was neutralized by a well-placed stick or stone hitting with considerable force. The non-lethal attacks, plus their efficiency at preventing any retaliatory response, served to increase Virgil's feelings of frustration to the level of panic.

As they ran, Bob kept up a steady stream of stones and sticks that struck Virgil like a plague of stinging insects. To add to the effect Bob hooted and hollered like a banshee.

Every so often he tossed in the occasional piece of helpful advice, "Run, run you can't escape fate. Run, run back to the gate." As Bob had explained to the orbs on more than one previous occasion, "Poetry helps to open the mind to new ideas."

Within a few minutes Virgil was reduced to a sobbing, panic-stricken wretch whose only thought was to get away. He tried to move away from the direction of the portal, but soon found that his pain intensified unless he went where Bob wanted him to. It wasn't long before he reached the portal, only to find that it would only allow one destination to be selected. With a final scream of defiance—ruined somewhat by sobbing and tears—Virgil accepted his fate and entered the transit film.

Bob skidded to a stop an arm's length away from the film and instructed the portal to terminate the connection. He stood there with his head bowed, hands on knees, sucking in lungfuls of air at a rapid rate. The orb came up to find Bob's shoulders quivering and his breathing ragged. Then he raised his head and the orb realized that he was laughing so hard that it was interfering with his breathing.

It took nearly a minute before he got himself under control. He wiped away tears as the laughter wound down. "Hoo. Haven't had that much fun in ages," he gasped. Then he looked at the orb and grinned. "Didn't use to tire me out quite so badly, though. Oh, let me catch my breath." It took a couple of minutes before his breathing returned to almost-normal and the laughter reduced to a broad smile.

The orb bobbed up and down, twirled, and made a wiping motion along the ground.

"Ah, aren't you the chatty one?" Bob said in a cheerful voice. "Yes, I am indeed going to destroy the portal. Well, set it to self-destruct and then leave. I'm getting rather good at this, you know." A shadow of sadness settled across his face, erasing his earlier merriment. His gaze was far away for a moment before he shook his head and looked at the orb. "I'm truly sorry about this, though. There's not many portals left and the universe will never see their like again. Certainly not the network that used to be."

Then his face hardened. "But there's a race of sentients on this planet. Primitive, yes, but I'll not leave a danger like this hanging over their heads."

He turned to look at the portal, and his eyes took on a distant look as he communed with it. Then his face took on a puzzled look and he muttered, "Strange. That's not right." The portal began to hum. Softly at first, but gradually increasing in pitch and volume.

"Oh, this is not good. Virgil's set the portal for destruction. Not total conversion, but still enough to cause a planetary catastrophe."

"Can you stop it?" came a soft, feminine voice from the orb. Her voice was strained, as if it took a great effort to speak at all.

Bob's head snapped around. "You can talk," he exclaimed.

"Can you stop it?" the orb repeated in an urgent tone.

"Uhm, not sure. Let me think."

"Run away."

"Shush. No. I told you, there are sentients on this planet." He continued to stare at the portal, trying to ignore the sounds coming from it. "I can't stop it, but I can minimize it. Higher yield than what I normally set them for, but not too bad."

At a wave of his hand whole sections of the portal vanished to reveal intricate patterns of energy. His sensorium fully extended, Bob walked from section to section beaming focused streams of energy into specific places.

"Bob, I can save you. Come with me."

He shook his head. "No. Have to finish this. I won't let innocents be harmed by our mistakes. Not ever again."

The sounds coming from the portal lowered to a

low-pitched moaning.

"What did you do?"

Bob grinned. "Something very clever. I can't stop the blast, but I've set things to deflect it upward and into subspace." He paused for a moment before adding, "Mostly."

"Meaning?"

"Meaning the jangle field is still active, can't be deactivated, and we need to run away as fast as we can." He spun around and began running as quickly as he could through the dense grove. The low moaning from the portal began to rise into a loud, tortured scream.

He'd only taken a few steps when the orb heard Bob say "oops" just before the portal exploded. Her own shields flared under the impact, but shrugged off the released energies without any problem. Bob, however, was not so protected. She saw his flaming body tossed and slammed through the trees, and finally into a large boulder some distance away. A ripple of energy ripped through the air as his implanted systems shattered and discharged. It was obvious that he was dead and damaged beyond any hope of resurrection.

The orb modified itself into the shape of a young woman which grew more solid in appearance. She knelt next to Bob's shattered body, a protective bubble of energy shielding them both from the fury unleashed by the explosion. Eventually the winds and the storm of debris died down. The portal grove was now a shallow crater, but the worst of the destruction was limited to just beyond where she knelt. Looking up she could see where a beam of energy had torn through the atmosphere. Bob's tinkering had, indeed, managed to force the worst of the blast upward. The sentients of this world would be safe, suffering only inclement weather for a few days as the shock wave rippled across the planet.

"Oh, my brother. What have you done?" she whispered.

The sun set, shining blood red through the dust. She sat

there all through the night and until the next morning, never leaving his side. As the sun rose, she came to her feet and with her hands dug a shallow grave next to the boulder where he fell. She put his remains into it and began piling stones around it. With each stone she paused to remember a pleasant memory about him. It took some time but eventually it reached the height of her chest. It was late in the afternoon when she finished and she had become covered in dirt and dust.

She stood beside his cairn looking drained. No longer capable of shedding tears, her sorrow was nonetheless deep. The sun was almost to the point of setting by the time she composed herself. Gathering her energies, she placed her hands on the stones, closed her eyes, and concentrated. The air around her rippled and the stones began to glow with heat. First a dull red heat then soon a nearly white heat that fused the stones, and what they covered, together. Only then did she stop and take a step back, oblivious to the heat.

"Farewell, brother. You never returned home for my Naming Day, but I never stopped loving you. You always watched over me and made me laugh. You protected me from the worst of the attentions of our siblings, even when that came at a cost to you. The least I can do is ensure that no-one will ever use your remains to create a shadow of you."

She paused as a wistful look came to her face. "I never stopped expecting you to return home. Every morning I would go to the water's edge and wait for the dawn boat to bring you home. But you never came. It took some time, but eventually I began to understand why. Even then I would still go to the water's edge every morning. I sent messages, of course, but Mother intercepted or destroyed them. I assume she did the same with any messages from you."

Then she smiled. "You would have enjoyed my Naming Day ceremonies, I think. The True Dragons sent a representative. Did you hear that I helped to broker a peace treaty between us? Their ambassador caused quite a stir when it arrived. Many self-important noses were put out of joint. Afterwards, your name was bandied about as a bad example. It was a fine time, but I missed you."

She stood upright and assumed a formal pose. "I see you. Hear me and see me. As our ancestors shaped us, as our actions define us, so our descendants shall know us. Know me by my chosen name—Ashira. Declared to be an adult, I assume my duties and responsibilities."

Her head bowed in sorrow for a moment before she regained control of her emotions. The drumbeat of many wings caused her to look up. Then came a cacophony of shrieking crows, a wide swath of them in the sky approaching her location. Her face became as emotionless as a stone image. Her voice had a matching chill to it as she spoke over the sound of the crows. "He beat you. Accept that. And accept this—if you desecrate his grave I will desecrate your home worlds. Both the First and Second Nests."

The sounds from the crows, if anything, increased in volume as they circled around the cairn.

In response she gave a grim smile. Her throat writhed while being reshaped from within. She opened her mouth and spoke in a harsh alien language that no human should have known, much less be able to pronounce. When she was done speaking, her throat returned to normal as she waited for a response.

The flocks continued to circle the cairn, but had become silent.

The air around her began to ripple as she spoke. "We know the locations of your home and colony worlds. Any who are on this world will assemble at the southern pole by this time tomorrow and we will arrange to return them. We know that it has been you tampering with the younger races as well as ourselves. We know that it was you who launched attacks on us. We will no longer tolerate your interference. We know you to be a blending between the Refuser Faction and the Ravens. If that is your chosen path, you are free to walk it. But you are to leave all human worlds and return to your own immediately or face extinction. This is the decision of the Conclave of Humanity."

The plaintive cry of a single crow broke the silence.

Her laughter was short and sharp. "Any of you who do not return will be exterminated as we find them. Did you really expect anything else? Now leave."

The flocks circled for one more circuit before heading away as fast as they could fly.

"Good choice," she said as the ripples around her subsided.

Then she looked once more at the cairn, her face now serene. "You missed a few portals, Bob. But don't worry, I'll finish cleaning up for you. And I'll make sure they know that it was you who sent me."

The air around her glowed with a heatless light that outshone the sun. After a few seconds it subsided and she was gone.

CHAPTER FOURTEEN
Whispers in the Dark

The signal twisted its way through the tortuous realms of the alternate spaces. Although so fast that it made the speed of light seem like a crawl, it still took years to arrive at its destination. Its initial powerful scream was now a faint whisper but that was enough for the receivers tuned to detect it. They, in turn, passed it on to the controller circuits. They in turn tasted and tested the signal before deciding that it was, indeed, what they'd been ordered to wait for. Mechanisms and devices were awoken from their slumbers, and the station brought to full alert status. The medical bay hummed into life, and after a full systems check set about its business.

Hours, days, and weeks passed. The station cared little about the passage of time, focusing only on what was being created in the medical bay. That facility had created a vat filled with specific mixtures of chemicals, bathed with specific radiations at specific times. Within that fluid environment an accretion of materials arose, slowly forming into bones and tissues. Eventually a human body was formed, gaunt and ill-defined. The fluids drained, the body was punctured by needles, and mechanisms poked and prodded to stimulate muscle growth. In time the body filled out and the mechanisms withdrew, as well as most of the needles.

Probes attached themselves to the bare skull and the room was bathed in the rippling lights as the control panels around the room flashed and flickered. Initially dormant, the body began to make small twitches. Those grew into full spasms that calmed into twitches after drugs were injected. Soon even the twitching ceased, and the body began to breathe of its own volition. The remainder of the probes and needles withdrew. The wounds left by them quickly healed. The breathing of the body was slow and steady, as if sleeping. The eyelids were shut, but the eyes moved as if dreaming.

The room issued soft sounds as it watched its creation. Then, at the appropriate moment, the structures around the body were withdrawn. The table supporting the body tilted until it was almost vertical, and began vibrating softly. The eyes of the creation flickered for several seconds, then opened. Its breathing quickened, becoming irregular as the creation softly groaned. The room crooned a series of soothing sounds and soon the creation's breathing evened out. Throughout all of this its eyes were darting about the room. The illumination level, initially quite dim, began to brighten. When the creation began making sounds of distress, the room darkened slightly.

There were loose-fitting restraints which the creation fumbled at in an attempt to free itself. The modest effort exhausted it, and several pauses were required before the restraints were unlatched. A nutrient tube was extended towards the face, and the contents were consumed with obvious relish. Soon thereafter, the creature spat the tube out, and it was retracted back into the table.

The eyes of the creation could better focus now, and it looked around the room as much as it could without raising its head. Soft sounds began to come out of its mouth. Not sounds of distress, but rather the exercising of long-unused vocal cords.

The room clucked and muttered to itself as a portion of

the wall cleared and a human image appeared upon it. "Hi. No doubt you're a bit confused by all this, so lay back and listen. If you're seeing this, then I died and you are my backup. I left details of where I was going in the control system, so you can look that up later. Hopefully the body was grown and my memories downloaded correctly. One can never be sure of these things when interfacing modern tech with something this old. Not sure what to call you, though. We're not brothers or clones. Of course, since I'm dead it really doesn't matter what I call you. Anyway, you're the new me, with one final chance to finish up what we ... I ... started. Take it easy for a while and let the automatic systems take care of you. I did some more calculations after I downloaded my essence, and your body is only good for two or three centuries. Make good use of your limited time. Remember that the Family will regard you as an abomination. Good luck, Bob." Then the image vanished.

Seeing the recording had caused a flood of memories to return. He remembered using his implants to download a copy of his personality into the station's memory banks ... a process unavailable to those ancient scientists. He remembered what he had planned to do, and where, after the download was complete, but that was the last thing he remembered.

Bob sighed. It was going to take a while to get used to this merely human body. There was work to do, but first he needed to ensure that his control of this new body was as good as it could be. There were some shortcuts he could take but it was still going to take a few years. Still, it was better than being dead. It occurred to him to wonder how long it had been since he had died and how it had happened. So many questions and mysteries remained to be looked into.

He shut his eyes and took several deep, calming breaths. Then he smiled. It was good to be alive.

Author's Afterword

Although authors are to blame for the final product, none of us are an island when it comes to inspiration and assistance.

The original inspiration came from pictures posted on Twitter as writing prompts ("write a sentence based on this picture"). I started making up strange and silly responses around a character named "Bob". I'd especially like to thank @DougWallace1973. He not only posted interesting pictures, he encouraged my silly micro-stories and jokes.

Many thanks to my beta readers : Janice, Lynn, and Trit. Your encouragement helped keep me going.

Thanks to Steve for his comments regarding the speech patterns in Wales.

A special thanks to Trit for making many editorial comments.

The cover image is from the NOAO (National Optical Astronomy Observatory) archive, credited to T.A. Rector/University of Alaska Anchorage, H. Schweiker/WIYN and NOAO/AURA/NSF

About The Author

Brian retired from the software development rat race to take up the carefree life of an author. He lives with his wife and two cats in Ontario, Canada.

For the latest news about this and forthcoming books, the occasional commentary on life, or to leave a comment (we love feedback), check out Brian's blog at

www.BrianGreiner.ca

Books by Brian Greiner

All books are available as e-books and paperbacks
from :

      kobobooks.com

      amazon.ca

      amazon.com

      overdrive.com

The Ascending Darkness series

    #1   Darkness Creeps Forth

    #2   Darkness Comes Reaping

The Accursed North series

    #1 The Werewolves of Winter

    #2 The Final Doom

The Saga of Bob series

    #1 Ancestors and Descendants

    #2 Dagger of Eons

Ancestors and Descendants

Bob has spent much of his life crisscrossing the galaxy trying to protect people from the ancient evils, horrors, and demons that lurk among the stars; fearsome creatures that consider humans as mere nothings, if they bother with humans at all.

Some call them monsters.

Bob calls them family.

Now he has discovered evidence of an insidious and corrupting influence spreading across the galaxy, threatening his family and all of humanity. Unsure of who he can trust, Bob must fight to uncover the truth and find a way to save everyone. He will discover there are no perfect solutions, and all come with a price.

Darkness Creeps Forth

A terrorist attack that leaves Toronto's financial district in shambles and the country's economy vulnerable. An investigative reporter who uncovers a major national scandal and then dies of apparent natural causes before his story can be published. Investigating these seemingly unrelated events draws small-time private investigator Yancey Franklin and his friends into a century-old web of corruption and deceit that threatens the security and independence of Canada. In a desperate race against time, Yancey and his friends rush to prevent an attack by a ruthless opponent on an ageing secret military facility in northern Ontario that holds a deadly secret.

Darkness Comes Reaping

Small-time investigator Yancey Franklin has thwarted the plans of a ruthless enemy to unleash biochemical weapons in Northern Ontario. Now he is on the run and trying to uncover the secrets behind a century-old web of corruption and deceit that strives to eliminate Canada as an independent nation. In a desperate race against time, Yancey and his friends struggle to stay alive as they rush to stop their enemy's latest plan – the deadly "Harvest of Souls".

The Werewolves of Winter

The werewolves were created by the Change Plague—the result of ill-considered biotechnology. It was only their annual winter die-off that saved humanity. But every spring the Change Plague returned to create a new and more deadly crop of werewolves.

People adapted and managed to carry on despite the increasingly precarious situation.

One man, trapped on his farm north of Toronto, began to piece together hints of a deeper and more dangerous threat. With werewolves closing in, time was running out in a desperate race to uncover answers.

A novel of modern horrors, ancient prophesies, data analysis, and nerds who save the world.

The Final Doom

Felix Kurtsius discovered that the Change Plague was being dispersed as part of a deliberate attack. Toronto appeared to be the epicentre for the infection, which targeted Canada preferentially. He escaped to Toronto after werewolves began purging the rural areas of humans, only to discover insidious forces at work. In a race against the clock, Felix and his friends must use all their skills to unravel the forces behind the werewolves, and prevent the destruction of humanity.

A novel of modern horrors, ancient prophesies, data analysis, and nerds who save the world.